C000255364

PAUL TEMPLE AND THE CONRAD CASE

Francis Durbridge

WILLIAMS & WHITING

Copyright © Serial Productions

This edition published in 2023 by Williams & Whiting

All rights reserved

This script is fully protected under the copyright laws of the British Commonwealth of Nations, the United States of America, and all countries of the Berne and Universal Copyright Convention. All rights including Stage, Motion Picture, Radio, Television, Public Reading and the right to translate into foreign languages are strictly reserved. No part of this publication may be lawfully reproduced in any form or by any means such as photocopying, typescript, manuscript, audio or video recording or digitally or electronically or be transmitted or stored in a retrieval system without the prior written permission of the copyright owners.

Applications for performance or other rights should be made to The Agency, 24 Pottery Lane, London W11 4LZ.

Cover design by Timo Schroeder

9781915887146

Williams & Whiting (Publishers)

15 Chestnut Grove, Hurstpierpoint,

West Sussex, BN6 9SS

Titles by Francis Durbridge published by Williams & Whiting

Murder At The Weekend – the rediscovered newspaper serials and short stories

Also published by Williams & Whiting:
Francis Durbridge: The Complete Guide
By Melvyn Barnes

Titles by Francis Durbridge to be published by Williams & Whiting

Kind Regards From Mr Brix – a novel

Paul Temple and the Alex Affair

Paul Temple and the Canterbury Case (film script)

Paul Temple and the Geneva Mystery

Paul Temple and the Margo Mystery

Paul Temple: Two Plays For Radio Vol 2 (Send For Paul Temple and News of Paul Temple)

The Face of Carol West – a novel

The Passenger

The Yellow Windmill – a novel

INTRODUCTION

Francis Durbridge (1912-98) began his career in 1933 as a prolific writer of stories and plays for BBC radio. He developed a reputation for light entertainments including short sketches and libretti for musical comedies, but a talent for crime fiction also became evident in his early radio plays *Murder in the Midlands* (1934) and *Murder in the Embassy* (1937). The *Radio Times* (11 February 1938) mentioned that he had by then written some one hundred radio pieces, and Charles Hatton commented in *Radio Pictorial* (28 October 1938) that "He is one of the very few people in this country who have succeeded in making a living by writing for the BBC."

Durbridge continued to write for BBC radio for many years, usually under his own name and occasionally using the pseudonyms Frank Cromwell, Nicholas Vane and Lewis Middleton Harvey, but in particular he became known for his creation of the novelist/detective Paul Temple and his wife Steve. The 1938 radio serial *Send for Paul Temple* attracted over 7,000 enthusiastic listeners' letters to the BBC, and Durbridge responded with sequels over several decades that built an impressive UK and European fanbase. In the autumn of 1938 the second serial *Paul Temple and the Front Page Men* was broadcast, followed from 1939 to 1968 by another twenty-six Paul Temple mysteries of which seven were new productions of earlier cases.

In the mid-twentieth century radio detectives were extremely popular, with Temple's rivals including Dick Barton (by Edward J. Mason), Philip Odell (by Lester Powell), Dr. Morelle (by Ernest Dudley), P.C. 49 (by Alan Stranks) and Ambrose West (by Philip Levene). In fact in the 1940s, in addition to the Temples, Durbridge wrote radio dramas featuring investigators Anthony Sherwood, Johnny Cordell, Amanda Smith, Gail Carlton, Michael Starr, André d'Arnell and Johnny Washington, and he even wrote a radio serial featuring the legendary Sexton Blake.

Then in 1952, while continuing to write for radio, Durbridge embarked on a series of BBC television serials that achieved enormous viewing figures until 1980. While his reputation since 1938 had rested largely upon the radio exploits of the Temples, it was his parallel television career in the 1950s that cemented his name in the history of popular culture – with such gripping serials as *Portrait of Alison, My Friend Charles* and *The Scarf.* And later, as his radio productions became fewer, his television career continued with serials such as *The World of Tim Frazer, Melissa, A Man Called Harry Brent* and *Bat out of Hell.* Indeed his popularity on the small screen was phenomenal, and for all his television serials from 1960 the BBC gave him the unprecedented accolade of the "Francis Durbridge Presents" screen credit before the title sequence of each episode.

Francis Durbridge was a multi-media writer. His radio career lasted until 1968 and was overlapped by his television career from 1952 to 1980, which in turn was overlapped by his career as a stage dramatist from 1971 in the UK and even earlier in Germany. His theatrical productions, all with twist-after-twist plots, included such plays as *Suddenly at Home, Murder with Love* and *House Guest.*

Paul Temple and the Conrad Case was broadcast on the BBC Light Programme in eight thirty-minute episodes from 2 March to 20 April 1959. Peter Coke (1913-2008) appeared as Temple for the sixth time, having taken over the role for *Paul Temple and the Gilbert Case* in 1954, and he remained for every other Temple serial until the concluding *Paul Temple and the Alex Affair* in 1968. Durbridge enthusiasts regard Coke and his co-star Marjorie Westbury (1905-89) as the definitive pairing of Paul and Steve Temple in their eleven serials, although Westbury excelled numerically as Steve with her twenty-two appearances overall. Before Coke, she had partnered Barry Morse in *Send for Paul Temple Again* (1945), Howard Marion-Crawford in *A Case for Paul Temple* (1946) and Kim Peacock on nine separate occasions from 1946 to 1953.

Paul Temple and the Conrad Case was repeated on the Light Programme from 3 July to 21 August 1959. Then very much later, unusually as a daily serial, it was repeated on BBC Radio 4 from Christmas Day 1986 to 1 January 1987. In fact, given its several 21st century outings on BBC Radio 7 and BBC Radio 4 Extra, it must rank among the most frequently broadcast Temple serials.

Unlike many of the Temple mysteries, *Paul Temple and the Conrad Case* has never been novelised. A recording of the original broadcast serial was, however, marketed on audiocassettes (BBC Audio, 1989) and CDs (BBC Audio, 2004) and later included in the CD box set *Paul Temple: The Complete Radio Collection: The Fifties 1954-1959* (BBC, 2016).

As well as their appeal at home the Temples acquired a huge European following, with translated radio versions broadcast in the Netherlands from 1939, Germany from 1949, Italy from 1953 and Denmark from 1954. *Paul Temple and the Conrad Case* was broadcast in the Netherlands as *Paul Vlaanderen en het Conrad mysterie* (27 September – 15 November 1959, eight episodes), translated by Johan Bennik (pseudonym of Jan van Ees) and produced by Dick van Putten, with Jan van Ees as Vlaanderen and Eva Janssen as Ina; in Germany as *Paul Temple und der Fall Conrad* (26 November 1959 – 21 January 1960, eight episodes), translated by Marianne de Barde and John Lackland and produced by Willy Purucker, with Karl John as Temple and Rosemarie Fendel as Steve; again in Germany as *Paul Temple und der Fall Conrad* (13 January – 3 March 1961, eight episodes), translated by Marianne de Barde and produced by

Eduard Hermann, with René Deltgen as Temple and Annemarie Cordes as Steve; and in Italy as *La ragazza scomparsa* (17 – 28 February 1975, ten episodes), translated by Franca Cancogni and produced by Umberto Benedetto, with Alberto Lupo as Temple and Lucia Catullo as Steve.

Although we have no novelisation of *Paul Temple and the Conrad Case* to read, we can now enjoy Durbridge's original radio script.

Melvyn Barnes
Author of *Francis Durbridge: The Complete Guide* (Williams & Whiting, 2018)

This book reproduces Francis Durbridge's original script together with the list of characters and actors of the BBC programme on the dates mentioned, but the eventual broadcast might have edited Durbridge's script in respect of scenes, dialogue and character names.

PAUL TEMPLE
AND THE
CONRAD CASE

A serial in eight episodes
By FRANCIS DURBRIDGE
Broadcast on BBC Radio
2nd March – 20th April 1959
CAST:

Paul Temple . . . . .Peter Coke
Steve, his wife . . . . .Marjorie Westbury
Charlie . . . . .James Beattie
Sir Graham Forbes . . . . . . Richard Williams
Herr Breckshaft . . . . Jeffrey Segal
English Waiter . . . . .John Graham
Roadman . . . . .John Hollis
Mrs Weldon . . . . .Virginia Winter
June Jackson. . . . . .June Tobin
German Waiter . . . . .John Hollis
Gerda Holman . . . . Hilda Schroder
Madame Klein . . . . . Dorothy Holmes-Gore
Denis Harper . . . . .John Bryning
Elliot France . . . . James Thomason
Elsa, Countess Dekker . . . . . Joan Matheson
Receptionist . . . . .John Graham
Dr Conrad . . . . .Rolf Lefebvre
Head Waiter . . . . John Cazabon
Joyce Gunter . . . . .Dorothy Smith
Fritz Gunter . . . . .George Hagan
Maid (Maria) . . . . .Judy Bailey
Hotel Maid . . . . .Beatrice Ormonde
Man, delivering wine . . . . . . .John Cazabon
Man, with Austrian accent . . .John Cazabon
2nd German Waiter . . . . .John Bennett

EPISODE ONE

THE MAN FROM MUNICH

OPEN TO: *The noise of a car engine.*
FADE down the noise to the background.
TEMPLE is driving the car.

STEVE: Paul, what time is it? The clock on the dashboard says twelve o'clock.

TEMPLE: I make it twelve twenty …

STEVE: I'd no idea it was as late as that.

TEMPLE: It's been quite an evening, hasn't it, Steve? I haven't danced so much in years.

STEVE: No, you haven't!

TEMPLE: I seem to detect a slight note of sarcasm in that remark!

STEVE: Well, really, darling, these modern dances aren't quite your cup of tea!

TEMPLE: Are you suggesting that I need a course of six easy lessons?

STEVE: Six!

TEMPLE: Considering it was a charity ball I think you might at least be a little more charitable about my dancing.

STEVE laughs.
The car slows down and eventually comes to a standstill.
TEMPLE switches off the car engine.

STEVE: Aren't you going to put the car away, Paul?

TEMPLE: (*With a yawn*) No, I'll let Charlie do it.

STEVE: Won't he be in bed?

TEMPLE: You've forgotten. It's his night out. He's probably been to the Palais, indulging in his weekly bout of rock n' roll.

STEVE: Now that's an idea!

TEMPLE: What?

STEVE: Maybe Charlie could give you six easy lessons!

They laugh.
FADE out.

FADE IN a door opening and shutting.

A pause.

TEMPLE: Ah, so you're still up, Charlie.

CHARLIE: Yes, Mr T.

TEMPLE: Did you have a good time?

CHARLIE: No! It was a proper washout! Old time night. Waltzes and foxtrots. Me and Beryl left soon after nine.

STEVE: Bad luck, Charlie! I've a feeling Mr Temple and I would have done better at the Palais.

TEMPLE and CHARLIE laugh.

TEMPLE: Any messages, Charlie?

CHARLIE: Yes, a chap telephoned – wanted to speak to you. But it was such a terrible line I haven't got a clue what it was all about.

TEMPLE: Didn't you get his name?

CHARLIE: Well, he said something about phoning from France and he'd ring again later.

STEVE: What part of France?

CHARLIE: (*Vaguely*) I don't know, Mrs Temple.

TEMPLE: Didn't he speak English?

CHARLIE: (*Still very vague*) Well, it sounded like English.

TEMPLE: (*Irritated*) Perhaps it was Hindustani.

CHARLIE: (*Taking TEMPLE seriously*) No, I don't think it was Hindustani, Mr Temple.

STEVE: Charlie, did you leave the light on in the drawing room?

CHARLIE: Oh, yes, Mrs Temple – there's somebody in there. They've been waiting over an hour.

TEMPLE: Well, who on earth …

CHARLIE: It's Sir Graham Forbes, sir, and a foreign gentleman. I told Sir Graham to help himself to a whisky and soda. I hope that was all right, Mr Temple?

4

TEMPLE: Yes, of course! Come along, Steve.
FADE.

FADE IN the voice of SIR GRAHAM FORBES.
FORBES: … You have to remember, Breckshaft, that
               our methods over here are rather different
               from yours in Western Germany. To begin
               with …
FORBES is interrupted by the opening of the door.
TEMPLE: Hello, Sir Graham! Sorry you've had such
               a long wait!
FORBES: Oh, here you are, Temple! Hello, Steve!
               Nice to see you both again!
STEVE: Good evening, Sir Graham – or is it good
               morning? Why on earth didn't you let us
               know you were coming?
TEMPLE: We've been out, tripping the light fantastic!
STEVE: Well, at least we've been tripping!
They all laugh.
FORBES: May I introduce Herr Wilhelm Breckshaft,
               of the Munich Police? Mr and Mrs Temple
               …
STEVE: How do you do, Herr Breckshaft?
BRECKSHAFT: (*A cultured German in his late forties, with
               only the merest trace of an accent*) I'm
               delighted to meet you, Mrs Temple – Mr
               Temple.
TEMPLE: (*Curious*) Delighted to meet you, Herr
               Breckshaft, but please let me get you
               another drink.
BRECKSHAFT: Not at the moment, if you don't mind, sir.
FORBES: Charlie told us to help ourselves. I hope you
               don't mind.

5

STEVE:	I should think so, after all these years, Sir Graham.
TEMPLE:	Would you like a drink, darling?
STEVE:	No thanks. I'll just sit down and massage my bruises.
FORBES:	(*Amused*) I can see you've made an impression this evening, Temple.
STEVE:	Are you here on holiday, Herr Breckshaft?
BRECKSHAFT:	(*Hesitantly*) Well – not exactly a holiday, Mrs Temple.
FORBES:	I picked Herr Breckshaft up at London Airport this evening. It's an unofficial visit – at least so far as the press are concerned.
BRECKSHAFT:	It is, however, a matter of some urgency, Mr Temple. My colleagues and myself are engaged upon an enquiry and I have come to ask for help from Sir Graham Forbes.
TEMPLE:	I see.
FORBES:	I know you're very busy on a new novel, Temple, but I thought perhaps we might persuade you …
STEVE:	(*Significantly*) I know, Sir Graham!
TEMPLE:	Is it a murder case, Herr Breckshaft?
BRECKSHAFT:	No, it concerns a well-known school near Garmisch-Partenkirchen in Bavaria.
STEVE:	A school? Not Weldon's?
BRECKSHAFT:	That is the place! You know it, Mrs Temple?
STEVE:	A great friend of mine was expelled from there. They were very strict in those days.
BRECKSHAFT:	They are still somewhat strict. That is why this affair is extraordinary. The young ladies are under close supervision, yet one of them has – disappeared.

TEMPLE:	Disappeared? What kind of school is this?
STEVE:	It's one of the best finishing schools on the continent, darling. Very exclusive.
FORBES:	Breckshaft tells me that it is owned and run by a widow – an Englishwoman – a Mrs Elizabeth Weldon.
BRECKSHAFT:	That's right. She was left a fortune by her husband and started the school just after the war. Her pupils come from all over Europe, indeed from all over the world.
TEMPLE:	How old are these girls?
BRECKSHAFT:	Oh – sixteen to nineteen.
TEMPLE:	And the missing girl?
BRECKSHAFT:	She's eighteen, Mr Temple.
FORBES:	And English. That's why Breckshaft is here.
BRECKSHAFT:	Her name is Betty Conrad. She's the daughter of a Harley Street psychiatrist.
STEVE:	Surely he's the man we've seen on television, Paul?
TEMPLE:	Yes. Go on, Breckshaft …
BRECKSHAFT:	The circumstances are most unusual. The girl seems to have vanished into thin air. My men have made many enquiries, but so far we have been unable to throw any light upon this strange affair.
TEMPLE:	I see. Well, are there any other facts?
BRECKSHAFT:	Facts? Ah, yes, there are many facts, Mr Temple. We discovered that Betty Conrad had been friendly with a young Englishman named Denis Harper.
TEMPLE:	Denis Harper?
BRECKSHAFT:	Yes, he works in the Anglo-Continental Bank at Munich. When the girl

disappeared, Harper was not to be found, and we thought they might have gone away together. But he returned a few days later – he had been on a motoring holiday in Austria and he knew nothing at all about Betty Conrad's disappearance. Indeed, he appeared to be genuinely upset when we told him about it.

STEVE: And what about Mrs Weldon? Was she upset?

BRECKSHAFT: Of course, Mrs Temple, she was most disturbed. Nothing like this had ever happened before at Weldon's. She told me that she allows her pupils a certain amount of freedom but at the same time they are under strict supervision.

TEMPLE: Did you question anyone else – besides Mrs Weldon and Denis Harper?

BRECKSHAFT: Yes, yes – it's over a week since the girl disappeared, so we have questioned many people. There's an English novelist named Elliot France. He frequently stays with a friend of his – a Countess Decker.

TEMPLE: Countess Decker?

BRECKSHAFT: Yes, she has an estate quite near the school. When France is staying with her she occasionally invites Mrs Weldon and some of the pupils to tea. Now and again she has a musical evening – poetry reading – that sort of thing.

TEMPLE: Elliot France? I think I've read some of his books.

BRECKSHAFT: Yes, I expect you have, Mr Temple. He's one of these international characters – travels about a great deal.

STEVE: Does Mr France come into this enquiry?

BRECKSHAFT: Yes, he does, Mrs Temple. You see, Betty Conrad shared a room with June Jackson, an American girl. On the day she disappeared she told June that she was going to Schreidenstein.

STEVE: Schreidenstein? Where's that?

BRECKSHAFT: That's the name of Countess Decker's estate.

STEVE: Oh, I see.

BRECKSHAFT: She told June that she was going there because she'd been invited to have tea with Elliot France. She was very thrilled about it.

TEMPLE: And did she keep the appointment?

BRECKSHAFT: She caught a bus outside the school and was seen to leave it at the main gates of the estate. Since then there's been no trace of her.

STEVE: And what did Mr France have to say about all this?

BRECKSHAFT: That's the peculiar part about it, Mrs Temple. He says he hardly knew the girl – certainly never gave her an invitation.

STEVE: Perhaps the Countess issued the invitation?

BRECKSHAFT: No – she denies ever having been in touch with Betty Conrad.

TEMPLE: Did Betty mention this invitation to any of the other girls? Or to Mrs Weldon?

BRECKSHAFT: No, only to her room mate, June Jackson.

STEVE: Miss Jackson could be lying, I suppose?

BRECKSHAFT: Yes – but why should she lie, Mrs Temple?

TEMPLE: Herr Breckshaft – tell me. Did this bank clerk – Harper – know that Betty was friendly with Elliot France?

BRECKSHAFT: They had never discussed him. But she wasn't friendly with him, Mr Temple. According to France he's only seen the girl two or three times – and that was in a party.

TEMPLE: I take it that Betty didn't mention the invitation to Mrs Weldon?

BRECKSHAFT: No, no, as I said, she didn't mention it to anyone except June Jackson.

STEVE: But surely she should have notified someone in authority that she was going to be out to tea?

BRECKSHAFT: She should have done, Mrs Temple – but she didn't.

FORBES: It would appear that she stepped off that bus and completely disappeared.

TEMPLE: I take it the girl's parents have been notified?

FORBES: Yes, and the girl's mother – well, actually, it's her step-mother – doesn't seem at all concerned; but the father's extremely worried.

BRECKSHAFT: I think perhaps Mrs Weldon is more worried than anyone else, Sir Graham. She's terrified that this affair might get into the newspapers. I've told her that we can't withhold it from the press indefinitely. We need the help of publicity to trace the girl's movements.

STEVE: I suppose she's frightened of what the other parents will think?

10

BRECKSHAFT: Exactly, Mrs Temple.

TEMPLE: And that's the entire story?

BRECKSHAFT: The entire story – so far.

TEMPLE: Well, it's interesting, Sir Graham, but there may be a perfectly simple explanation for all this.

BRECKSHAFT: Well, if there is – we'd like to know what it is, Mr Temple!

TEMPLE: Yes, well, I'm afraid I can't express an opinion without first talking to the people concerned.

FORBES: That's exactly what we'd like you to do, Temple.

TEMPLE: (*Laughing*) But I can't possibly rush off to Garmisch at a moment's notice.

STEVE: Why not? You always said you liked Bavaria.

TEMPLE: Yes, I do. But you know jolly well I've got … (*He stops, surprised*) Steve, do you want to go to Bavaria?

STEVE: Well, it might be interesting to see the school where they had the temerity to expel Angela Turnbull.

TEMPLE: But I've never known you want to get mixed up in a case before! By Timothy, this is extraordinary!

FORBES: (*Amused*) Well, Temple?

TEMPLE: I'll sleep on it, Sir Graham. Give me a ring tomorrow morning …

STEVE: (*With a yawn*) This morning, darling!

FADE.

FADE UP STEVE talking to TEMPLE.

11

STEVE: (*Still yawning*) Oh dear – it's one o'clock! You'd better lock up the front door, Paul.

TEMPLE: I think Charlie's done it. (*A pause*) Steve, do you really want me to get involved in this case?

In the background the sound of the doorbell ringing.

STEVE: No …

TEMPLE: But you said …

STEVE: But I know what will happen if you don't! You'll start work on another book and I shan't see you for weeks – months, in fact. Look what happened when you wrote "The Tyler Mystery". You even had your meals in your study!

TEMPLE: (*Laughing*) Yes, I know, but – this doesn't seem a very interesting case to me. Too straightforward. Now if there was something unusual about it – some intriguing little thing …

TEMPLE stops speaking as the door opens.

CHARLIE: Excuse me, sir – Mr Breck – Breck …

BRECKSHAFT: I beg your pardon, Mr Temple.

TEMPLE: Oh – come in, Herr Breckshaft!

BRECKSHAFT: I'm afraid I've left my valise somewhere. I put it down near the sofa … Oh, there it is!

TEMPLE: I'll get it for you!

A pause.

TEMPLE: There you are!

BRECKSHAFT: Thank you – it's most kind of you. Goodnight, Mrs Temple.

STEVE: Goodnight.

BRECKSHAFT: (*After a tiny pause*) Oh, there's one small point I forgot to mention. It's not really important – at least I don't think so, but when my men searched Betty Conrad's room at the school, they found a small stick in her desk.

TEMPLE: Stick? You mean a walking stick?

BRECKSHAFT: (*With a little laugh*) No! No, I mean a little cocktail stick, the kind you have in – a gin and Italian, perhaps. You know the sort of thing I mean. A tiny stick – usually it's got a cherry on the end.

TEMPLE: Go on.

BRECKSHAFT: This stick was rather unusual because the top represented the head of a dog – an Alsatian dog. You know what these sticks are like. Sometimes they have a coat of arms on them – or a cockerel – or something like that.

TEMPLE: Yes, I know what you mean. But why shouldn't she?

BRECKSHAFT: I didn't think it was important – indeed, I still don't think so – but some days after we found it I took my family for a run into the country. We stopped at an inn for a drink. It was about twenty miles from the school. They had identically the same type of cocktail stick that we'd found in Betty Conrad's desk. They assured me the sticks were exclusive to that particular inn – the proprietor was very proud of them, in fact.

TEMPLE: Did you describe Betty Conrad to him?

BRECKSHAFT: Yes, yes, and showed him a photograph of her. But neither he nor his staff recognised her. So I telephoned Mrs Weldon and asked her if she had any rules on this matter. She said the girls were not allowed outside a

13

	five mile radius of the school unless they were accompanied by their parents.
STEVE:	Then how could she have got that cocktail stick?
TEMPLE:	Someone could have taken one for a souvenir, I suppose – and given it to her.
BRECKSHAFT:	That's a possibility, of course.
STEVE:	Yes, it's a possibility.
BRECKSHAFT:	So, Mr Temple, do you think you will be able to help us?
TEMPLE:	I'm afraid I still haven't decided, Herr Breckshaft – but as I told Sir Graham, I'll sleep on it.
BRECKSHAFT:	Very well. Now I mustn't detain you any longer. Goodnight, Mrs Temple.
STEVE:	Goodnight.
TEMPLE:	I'll see you to the door …
FADE.	

FADE UP the noise of a breakfast table.

TEMPLE:	Steve, I wish you'd speak to Charlie about the toast.
STEVE:	He blames that new machine you bought. He says it's out of adjustment, or something.
TEMPLE:	He's out of adjustment, if you ask me! I'll buy him a toasting fork.
STEVE:	(*Laughing*) Oh, darling, you sound very grumpy this morning.
TEMPLE:	I'll have some more coffee, please.

STEVE pours the coffee.
In the background, the telephone starts to ring.

STEVE:	Paul …
TEMPLE:	Yes?

STEVE: You've slept on it.

TEMPLE: Slept on what?

STEVE: Here's your coffee … You know perfectly well what I mean. Are we going to Germany?

TEMPLE: No, darling, we're not. It's no use, Steve, I've got far too much work to do. I've got that new novel to write and by the end of next month I've promised … Why on earth doesn't Charlie answer the telephone?

The telephone stops ringing.

STEVE: (*Laughing*) He has answered it!

TEMPLE: Yes. And I can just imagine what's going on!

STEVE: Well, really, you are in a mood.

A pause.

The door opens.

CHARLIE: Mr Temple, that man's on the phone again – the chap that telephoned last night. But I got it wrong, sir – he wasn't talking from France, his name's France.

TEMPLE: Oh!

STEVE: It must be Elliot France, darling.

TEMPLE: Yes. All right, Charlie, I'll take it. (*To STEVE*) You'd better listen on the extension, Steve.

STEVE: Yes, all right. (*To CHARLIE*) Clear the table, will you, Charlie, please?

FADE on CHARLIE removing the dishes from the table.

FADE UP on TEMPLE lifting the telephone receiver.

TEMPLE: (*On the phone*) Hello, Paul Temple speaking.

MAN: (*On the other end of the line*) Oh, good morning, Mr Temple. My name is France. I telephoned you last night, but unfortunately you were out.

TEMPLE: Yes, I got your message, Mr France – but I couldn't ring you back because you didn't leave a number.

MAN: No, I'm only in England for a few days.

TEMPLE: Well – what can I do for you?

MAN: I rather wanted to have a word with you, Mr Temple – if you could spare me a moment or two.

TEMPLE: Yes, certainly. I'd be delighted to meet the author of "Zero is Tomorrow".

MAN: Thank you.

TEMPLE: But couldn't you give me some idea what it's all about?

MAN: (*Hesitantly*) It's about – Betty Conrad.

TEMPLE: Betty Conrad! But when you telephoned last night I hadn't even heard of the girl!

MAN: Yes, I know. I also know about Herr Breckshaft's visit to your flat last night.

TEMPLE: Really? Well, I shall be here all the morning, Mr France, if you care to call.

MAN: No, I'm afraid I can't do that.

TEMPLE: Why not?

MAN: You see, I'm staying out of town and if you wouldn't mind … (*Suddenly*) Look, Mr Temple, do you know Pointers Hotel near Godstone?

TEMPLE: Pointers? Yes, I do.

MAN: Do you think we could possibly meet there for lunch?

TEMPLE: Today?

MAN: Yes.

TEMPLE: Well – if you can make it fairly late – say one thirty?

MAN: That will do admirably. I shall look forward to –

16

TEMPLE:	(*Interrupting the MAN*) Oh – er – would you have any objection if my wife came along?
MAN:	No, of course not. I'd be delighted.
TEMPLE:	Good. Well – one thirty, then …
MAN:	Yes. Goodbye, Mr Temple.
TEMPLE:	Goodbye.

TEMPLE replaces the receiver.
FADE SCENE.

FADE UP the sound of a car.
It is travelling fairly fast.
TEMPLE is driving.

STEVE:	Paul, you really are extraordinary! Here we are dashing down to Godstone and yet you say you're not going to get mixed up in this affair.
TEMPLE:	I didn't say I wasn't going to get mixed up in it. I said I had a great deal of work to do. Anyway, I must confess, the whole thing sounds a little more intriguing.
STEVE:	You mean since Elliot France telephoned?
TEMPLE:	Yes!
STEVE:	By the way, he doesn't write many novels, does he?
TEMPLE:	No, but those he does write sell like mad pretty well all over the world.
STEVE:	I've never read one of them. I've always thought they were obscure and terribly highbrow.
TEMPLE:	A lot of people seem to like them. Still, it wouldn't worry him very much if they didn't. I'm told he's got an enormous private income.
STEVE:	Has he? Well, we shall probably have a jolly interesting lunch. Although, it's going to be a bit awkward if he asks me if I've read any of his books. I'll tell you what, Paul, you tell me the

17

	plot of that one you mentioned. What was it? – "Zero is Tomorrow". If you can remember the plot, of course.
TEMPLE:	Oh, I can remember it all right. Remember it very well. "Zero is Tomorrow" happens to be the title of my next novel.
STEVE:	<u>Your</u> next novel?
TEMPLE:	Yes.
STEVE:	But why did you mention it to Elliot France?
TEMPLE:	I suddenly had a hunch. I wanted to discover if the gentleman on the telephone really was Elliot France.
STEVE:	And wasn't he?
TEMPLE:	No, he wasn't! (*Faintly amused*) You know, you're quite right, Steve, I think it is going to be a jolly interesting lunch!

FADE IN incidental music.

FADE music.
FADE IN STEVE speaking.

STEVE:	I hope we can get a table, Paul – the hotel seems very busy.
TEMPLE:	Well, I presume our host has taken care of that.
STEVE:	Here's the head waiter …
TEMPLE:	Perhaps I'd better have a word with him.
WAITER:	(*Approaching*) Yes, sir? You've reserved a table?
TEMPLE:	I think Mr France has already booked …
WAITER:	Ah, yes, of course! Mr and Mrs Temple!
TEMPLE:	That's right.
WAITER:	Mr France has just phoned to say he'll be down in a few moments, sir.
TEMPLE:	(*Faintly surprised*) You mean Mr France is staying here?

WAITER: Yes, sir. He's been here for several days. He has asked me to serve cocktails on the terrace, Mr Temple. Will you come this way, please?

FADE to terrace.

FADE UP background noises of the river.
Occasional background sounds of river traffic are heard.

STEVE: Well, we've got the terrace to ourselves.

TEMPLE: And very pleasant, too.

STEVE: It's a heavenly view.

TEMPLE: It certainly is on a day like this.

A pause.

TEMPLE: You haven't finished your drink, darling.

STEVE: No, I'm not very keen on it.

TEMPLE: Too much gin?

STEVE: Yes … (*After a moment, quietly*) Paul, you've noticed the sticks – the cocktail sticks?

TEMPLE: Yes …

STEVE: They're exactly like the one that Breckshaft found in Betty Conrad's room.

TEMPLE: Yes, I know. (*Calling out*) Waiter!

WAITER: Yes, sir?

TEMPLE: Mr France is rather a long time – we've been here twenty minutes.

WAITER: Yes, I'm sorry, sir. He must have been detained.

TEMPLE: Well, could you get us some olives?

WAITER: Yes, certainly, sir …

TEMPLE: Oh, and, waiter …

WAITER: Mr Temple?

TEMPLE: These cocktail sticks – they're rather unusual, aren't they? How long have you had them here?

WAITER: (*Laughing*) No time at all, sir. Mr France said you'd be amused …

STEVE: Did Mr France supply them, then?

19

WAITER:	He did indeed, madam. He insisted I used them for your cocktails. I gathered it was some kind of a private joke, sir?
TEMPLE:	A private joke? Oh, yes. Yes, of course! Thank you, waiter – don't forget the olives.
WAITER:	Right away, sir.

A slight pause.

STEVE:	Our host seems to have a rather strange sense of humour.
TEMPLE:	(*His thoughts elsewhere*) Yes …
STEVE:	These sticks are rather attractive, aren't they? The Alsatian's awfully well carved.
TEMPLE:	Hm …
STEVE:	What are you thinking about, darling?
TEMPLE:	You know, Steve, I think there's more to this business than just the disappearance of a school girl. I think that when Breckshaft contacted Sir Graham Forbes, he knew perfectly well that …

TEMPLE breaks off speaking as the WAITER returns.

WAITER:	Excuse me, sir, Mr France sent this note down for you.
TEMPLE:	A note? Oh, thank you.

TEMPLE opens the envelope.

There is a pause.

TEMPLE:	All right, thank you, waiter.
WAITER:	Yes, sir.
STEVE:	What does it say, Paul?
TEMPLE:	(*Reading*) "I am extremely sorry I have been unable to keep our appointment, but I have been urgently summoned to see a friend in Oxted. I shall be most offended, however, if you do not stay for lunch – the waiter has his instructions. Perhaps you could look in at my

	friend's cottage on your way back to town. The address is Bankside Cottage, Faraday Lane, Oxted. Elliot France. P.S. I will explain my shaggy dog joke when I see you." Well, what do you make of that, Steve?
STEVE:	What does he mean by shaggy dog joke?
TEMPLE:	Presumably, the cocktail sticks.
STEVE:	Oh yes. (*A pause*) Well – what do we do now, Mr Temple?
TEMPLE:	(*Almost tense*) There's only one thing we can do, Steve.
STEVE:	(*Capturing TEMPLE's tenseness*) What's that?
TEMPLE:	(*Lightly*) Have lunch, darling.

FADE IN incidental music.

FADE DOWN the music.
FADE UP the sound of the car.
TEMPLE is driving.

STEVE:	Paul, we've been going round in circles – I think you ought to ask someone where this place is.
TEMPLE:	Yes, there's a chap working on the road over there. I'll ask him.
STEVE:	I'll bet he's a stranger in these parts!

The car draws to a standstill.

TEMPLE:	Excuse me. Could you direct me to Bankside Cottage? It's in Faraday Lane.
ROADMAN:	Yes, sir – you mean Dr Conrad's place?
TEMPLE:	Dr Conrad?
ROADMAN:	That's right. He's a big London doctor. Comes down here at weekends.
STEVE:	(*Aside*) That must be Betty Conrad's father.

| ROADMAN: | You keep straight down here to the crossroads, sir, then you turn left and take the second road on the right. That's Faraday Lane. The house you want is right at the end, just past the little pond. |
| TEMPLE: | I see. Thank you very much. |

The car slowly drives away.

STEVE:	(*Quietly*) Paul, what does this mean? What do you think this man who calls himself Elliot France has got to do with Dr Conrad?
TEMPLE:	He could be a patient, I suppose.
STEVE:	Yes, but if he was a patient, surely he wouldn't … (*Suddenly*) This looks as if it might be the place, darling!
TEMPLE:	But it isn't a cottage at all. It's a house.

The car slows down.

| STEVE: | It says Bankside Cottage on the gate. |
| TEMPLE: | Yes, it does. This is it all right. |

The car draws to a standstill.
FADE OUT.

FADE IN the sound of a wicket gate opening and closing.

STEVE:	The garden's rather neglected.
TEMPLE:	Yes. The lawn could certainly do with a trim.
STEVE:	It's all very quiet, darling. I don't think there's anyone in.
TEMPLE:	There never is. I'll try the bell.

The bell rings inside the house.

STEVE:	If the doctor only comes at weekends …
TEMPLE:	But the note distinctly said that the man who called himself France had an urgent summons here.
STEVE:	Yes, but I still think that there's no one in, darling.

The bell stops ringing.
There is a pause.

STEVE: If there is, they're certainly not hurrying themselves.

TEMPLE: Stay here, and I'll go round the back.

STEVE: Oh no! No, don't do that! Let's wait a few more minutes, Paul.

TEMPLE: (*With a little laugh*) Are you nervous, Steve?

STEVE: Yes.

TEMPLE: Why?

STEVE: I don't know why, I'm sure!

TEMPLE: All right, darling, you come with me. We'll see if we can make anyone hear at the back door.

FADE OUT.

FADE IN TEMPLE knocking on the back door.
He continues to knock for some little time but there is no reply.

STEVE: The place is empty, Paul!

TEMPLE: Yes, I think it must be.

TEMPLE tries the door handle and discovers that the door is unlocked.

TEMPLE: This door's not locked! Come on, let's go in.

TEMPLE and STEVE enter the kitchen of the house.

STEVE: It's a pretty big kitchen, Paul.

TEMPLE: Yes, and a pretty dirty one. I think this is the way to the hall.

We hear a door opening as TEMPLE and STEVE enter the hall.

STEVE: It looks a much bigger place from the outside.

TEMPLE: Yes.

STEVE: Oh look, there's some letters on the floor – by the front door.

TEMPLE: Yes, I'd just noticed them.

TEMPLE crosses and picks up the letters.

TEMPLE: Circulars ... Detergent coupons ... Hello, here's a post card ...

A pause.

STEVE: What does it say?

TEMPLE: It's addressed to Mrs Ruth Conrad ... it's from a tailor by the look of things; but there's no name on it and no address.

STEVE: Well – what does it say?

TEMPLE: (*Reading*) "Dear Madam ... Your coat – the blue coat – will be ready on Friday, the 18th, at four o'clock ..."

STEVE: Friday, the 18th ...

TEMPLE: Yes, that's next Friday.

STEVE: Yes. Well, at any rate it looks as if <u>Mrs</u> Conrad spends some time here.

TEMPLE: Yes, that's just what I was thinking. Steve, I'm going to have a good look round this place. Are you sure you wouldn't like to go and wait in the car?

STEVE: No! I'm coming with you!

TEMPLE: All right, but for heaven's sake don't be so jumpy!

STEVE: I won't if there's nothing to be jumpy about.

TEMPLE opens a door.

TEMPLE: We'll start here. This looks as if it might be the drawing room.

There is a pause, then STEVE suddenly gives a little scream.

STEVE: Paul, just look ...

TEMPLE: By Timothy! What a shambles! There's been a devil of a struggle in here ... (*Suddenly*) Steve, stay where you are!

STEVE: What is it, Paul?

TEMPLE: There's someone on the floor at the back of the settee. No, don't move, darling – stay where you are!

A pause.

STEVE: Who is it?

TEMPLE: I don't know.

STEVE: Do you think it's the man who telephoned you? The man who pretended to be Mr France?

TEMPLE: (*Interrupting STEVE*) It could be, I suppose …

STEVE: (*Extremely nervous*) He's dead, isn't he?

TEMPLE: Yes, Steve – he's dead all right. And there's the knife …

FADE IN incidental music.

FADE IN the voice of SIR GRAHAM FORBES.

FORBES: Well, you've certainly had quite a day, Temple! Quite a day!

TEMPLE: Haven't the police any idea who the murdered man might be, Sir Graham?

FORBES: No, Temple, but they're sure of two things. One, that's he's not Elliot France – two, that he's the man who stayed at Pointers and called himself France. But as to how he knew so many facts about this particular case, we just can't imagine. Unless Breckshaft can throw some light on the matter?

BRECKSHAFT: I regret, Sir Graham, that I know nothing about this man.

TEMPLE: Did you see Dr Conrad, Sir Graham?

FORBES: Yes, I went round as soon as you telephoned. There again, I'm afraid we seem to have struck a dead end. He knew nothing about the man, either, and had no idea how he got into the house.

TEMPLE: The man who killed him must have got into the house as well, Sir Graham. What were they after, do you think?

FORBES: I don't know – and Dr Conrad can't throw any light on it, either. He told me he hardly uses the house now and was thinking of selling it. It seems his wife doesn't very much care for the country.

TEMPLE: Does Mrs Conrad know anything about the dead man?

FORBES: Apparently not. She was present when I gave her husband the description and she said she had no idea who he could be.

TEMPLE: I see. I found this post card, Sir Graham. It's addressed to Mrs Conrad – it was on the mat near the front door.

There is a slight pause whilst SIR GRAHAM looks at the card.

FORBES: (*Thoughtfully*) … Blue coat … Friday the 18th … Why should she give them her country address if she's hardly ever there?

TEMPLE: Exactly!

BRECKSHAFT: I may be wrong, but I have a feeling that Dr Conrad is withholding information, Sir Graham.

FORBES: Yes, well, I'm afraid there's nothing we can do about that at the moment.

BRECKSHAFT: Mr Temple, forgive me for raising the question again, but – have you reached a decision about this case?

TEMPLE: Yes. If you think I can be of any help to you, Herr Breckshaft, I'm at your disposal.

BRECKSHAFT: Thank you, Mr Temple. Could you and Mrs Temple fly to Munich with me tomorrow?

TEMPLE: Yes, I think that can be arranged.

BRECKSHAFT: I'm leaving at ten thirty, Sir Graham. Do you think you can make arrangements for Mr and Mrs Temple to be on the same plane?

FORBES: Yes – don't worry. That'll be all right. Well, goodnight, Temple. Goodnight, Steve. Take care of yourselves.

TEMPLE: We'll try, Sir Graham.

BRECKSHAFT: I'll ring you early tomorrow morning, Mr Temple.

FADE.

FADE IN TEMPLE speaking.

TEMPLE: Are you asleep, Steve?

STEVE: No …

TEMPLE: What are you thinking about?

STEVE: You.

TEMPLE: Me?

STEVE: Yes, you, darling. Paul, you never said a word to Breckshaft about the cocktail sticks.

TEMPLE: The cocktail sticks?

STEVE: Yes – at Pointers.

TEMPLE: Didn't I?

STEVE: (*Significantly*) No, you didn't.

TEMPLE: By Timothy! You're quite right, I didn't. I forgot all about it.

STEVE: Oh yes?

TEMPLE: What do you mean – oh yes?

STEVE: (*With a little laugh*) Come off it, Paul! Goodnight, dear.

27

TEMPLE: (*Faintly amused*) Goodnight, Steve.
FADE IN incidental music.

FADE IN the sound of a car.
TEMPLE: I must say, this German car goes like a
               bomb.
STEVE: Was it very expensive to hire?
TEMPLE: Yes – it was! I shall charge it up to Sir
               Graham!
STEVE laughs.
A slight pause.
STEVE: Oh, look, that must be the school, Paul!
TEMPLE: By Timothy! It's quite a place, isn't it? I
               didn't think it would be quite as
               impressive as that!
STEVE: Neither did I!
The car slows down.
STEVE: Paul, why didn't Herr Breckshaft come
               with us?
TEMPLE: I didn't particularly want him. I thought it
               would be less embarrassing for Mrs
               Weldon if we had a little chat off the
               record, as it were.
STEVE: Was that the only reason?
TEMPLE: Yes, darling – the only reason!
STEVE: (*Disbelievingly*) Um!
The car slows down to a standstill.
TEMPLE: Well, here we are!
FADE.

FADE IN the voice of MRS WELDON.
MRS WELDON: (*She is middle-aged, is cultured, and
               charming*) I'm delighted to meet you, Mr
               Temple, and it's most kind of you to

	interest yourself in our little storm in a teacup.
TEMPLE:	Let's hope it is a storm in a teacup, Mrs Weldon.
MRS WELDON:	Do sit down, Mrs Temple – over by the window – it's a rather pleasant view.
STEVE:	This is a lovely place, Mrs Weldon.
MRS WELDON:	Yes, it is, isn't it? Particularly at this time of the year.
TEMPLE:	It's surprising that a girl should want to run away from such agreeable surroundings.
MRS WELDON:	Yes, it is. Dear – oh dear – this is a most irritating affair.
STEVE:	You still haven't heard anything from the young girl, I take it?
MRS WELDON:	No, not a word. I do wish the silly girl would telephone or write.
STEVE:	What's your opinion of all this, Mrs Weldon?
MRS WELDON:	Well, I can't help feeling that she's lost her head over some man or other – she's at a very susceptible age, you know.
STEVE:	Do you think she might have had a crush on Elliot France?
MRS WELDON:	Well, that's possible, of course. Apparently she was very thrilled at the thought of going to tea with him. But I don't think for a minute that Mr France is involved in any way, if that's what you mean, Mrs Temple.
TEMPLE:	And Countess Decker?
MRS WELDON:	Oh, quite beyond suspicion, Mr Temple. I've known Elsa – the Countess – for

29

some time. We're great friends; she's entertained the girls almost since the school started.

TEMPLE: Well, I hope we'll be able to find this girl, Mrs Weldon – but there seems to be very little to go on at the present moment.

MRS WELDON: Are you staying in Garmisch or in Munich, Mr Temple?

TEMPLE: In Garmisch, at the Partenkirchen Hotel. We flew from London this morning.

MRS WELDON: Well, you'll have the full co-operation of everyone here, I assure you. Anything you care to suggest …

TEMPLE: Thank you. Perhaps it might be a good idea if I had a talk with Betty Conrad's roommate. I understand she shared a room with an American girl called June Jackson?

MRS WELDON: Yes, but I'm afraid you won't get much sense out of June just at the moment.

TEMPLE: Oh, indeed? Why's that?

MRS WELDON: She's been in bed since yesterday afternoon with a very bad headache. I called the doctor but he couldn't find anything seriously wrong.

STEVE: Perhaps it would be a better idea if I talked to her? I'm not quite so terrifying as my husband.

MRS WELDON: (*After a momentary hesitation*) Well, I see no objection to that, Mrs Temple. As long as you make it a fairly short visit. The poor girl really does seem to be under the weather.

FADE.

FADE IN the voice of JUNE JACKSON.

JUNE is about 17, and has a distinct but quite pleasant, American accent.

JUNE: I'm afraid that chair isn't very comfortable, Mrs Temple.

STEVE: I'm quite comfortable, thank you. I'm sorry you're not feeling very well, June.

JUNE: I'll be okay.

STEVE: Do you think you should be reading if you have a bad headache?

JUNE: I wasn't really reading – just kind of skipping, I guess.

STEVE looks at the book.

STEVE: "The Third and Fourth Generation" by Elliot France …

JUNE: It's one of Betty's books. Can't say I go for him myself.

STEVE: Betty's rather young to be reading Elliot France, isn't she?

JUNE: I doubt she understands half of it – I'm sure I don't. But she's crazy about him – as a person, I mean.

STEVE: Well, it makes a change from the Games Mistress.

JUNE: (*Laughing*) I guess you're right at that!

STEVE: You're fond of Betty, aren't you?

JUNE: We've shared a room for two years. Hardly had a row. I guess that's a record. Yes, I'm fond of her. She's a nice kid.

STEVE: Aren't you worried about what's happened to her?

JUNE: I don't mind telling you I'm very worried, Mrs Temple. At first I thought it was some kind of a joke.

31

STEVE: Why? Does she play jokes?

JUNE: Well, yes – sort of.

STEVE: But you believe her when she said she was going to tea with Elliot France?

JUNE: Of course I believed her. She was so thrilled about it. I told you, she really has a crush on him. You should have seen her face when she came running in here to say she'd actually been talking to him on the telephone and he'd asked her to tea.

STEVE: Mr France says he knows nothing about the telephone call.

JUNE: What do you mean?

STEVE: He says he didn't phone her.

JUNE: Well, somebody did. If it wasn't France then someone impersonated him.

STEVE: Yes …

JUNE: Do you think that's a possibility, Mrs Temple?

STEVE: Yes, I do. The man on the phone must have known she had a crush on France and that she'd be sure to turn up if he invited her out to tea. He could have intercepted her at a certain place, at a fixed time … Yes, I think it's a possibility, June. Have you met Mr France?

JUNE: Yes, we've all met him – all the girls – at some time or other.

STEVE: Would you say that he had encouraged Betty at all?

JUNE: No, I don't think so.

STEVE: Do you think she'd have told you if he had?

JUNE: Oh, sure – she'd have told me all right! She chattered about her boyfriends for hours.

STEVE: Was Betty happy at school? Can you think of any reason why she should run away?

JUNE: No, I guess she was one of the happiest girls here. Happier than she was at home, I'm sure of that. After all, they're not very strict here, you know – we get lots of freedom.

STEVE: Well, it's certainly a mystery, June.

JUNE: It sure is. I wish I could think of something, Mrs Temple. I've been lying here thinking and thinking – guess that's what's brought on this headache. But if there's anything I can do, Mrs Temple, you've only got to say the word.

STEVE: Yes, of course. Thank you, June. By the way, I suppose there haven't been any letters or messages for Betty since she disappeared?

JUNE: No – nothing. (*Casually*) Only a post card from a shop in Garmisch. It should be here somewhere … Oh, yes, there it is, behind that vase.

STEVE takes the card.

STEVE: Thank you.

JUNE: (*Casually*) What does it say, I forget?

STEVE: (*Reading*) "Dear Madam … Your coat – the blue coat – will be ready on Friday the 18th, at four o'clock…"

END OF EPISODE ONE

EPISODE TWO

CONCERNING
ELLIOT FRANCE

OPEN TO: *FADE IN the voice of STEVE.*

STEVE: By the way, I suppose there haven't been any letters or messages for Betty since she disappeared?

JUNE: No – nothing. (*Casually*) Only a post card from a shop in Garmisch. It should be here somewhere … Oh, yes, there it is, behind that vase.

STEVE takes the card.

STEVE: Thank you.

JUNE: (*Casually*) What does it say, I forget?

STEVE: (*Reading*) "Dear Madam … Your coat – the blue coat – will be ready on Friday the 18th, at four o'clock…"

JUNE: Oh yes, of course. I remember now. Betty was having a new coat made at Brenner's …

STEVE: Brenner's?

JUNE: Yes. It's the best dress shop in Garmisch.

STEVE: Is Betty a regular customer there?

JUNE: No, I don't think so. Countess Dekker recommended her – she was very thrilled. The Countess gets most of her clothes there.

STEVE: (*Surprised*) What – in Garmisch?

JUNE: Yes. You seem surprised, Mrs Temple.

STEVE: Well, I am rather. I thought Countess Dekker was an extremely wealthy woman.

JUNE: She is.

STEVE: Well, surely she'd buy her clothes in Paris, or Rome – or Munich, even.

JUNE: Well, I'm only repeating what Betty told me. But why are you interested in that card?

STEVE: My husband and I are trying to find out what's happened to Betty Conrad. Even the most ordinary object might be an important clue –

37

JUNE: Well, I've told you everything I know, Mrs Temple. I'm sorry not to have been more helpful.

STEVE: You've been very helpful, and I'm most grateful. Tell me – would you say that Betty was a serious sort of girl?

JUNE: Well, yes, I suppose I would. She was always reading T.S. Eliot – Bernard Shaw, that kind of thing.

STEVE: Yet she had a crush on Elliot France?

JUNE: Well, he's an attractive personality.

STEVE: Did Betty talk to you much about him?

JUNE: Well, yes, she did. She was a great admirer of his. She said he understood the problems of modern youth.

STEVE: What are the problems of modern youth?

JUNE: (*With a laugh*) Don't ask me, Mrs Temple – I guess they're the same as they've always been.

STEVE: Did Betty see a great deal of Mr France?

JUNE: No, I don't think so – although, come to think of it, she saw quite a lot of Countess Dekker. She went over to Schreidenstein several times this term.

STEVE: I see … June, tell me, was Betty very attached to her parents?

JUNE: How do you mean?

STEVE: Did she write home frequently?

JUNE: I wouldn't know about that.

STEVE: Why? You shared the same room – you must have talked a great deal. Betty must have mentioned her parents to you.

JUNE: (*Hesitantly*) Well – I suppose I shouldn't say this – but Betty didn't get on too well with her stepmother and even her father …

STEVE: Yes?

JUNE: I don't think he had a lot of time for Betty. He's a pretty busy man.

STEVE: Well, at the moment he's a pretty worried man. I can tell you that.

JUNE: Because of what's happened to Betty?

STEVE: Yes.

JUNE: What's he like, Mrs Temple?

STEVE: Dr Conrad?

JUNE: Yes.

STEVE: We haven't met – not yet.

JUNE: When you do meet him you won't let on that I …

STEVE: No, everything you've told me is in confidence, and I'm very grateful to you, June.

JUNE: That's okay, and if there's anything I can do to help you, Mrs Temple …

STEVE: I'll remember that. Now I'll take this card, if you don't mind. If Betty turns up I'll let her know about the coat.

JUNE: Sure – a phone call will fix that.

STEVE: Goodbye, June! I hope your headache will soon be better.

JUNE: It's practically gone now, Mrs Temple. Goodbye …

FADE.

FADE UP background noises of a small hotel orchestra and dining-room atmosphere.

STEVE: I must say the food's very good here.

TEMPLE: Yes – it's a very good hotel altogether. It's a pity we're not here on holiday.

A slight pause.

STEVE: Yes. Well – did you get anything else out of Mrs Weldon?

TEMPLE: Nothing that seemed important. She's still anxious to keep this matter out of the papers. But I warned her there's bound to be publicity sooner or later.

STEVE: Yes.

TEMPLE: I wish Breckshaft would turn up. There are several things I want to discuss with him.

STEVE: You think he might know something about Brenner's?

TEMPLE: Brenner's? Oh – the dress shop. Yes, it's possible, I suppose.

STEVE: You know those two post cards – the one we found in Oxted addressed to Mrs Conrad – and now this one addressed to Betty Conrad, aren't just a coincidence, Paul.

TEMPLE: Yes, I agree. You said June Jackson knew that Betty had ordered a coat from Brenner's?

STEVE: No, she didn't exactly say she knew about the coat. She said she knew Betty had been to Brenner's and had been recommended to go there by Countess Dekker.

TEMPLE: I see.

STEVE: You know, Paul, I think we made a mistake in coming to Bavaria without …

TEMPLE: Well, by Timothy, I like that! It was entirely your idea that we came to Bavaria!

STEVE: Let me finish, darling! I was going to say we made a mistake in coming here without first seeing Dr Conrad.

TEMPLE: Why do you say that?

STEVE: June seemed to think that things weren't too happy with the Conrads.

40

TEMPLE:	Sir Graham saw Dr Conrad – on more than one occasion – he seemed to be perfectly satisfied.
STEVE:	Yes, I know. But if Betty had an unhappy home life …
TEMPLE:	Did Betty tell June that her home life was unhappy?
STEVE:	Not in so many words, but –
WAITER:	Excuse me, sir. Herr Breckshaft wishes to speak to you. He's waiting in the lounge. He says he'll remain there until you have finished dinner.
TEMPLE:	Thank you, waiter. We'll take our coffee in the lounge then … Coffee for three.
WAITER:	Yes, Mr Temple …

FADE.

FADE UP background noises of the hotel lounge.

BRECKSHAFT:	Ah, good evening, Mrs Temple – Mr Temple. I'm so glad I found you in.
TEMPLE:	I've ordered some coffee, Breckshaft. Or perhaps you would prefer something else?
BRECKSHAFT:	No – no, coffee will be most acceptable, thank you.
STEVE:	We rather wondered what had happened to you, Herr Breckshaft?
BRECKSHAFT:	I've been so busy since I got back, Mrs Temple. My work fell behind when I was in England.
TEMPLE:	Are there any new developments in the Conrad case?
BRECKSHAFT:	Not so far as I'm concerned. I was going to ask you the same question.

TEMPLE: No, there's nothing of any real importance,
                   I'm afraid. We've been to the school and
                   talked to several people, of course, but
                   things are still very much in the air. By the
                   way, I think it might be a good idea if my
                   wife and I went to that inn you were telling
                   us about where you found the cocktail
                   sticks.

BRECKSHAFT: Yes, I agree. It's at Oberammergau – the
                   Hotel Reumer. It's just outside the village
                   on the road to Garmisch. It's very easy to
                   find.

STEVE: Herr Breckshaft, do you know a dress shop
                   in Garmisch called Brenner's?

BRECKSHAFT: Why, certainly. They have several branches
                   in Bavaria – a very reputable firm. But why
                   are you interested in Brenner's, Mrs
                   Temple?

TEMPLE: My wife found this post card in Betty
                   Conrad's room at the school …

STEVE: I didn't find it, darling. June Jackson gave
                   it to me.

BRECKSHAFT: (*After a moment; reading from the card*) "A
                   blue coat … Friday, the 18th …"

TEMPLE: You remember the card we found at Oxted,
                   addressed to Mrs Conrad.

BRECKSHAFT: I do, I do indeed, Mr Temple. That too
                   referred to a blue coat and Friday the 18th
                   … It's a curious coincidence.

TEMPLE: Is it a coincidence?

BRECKSHAFT: The other card had no name and no address
                   on it – if I remember rightly.

STEVE: And it was addressed to Mrs Conrad.

BRECKSHAFT: Yes … (*After a moment*) I saw Mrs Conrad
when I was in London. She seems a strange
woman …

TEMPLE: Strange? In what way?

BRECKSHAFT: Well – she's – what do you say in English?
Cold? Cold and rather distant, if you know
what I mean. She didn't appear unduly
perturbed by the disappearance of her
stepdaughter.

STEVE: Perhaps she wasn't perturbed, Herr
Breckshaft.

BRECKSHAFT: (*Thoughtfully*) No – no, perhaps she wasn't,
Mrs Temple. (*Suddenly, almost changing
the subject*) But tell me, what do you think
of Mrs Weldon?

TEMPLE: Well, she was obviously upset when we
saw her. I like her – she seems a nice
person. Very intelligent. Although she
could be pretty strict, I imagine, if she
wanted to be.

BRECKSHAFT: Yes, she can be strict all right – but the girls
like her. Most of them seem to be very
happy at Weldon's.

STEVE: I can imagine it. It's such a lovely place –

BRECKSHAFT: Yes. You know, Mr Temple, I doubt if I
shall be able to keep this case from the
newspapers very much longer.

TEMPLE: Yes, I agree.

BRECKSHAFT: Naturally, Mrs Weldon is anxious for the
reputation of her school, but there are many
other considerations … Who knows?
Perhaps some publicity would be useful to
us in this affair …

TEMPLE: Yes, perhaps it might be.

WAITER: (*Approaching*) Coffee, madame …

STEVE: Thank you, waiter.

TEMPLE: (*Pleasantly; aside*) Would you care for a cigar, Herr Breckshaft? I've got one here …

FADE.

FADE IN the sound of a clock chiming the hour.
It is two o'clock.
A pause.

TEMPLE: Steve, are you awake?

STEVE: Yes, darling. I can't get to sleep. I don't know why, I'm sure. It's a very comfortable bed.

TEMPLE: I suppose you were thinking about Betty Conrad.

STEVE: Yes, I was as a matter of fact. Paul, in the dim and distant past, when I was in Fleet Street, it was part of my job to visit the local police stations. I'm pretty sure that if a schoolgirl had mysteriously disappeared they'd have given me the story. Don't the police work that way over here?

TEMPLE: Yes, I should imagine so.

STEVE: Then why hasn't some reporter got hold of this story?

TEMPLE: Simply because Mrs Weldon went straight to the top and asked for it to be kept out of the newspapers.

STEVE: I suppose if Betty Conrad had been a local girl it would have been in the headlines days ago.

TEMPLE: Yes – and I'm not sure it wouldn't have been a very good thing.

STEVE: You know, Paul – I just can't weigh up Breckshaft.

TEMPLE: What do you mean?

STEVE: Oh, I don't know – there's something about him.

TEMPLE: He's a very worried man, darling. After all, it should be a comparatively easy matter for him to find an English girl in Bavaria. That's probably why he agreed with Mrs Weldon that the matter shouldn't be publicised. He thought that somebody would be bound to report to the local police the appearance of an English girl.

STEVE: Yes, well it hasn't worked out that way.

TEMPLE: It certainly hasn't. (*A moment*) Steve, will you do something for me tomorrow?

STEVE: (*Yawning*) What?

TEMPLE: I want you to go to that dress shop – Brenner's.

STEVE: Delighted, Mr Temple! And what do I buy myself when I get there?

TEMPLE: You don't buy yourself anything, darling. (*With a little laugh*) No, seriously, this is what I want you to do. I want you to tell everyone in the shop about the Conrad case. I want you to give the impression …

COMPLETE FADE.

FADE UP background noises of a busy dress shop.

GERDA: (*An attractive girl in her late twenties*) Can I show you something, madame?

STEVE: (*With an affected, faintly scatter-brained manner*) Oh! Oh, yes, of course! How did you know I was English?

GERDA: I can always tell, madame. I worked in Bond Street for two or three years. Is there anything I can show you?

STEVE: Oh, really – in Bond Street? Well, how extraordinary! It's a small world, isn't it?

GERDA: (*Faintly puzzled by STEVE*) Yes, madame.

45

STEVE: How long have you been here – at Brenner's – in Garmisch?

GERDA: For three years I was at our Munich shop. I came here last year. What can I show you, madame?

STEVE: Those lace blouses … I think they're most intriguing – but frightfully expensive, I suppose?

GERDA: Not so expensive, madame. Just under – now let me see – just under twelve pounds …

STEVE: Oh, really! Just under twelve pounds – quite reasonable. I admire the colours … I don't know which would suit me best … I think perhaps the beige, or the pale chiffon – I'm not really sure.

MADAME KLEIN arrives on the scene.

She is about forty and has hardly any trace of an accent.

KLEIN: Perhaps I can help, madame?

STEVE: (*Turning, apparently surprised*) Oh! Oh, thank you …

KLEIN: (*Dismissing GERDA*) All right, Gerda.

GERDA: Yes, Madame Klein.

KLEIN: Now, madame – the grey one would be a perfect match for the skirt you're wearing. If you intend to wear it with that skirt, of course.

STEVE: Well, actually I thought … Yes, it is nice, isn't it? … Do you know, I believe you're quite right …

KLEIN: Perhaps you'd like to try it on?

STEVE: No, I don't really think that's necessary, do you? …

KLEIN: I'm sure it would fit you, madame.

STEVE: Yes … It's a lovely colour …

KLEIN: Shall I send it, madame – or would you like to take it with you?

STEVE: Well – I haven't quite made up my mind yet, I thought perhaps … (*Suddenly*) I'll take it. No, on second thoughts … No, I'll take it with me.

KLEIN: Very good, madame.

STEVE: (*Changing her mind*) No, I won't! You can send it to the hotel. My husband and I are staying at the Partenkirchen.

KLEIN: At the Partenkirchen. And the name?

STEVE: Mrs Paul Temple …

KLEIN: (*A moment*) Mrs Paul Temple?

STEVE: Yes …

KLEIN: Are you on holiday in Garmisch, Mrs Temple?

STEVE: Well – not exactly a holiday. My husband's investigating the disappearance of that schoolgirl – you know, the English girl who disappeared from Mrs Weldon's.

KLEIN: (*Apparently puzzled*) Girl who disappeared?

STEVE: Oh, haven't you heard?

KLEIN: No.

STEVE: I thought everyone in Garmisch knew about it. Goodness knows Paul – my husband – has talked to dozens of people since we got here. In fact he's never stopped talking. Not a bit like me, you know. I'm the quiet one. Oh, and that reminds me – someone told me that the missing girl – Betty Conrad – was a customer of yours.

KLEIN: Betty Conrad?

STEVE: Yes, I believe she ordered a coat from you – a blue coat.

KLEIN: Betty Conrad? I'm afraid I don't recall the name, Mrs Temple.

STEVE: Her father's a doctor – or psychiatrist – or chiropractor, or something like that.

KLEIN: Here in Garmisch, Mrs Temple?

47

STEVE: No, no, no, of course not. I told you, she's
            English. He practises in Harley Street.

KLEIN: I don't recall the name, Mrs Temple. But wait a
            moment, I'll look in my day book …

STEVE: (*Almost to herself, babbling away*) Thank you so
            much. Of course the girl must be somewhere –
            she can't have completely disappeared. It's my
            opinion … (*Watching MADAME KLEIN*) Have
            you found something?

KLEIN: (*Slowly, looking at the book*) Yes, I have. You're
            quite right, Mrs Temple. We have a customer
            called Betty Conrad … She was recommended
            by Countess Dekker. Ah! Now I remember the
            girl – very pretty – English. Of course I
            remember.

STEVE: I thought you would. And she ordered a coat
            from you.

KLEIN: Yes, she did. A blue coat. It's quite ready; or
            rather it will be by Friday. We've sent her a card
            to that effect. But you say this girl has
            disappeared, Mrs Temple?

STEVE: Yes. Completely. That's why my husband is
            here – in Garmisch. He's helping the police –
            unofficially, of course. A man called Breckshaft
            consulted Scotland Yard and they decided …
            (*Suddenly*) Oh, dear! Perhaps I shouldn't have
            told you that …

KLEIN: That's all right, Mrs Temple.

GERDA: The parcel for madame …

KLEIN: Mrs Temple wishes it to be sent to the
            Partenkirchen …

STEVE: No. No – now it's ready I'll take it with me. It's
            only a small parcel.

STEVE takes the parcel.

48

STEVE: Thank you.

GERDA: Thank you, madame.

KLEIN: Goodbye. (*A little cough*) Madame, the blouse was a hundred and fifty Deutschmarks.

STEVE: (*Stopping in her tracks*) Oh! Oh, yes of course! How stupid of me! How very stupid …

FADE.

FADE UP background noises of a fairly busy street.
FADE UP the sound of a car approaching.
The car draws to a standstill.

TEMPLE: (*Calling from the car*) Steve! Hi! Steve!

STEVE: (*Approaching*) Oh, there you are, Paul!

The car door opens and STEVE gets into the car.

STEVE: I'll just put this on the back seat …

The car drives away during the following dialogue.

TEMPLE: Well – how did you get on?

STEVE: Well, apart from giving the performance of my life as a complete nit-wit – I bought a very nice blouse.

TEMPLE: (*Laughing*) Never mind the blouse. What happened? Who did you see?

STEVE: There was a young salesgirl named Gerda who's apparently worked in Bond Street and spoke passable English. Then there was the manageress, or chief saleswoman – a Madame Klein …

TEMPLE: German?

STEVE: Yes. Extremely competent. Hardly a trace of an accent.

TEMPLE: How did she react to the information you gave her?

STEVE: Absolutely poker face. But her eyes rather gave her away, I'm afraid.

TEMPLE:	She knew Betty Conrad?
STEVE:	At first she said she didn't know her, then she made a great show of looking her name up in some accounts book. Then she said she remembered the girl – and that she was expecting her in on Friday.
TEMPLE:	Well, that seems all right – that seems to tie up.
STEVE:	Yes, I know, but …
TEMPLE:	I gather you didn't take to Madame Klein?
STEVE:	No, I didn't. Anyway, I did what you wanted, Paul.
TEMPLE:	You don't think she suspected anything?
STEVE:	I don't know. Perhaps I overdid it – it's awfully difficult to tell when you're putting on an act.
TEMPLE:	Well, it doesn't matter much either way, really.
STEVE:	Except that if she didn't see through me then she underestimates the opposition, which is always useful.
TEMPLE:	Yes, that's true. Well, we shall see …
STEVE:	Paul, where are we going? This isn't the road to Oberammergau.
TEMPLE:	Good Lord, I almost forgot! Elliot France telephoned me soon after you left. He wants to see me. That's where we're going, darling – to Schreidenstein – Countess Dekker's place.
STEVE:	What was Mr France like?
TEMPLE:	Oh, smooth … sympathetic … apparently concerned about Betty Conrad. Much as I expected.
STEVE:	You don't sound very enthusiastic.
TEMPLE:	I'm reserving judgement on Mr France until we've met.

A pause.

STEVE:	This isn't a very good road, is it?

TEMPLE: No, it isn't … it's surprisingly bad for Bavaria.

STEVE: It's not very wide, either …

We hear the sound of a car approaching from behind, followed by the noise of a horn.

TEMPLE: Hello! Somebody's in a hurry …

STEVE: (*Turning*) It's a sports car – an enormous thing …

The sound of the horn from the background is heard again.

TEMPLE: Yes – I can see it in the mirror. It's one of those fuel injection jobs … A hundred and fifty miles an hour.

STEVE: Ye gods!

The car horn sounds again.

STEVE: He's trying to pass you …

TEMPLE: The fool – he can't pass now, there's a railway arch ahead …

STEVE: (*Alarmed*) Pull over, Paul!

TEMPLE: There's no room, I can't possibly … By Timothy, what's he trying to do?

STEVE: Paul!

TEMPLE applies the brakes and there is a crash as TEMPLE's car skids into a ditch.

The sports car roars away into the distance.

TEMPLE: (*Slightly winded*) Steve, are you all right?

STEVE: Yes, I'm a bit shaken, that's all …

TEMPLE: Another ten yards and we'd have been into that wall … Come on, I think we can get out this side.

STEVE: Why didn't he stop? He could easily have stopped because … (*A sudden thought*) Paul, you don't think …

TEMPLE: I don't know, Steve. Did you get a look at the driver?

STEVE: He was wearing a white crash helmet and sun glasses. But how could it have been planned,

51

	Paul? I mean, who knew we were going to be here this morning?
TEMPLE:	Elliot France, for one.
STEVE:	But surely you don't think ...
TEMPLE:	I don't think anything at the moment. We mustn't jump to conclusions. Our telephone conversation might have been overheard, for instance – or Elliot France might have mentioned it to someone – or our car could have been followed ... I say, darling, you look rather pale – are you sure you're all right?
STEVE:	Yes, I'm just a bit shaken, that's all. What about the car, Paul?
TEMPLE:	I think it'll probably be all right – unless something's got jammed. Thank goodness it's an open car – we can get out. Give me your hand. That's it!

TEMPLE and STEVE get out of the car.

TEMPLE:	The question is, how do we get the car out of the ditch?
STEVE:	We'll never do it without some help.
TEMPLE:	I wonder if there's a telephone box around here.

We hear the sound of an approaching car in the background.

| STEVE: | Paul, there's a car coming! |
| TEMPLE: | (*Quickly*) Wait here, darling. I'll try and stop him! |

The car quickly approaches and slows down.

| STEVE: | I hope you can make him understand, darling. |
| TEMPLE: | He'll understand all right, when he sees the car. |

The car draws to a standstill.

| TEMPLE: | (*In halting German*) Goedemorgen, het spijt me dat ik u stoor, maar... |
| HARPER: | (*A pleasant Englishman in his early thirties*) Good afternoon, Mr Temple. |

TEMPLE: You're English!

HARPER: That's right – my name's Denis Harper. I expect you're Mrs Temple?

STEVE: Yes, but –

TEMPLE: But how did you recognise us?

HARPER: I've just been reading a German edition of The Tyler Mystery, Mr Temple. There's a large photograph of you on the back of the jacket.

TEMPLE: (*A little taken aback*) Well, you certainly have a good memory, Mr Harper.

HARPER: And actually I knew you were in Garmisch.

TEMPLE: Do you happen to remember seeing a cream sports car driven by a man in a crash helmet?

HARPER: Why no! I haven't seen anyone in the last two or three minutes. Of course, the road forks about half a mile from here.

TEMPLE: (*Quietly*) No doubt that explains it.

HARPER: What's happened? Have you had an accident?

STEVE: Yes – the sports car forced us into the ditch, although I don't think that was his intention.

HARPER: What do you mean, Mrs Temple?

TEMPLE: He intended to force us into the railway arch.

HARPER: Good Lord! I say, who was this customer? They're usually pretty good drivers over here, you know.

TEMPLE: We don't know who it was. We only just caught a glimpse of him. However, there's no great damage done if we can get the car out of the ditch.

HARPER: Oh, we'll soon fix that. I've got a rope in the boot of my car.

TEMPLE: Oh, good!

HARPER:　Just hold on and I'll fetch it … I say, Mrs Temple – are you all right? You look pretty shaken to me …

STEVE:　(*Obviously not feeling too well*) I'm all right, Mr Harper, thank you.

TEMPLE:　(*Aside to STEVE*) I should sit down, darling. This is going to take some time …

STEVE:　Yes, I'll be glad to.

FADE.

FADE IN the noise of HARPER's car pulling TEMPLE's car out of the ditch.

There is the constant sound of an engine revving, etc.

HARPER:　(*Over the noise of his car*) All right! Let her come!

TEMPLE:　(*From his car, in the background*) Steady now, or you'll snap the rope …

HARPER:　She's coming! Keep her straight …

TEMPLE:　Easy now …

HARPER:　Here she comes … Steady now! Steady …

TEMPLE:　That's all right! All clear, Harper …

HARPER:　Jolly good show!

HARPER switches off his car engine.

STEVE:　The wheels still go round, anyway, darling!

HARPER gets out of his car.

HARPER:　I'm afraid that front mudguard is pretty badly bent. There's a dent in the radiator, too. Doesn't seem to be leaking, though.

TEMPLE:　(*Approaching*) We're really most grateful to you, Harper.

HARPER:　Not at all. Only too glad to help. As a matter of fact I was coming to see you anyway, after I'd finished my business in Garmisch.

TEMPLE:　You were?

HARPER: Yes, I wanted to talk to you about Betty Conrad.

TEMPLE: Betty Conrad?

STEVE: Why, of course! You're the young man that she was friendly with – the young man who works in the bank in Munich.

HARPER: Yes, that's right – the Anglo-Continental Bank. I'm on my way to our branch in Garmisch to check some securities and I thought it would be a good idea if I …

TEMPLE: (*Interrupting HARPER*) But how did you know I was at Garmisch?

HARPER: Well, I've been questioned quite a lot by the Munich police since I got back from my holidays. During one of the sessions Herr Breckshaft came in and spoke to the officer who was questioning me. I gathered that he'd just come back from England and brought you with him, Mr Temple.

TEMPLE: I see.

STEVE: Were you a great friend of Betty Conrad's, Mr Harper?

HARPER: (*Hesitantly*) Well, I don't know exactly whether you'd call us great friends, exactly.

TEMPLE: Where did you meet?

HARPER: At the Queen's Club Ice Rink about six months ago. That was before I was posted to Munich, of course.

TEMPLE: Do you like working in Germany?

HARPER: Oh, rather! Wouldn't go back for anything! I don't mind telling you I had to pull a few strings to get here in the first place. But it was jolly well worth it. Wouldn't go back for all the tea in China …

STEVE: But what about this Conrad case, Mr Harper?

55

HARPER: (*Nervously*) Well – what about it?

STEVE: Hasn't it worried you at all?

HARPER: Well, I haven't exactly liked all these
             confounded questions the police have been
             asking me, if that's what you mean, Mrs
             Temple?

STEVE: No. I meant aren't you worried at all at the
             thought that Betty's completely disappeared?

HARPER: (*A shade uncomfortable*) Well, yes and no. You
             see I haven't seen Betty for two or three weeks
             – since just before I went on my holiday – so I
             really haven't a clue as to why she should have
             completely vanished like this.

STEVE: I see.

HARPER: Of course, it's going to be jolly awkward if she
             doesn't show up. If she's involved in any sort of
             crime and I'm associated with her, however
             innocently – well, you know how banks are
             about these things.

TEMPLE: (*With a note of sarcasm*) I'm afraid our
             knowledge of banks is confined to the
             customers' side of the counter.

HARPER: Yes. Well, banks are still pretty old fashioned,
             you know. They don't like their staff being
             questioned by the police.

TEMPLE: Yes, well I'm afraid in a case of this kind the
             police have very little alternative. But tell me,
             you said you wanted to see me – that you
             intended to visit me in Garmisch? Why?

HARPER: Yes. I was going to ask you to speak to this
             Breckshaft person and assure him I know
             nothing at all about this business. Naturally I
             don't want to be mixed up in anything, and

56

anyhow I'm sure Betty's all right – I'm sure there's a perfectly simple explanation of all this.

STEVE: How often did you see Betty, Mr Harper – once or twice a week?

HARPER: Good heavens, no! Once a month at the outside.

STEVE: Where did you take her – restaurants – cinemas?

HARPER: Well – yes …

TEMPLE: Did you ever go to the Hotel Reumer at Oberammergau?

HARPER: No. We only went to Oberammergau once, that was many months ago. We didn't stay long because the village was crowded. Betty wasn't supposed to go there, you know. It was out of bounds.

TEMPLE: Yes, I know. Harper – tell me – did Mrs Weldon ever question you about … Steve, are you all right?

HARPER: Mrs Temple!

STEVE: I feel a little faint, I think …

TEMPLE: (*Taking hold of STEVE's arm*) It's all right, darling … I've got you …

HARPER: It's delayed shock, I should imagine …

TEMPLE: Yes.

STEVE: (*Weakly*) It's all right, Paul, there's nothing to worry about …

TEMPLE: Steve, I think you should go back to the hotel and lie down for a little while. There's no point in coming with me, darling.

HARPER: Why not come back to Garmisch with me, Mrs Temple? I can drop you at your hotel. (*To TEMPLE*) Which one is it, sir – the Partenkirchen?

TEMPLE: Yes. I should do that, darling, if I were you …

STEVE: (*Quietly*) Yes, all right, Paul …

HARPER opens the door of his car.

TEMPLE: Don't forget your parcel, darling – here you are
         …

STEVE: Thank you.

TEMPLE: I'd better see if my car will start, first, Harper …

TEMPLE presses the self-starter and the engine starts immediately.

TEMPLE: Good … Now are you sure you'll be all right, Steve?

HARPER: I'll take good care of her, sir.

TEMPLE: Perhaps you'll dine with us this evening, Harper?

HARPER: I'd like to, but it may be a little difficult …

TEMPLE: Well, drop in to the hotel for a drink – any time during the evening.

HARPER: That's very kind of you. I'll phone you later, if I may.

TEMPLE: Yes, of course.

HARPER: Now we'll just wait and see you get away, Mr Temple – then we'll be moving.

TEMPLE: Yes – all right.

TEMPLE changes gear and the car moves away.

TEMPLE: (*Calling to STEVE*) I shan't be long, darling. See you at the hotel …

STEVE: Yes, all right, Paul … Don't worry, dear. I feel much better now.

HARPER: (*As TEMPLE's car disappears*) Now we'll be off, Mrs Temple. Let me take your parcel.

FADE IN incidental music.

FADE music.

FADE IN the voice of ELLIOT FRANCE.

FRANCE: But why should anyone wish to impersonate me, Mr Temple?

TEMPLE: I have no idea, Mr France, but the gentleman in question certainly paid for his impersonation.

FRANCE: He certainly did if, as you say, he was murdered.

TEMPLE: He was murdered all right.

FRANCE: But who was this man who impersonated me?

TEMPLE: We don't know. Not yet.

FRANCE: Do you think the murderer was under the impression that it was actually me whom he'd murdered?

TEMPLE: No … somehow I don't think so.

FRANCE: We all of us feel like murdering somebody at some time or other. Perhaps someone felt that way about me. Still, I find this considerably less disturbing than these continual visits from the police. If I've told them once I've told them twenty times that I didn't invite this girl to tea.

TEMPLE: Yes, but you can't blame the police. They've established that she was seen getting off the bus at the entrance to this estate, and her friend – June Jackson – says that Betty told her that you did invite her to tea.

FRANCE: (*Irritated*) Why on earth should I invite a schoolgirl to have tea with me? Good heavens, Temple, you must realise …

TEMPLE: Betty Conrad wasn't exactly a schoolgirl. Mrs Weldon's isn't a conventional school. It's a finishing school, and Betty was eighteen and very attractive.

FRANCE: <u>Was</u> eighteen? Why do you use the past tense?

TEMPLE: I didn't mean it that way, I merely … Mr France, I'm a little puzzled by all this.

FRANCE: So am I! Puzzled is putting it lightly.

TEMPLE: Yes, but you haven't told me why you wanted to see me. If you've told the police everything you know, then why should you send for me?

FRANCE: There's something I haven't told the police. (*Pause*) Perhaps it isn't important, but …

FRANCE is interrupted by the opening of a door.

ELSA: (*An attractive woman in her forties, with the suggestion of an accent*) Oh, I beg your pardon, Elliot, I didn't know you had someone with you.

FRANCE: That's all right, Elsa! Come in, my dear! Mr Temple, may I introduce Countess Dekker? I expect you've heard of Mr Temple, Elsa.

ELSA: Yes, indeed. I heard that you were in Garmisch, Mr Temple. Are you going to solve all our problems for us?

TEMPLE: I shall do my best.

ELSA: I can't understand why an Englishman is expected to find this girl when the entire Bavarian police force have failed.

TEMPLE: The missing girl does happen to be English, and I know something of her background. And I am working in co-operation with the Munich police, it was at their invitation that I came here.

ELSA: Yes, of course, I realise that. Forgive me if I sounded a little – a little abrupt. This business is so irritating. So many questions are being asked. So many unnecessary questions. It's perfectly obvious what's happened. The girl got tired of the school and just decided to – disappear.

TEMPLE: Yes, but where did she disappear to, Countess?

ELSA: That's for you to find out, Mr Temple. (*To FRANCE*) Elliot, I thought we'd have tea on the lawn, since it's such a lovely afternoon …

FRANCE: Yes, of course, Elsa.

ELSA: You'll join us, of course, Mr Temple?

TEMPLE: Thank you. Mr France, there's just one question
            I'd like to ask – forgive me if it sounds a little
            impertinent.

FRANCE: If it's about Betty Conrad – go ahead. The
            chances are I've already been asked the question
            a thousand times already.

TEMPLE: Would you say that Betty was infatuated with
            you?

FRANCE: Good heavens, no! I've told you I only saw the
            girl …

ELSA: Of course she was infatuated with you, Elliot.
            All the girls at Weldon's are.

FRANCE: Oh, that's absurd. Why should they be infatuated
            with a middle-aged novelist?

ELSA: Because you are good-looking and you write the
            sort of books those schoolgirls shouldn't read.

TEMPLE: (*Laughing*) Thank you, Countess, you've
            answered my question.

ELSA: Now, shall we have tea – or are there any more
            questions, Mr Temple?

TEMPLE: Just one. Did you recommend Brenner's to Betty
            Conrad?

ELSA: Brenner's?

TEMPLE: The dress shop, in Garmisch.

ELSA: Why, no – I don't think so. Why do you ask?

TEMPLE: I wondered, that's all.

FRANCE: (*Slowly, watching TEMPLE*) Let's have tea,
            Elsa.

FADE IN incidental music.

FADE music.
FADE UP footsteps on a gravel path.
There is a background of outdoor noises.

61

FRANCE: I hope you haven't got the wrong impression of Elsa, Mr Temple. She's not usually a difficult person.

TEMPLE: I didn't think she was difficult this afternoon. A little worried, perhaps, but under the circumstances, that's only natural.

FRANCE: Yes – this Conrad business has worried her quite a bit, you know. More than she admits. You see she's friendly with quite a lot of the Weldon girls.

TEMPLE: What do you mean – friendly?

FRANCE: Well, they come to tea, and listen to Elsa laying the law down about clothes and politics, and the cost of living, and that sort of thing. She's a bit of a demigod in a way, you know. What the Americans call a line-shooter.

TEMPLE: How long have you known her?

FRANCE: Elsa? Oh donkeys' years. We're very old friends. (*Suddenly*) I say, is this your car?

TEMPLE: Yes.

FRANCE: My word, you did have a smash-up, didn't you?

TEMPLE: Yes. I told you about it. Don't you remember, I …

FRANCE: Yes – yes, I know. I was just looking at the car. Is Mrs Temple all right?

TEMPLE: She was rather badly shaken. That's why she went back to the hotel.

FRANCE: Yes, I can well believe it.

TEMPLE: Mr France, before we had tea – before we were interrupted – you said there was something you wanted to tell me.

FRANCE: Yes …

A pause.

TEMPLE: Well? What was it?

62

FRANCE: (*Hesitantly*) Once, a long time ago, I met Betty Conrad's father.

TEMPLE: Where?

FRANCE: In Harley Street …

TEMPLE: You mean – you consulted him?

FRANCE: Yes. He's a psychiatrist, you know.

TEMPLE: Yes, I know that.

A moment.

TEMPLE: Go on.

FRANCE: Well – I just wanted to ask you … (*He hesitates, then:*) Are these professional men – men like Mr Conrad – are they bound by an oath of secrecy?

TEMPLE: An oath of secrecy – what do you mean?

FRANCE: Well, I mean – would Dr Conrad discuss his patients with anyone, for instance?

TEMPLE: I very much doubt it.

FRANCE: Not even with the police?

TEMPLE: I think that would rather depend on the circumstances.

FRANCE: And the patient?

TEMPLE: Yes – and the patient.

FRANCE: (*Almost dismissing TEMPLE*) Well, thank you, Mr Temple. It's been very nice meeting you. I hope I shall have the pleasure again.

TEMPLE: Mr France, why did you consult Dr Conrad?

FRANCE: (*Apparently casual*) I was very ill at the time. Very ill.

FADE IN incidental music.

FADE music.

FADE IN background noises of a hotel foyer.

RECEPTIONIST: Good afternoon, Mr Temple.

TEMPLE: Good afternoon. May I have my key, please?

RECEPTIONIST: Mrs Temple's upstairs, sir – she went up about half an hour ago.

TEMPLE: Oh, thank you.

RECEPTIONIST: This note came for you by messenger, Mr Temple.

TEMPLE: Oh, thank you.

A moment whilst TEMPLE reads the note.

TEMPLE: When did this arrive?

RECEPTIONIST: Just after lunch, sir.

TEMPLE: I see. Well, in future, it's perfectly all right to give my wife any letters that are addressed to me.

RECEPTIONIST: Very good, Mr Temple. Thank you, sir.

FADE.

FADE UP the opening of a door.

STEVE: (*Quickly*) Who's that?

TEMPLE: It's all right, darling – it's only me!

STEVE: Oh, hello, Paul.

TEMPLE: How are you, Steve? Are you feeling any better?

STEVE: Yes, I feel fine. Denis Harper brought me back to the hotel and I had a rest for an hour or so. I felt so much better when I woke up I decided to go out and have some tea.

TEMPLE: Did you find out something about Mr Harper?

STEVE: (*Innocently*) What do you mean?

TEMPLE: Darling, I know you were pretty badly shaken – but you weren't that bad! (*Laughing*) You don't think you took me in with that corny fainting act!

STEVE: Well, I had a hunch about Denis Harper. I wanted to find out whether …

TEMPLE: I know – that good old intuition!

STEVE: You can laugh – but it's paid off, anyway.

TEMPLE: What do you mean?

STEVE: Well, after I'd had a sleep, I decided to go out to tea. I found a wonderful little café with an unpronounceable name, just off the main street. It was bristling with period bits and pieces, and the most wonderful pastries you've ever seen.

TEMPLE: I thought you were supposed to be on a diet, darling?

STEVE: I just got myself nicely settled in a corner with two of the largest meringues you've ever seen, when in walked Denis Harper.

TEMPLE: Well, what's extraordinary about that – if it was tea time?

STEVE: Mr Harper wasn't alone, darling.

TEMPLE: Oh?

STEVE: You remember that woman I told you about – at Brenner's, the dress shop?

TEMPLE: Madame Klein?

STEVE: Yes. Well, Mr Harper and Madame Klein had tea together – and it wasn't the first time they've had tea together, either, if you ask me.

TEMPLE: Oh … This interests me, Steve.

STEVE: Yes. I thought it would. Now what happened to you this afternoon – how did you get on at Countess "What's-her-name's?"

TEMPLE: Oh, very well. Elliot France is more or less what I expected.

STEVE: And the Countess?

TEMPLE: A strange mixture of Teutonic sophistication.

STEVE: And what about the estate – Schreidenstein?

TEMPLE: Oh, a wonderful place. It would gladden the heart of any National Trust.

STEVE: Did they tell you anything new about Betty Conrad?

TEMPLE: Nothing very much, I'm afraid. But there's one interesting point, Steve. Apparently France was once a patient of Dr Conrad's.

STEVE: He was?

TEMPLE: Yes.

STEVE: Did France tell you that himself?

TEMPLE: Yes. Incidentally, I've had a note from Dr Conrad – he's in Garmisch. He's calling round to see me this evening.

STEVE: Is he?

TEMPLE: Now what do you mean – "is he?" You sound very mysterious.

STEVE: Paul, what does Dr Conrad look like?

TEMPLE: Well, I've never actually seen him, but judging from his photographs he's a dapper little man with a grey beard …

STEVE: … And glasses – rimless glasses?

TEMPLE: Yes, I think so.

STEVE: He was in the café.

TEMPLE: With Harper?

STEVE: No, he was at the cash desk just as I walked in. I must have seen the photograph of him myself, somewhere, because I recognised him without actually knowing who it was.

TEMPLE: Was anyone with him?

STEVE: No, he appeared to be on his own.

The telephone rings and TEMPLE lifts the receiver.

TEMPLE: (*On the phone*) Hello?

RECEPTIONIST: (*On the other end of the phone*) Herr Temple?

TEMPLE: Yes.

RECEPTIONIST: Reception Desk here, sir. A Dr Conrad is asking for you …

TEMPLE: Thank you. I'll be right down.

TEMPLE replaces the receiver.

STEVE: Who is it, darling?

TEMPLE: It's Conrad. I shan't be long, darling.

STEVE: Yes, all right, Paul. Will you take the key? I shall probably have a bath …

FADE.

FADE IN the voice of DR CONRAD.

CONRAD: (*He is nervous and agitated*) Believe me, Mr Temple, I'd have been here several days ago, but it's extremely difficult for me to leave my patients for any length of time.

TEMPLE: I should have thought that this matter would have taken priority over even your patients, Dr Conrad.

CONRAD: You don't understand – some of them are very ill. Not just physically ill, but …

TEMPLE: Was Mr France very ill?

CONRAD: (*A moment*) You know about Mr France – you know that he consulted me?

TEMPLE: Yes.

CONRAD: Who told you?

TEMPLE: He told me himself.

CONRAD: Did he tell you what was wrong with him?

TEMPLE: No, and I'm not going to ask you to divulge professional confidences, Dr Conrad …

CONRAD: I've told Sir Graham – I suppose there's no reason why I shouldn't tell you. I imagine you can be trusted.

TEMPLE: Well, I've come here at some trouble and personal expense to try and solve this case, Dr Conrad …

CONRAD: Yes – yes, of course. Excuse me. I didn't mean to be rude. Elliot France was a pretty bad psychopathic case. He has obsessional tendencies.

TEMPLE: Obsessional tendencies?

CONRAD: Yes. Particularly with regard to young women.

TEMPLE: I'm afraid I don't quite follow you, doctor.

CONRAD: Once, a long time ago, France tried to murder someone. A young girl, a complete stranger to him. But I'd rather not say any more about it, Mr Temple.

TEMPLE: And you were able to help him?

CONRAD: Yes, I was able to help him. He was extremely grateful, I'll say that for him. So grateful in fact that he gave me this cigarette case.

TEMPLE: M'm – quite touchingly inscribed. "In memory of a successful cure".

CONRAD: (*Almost to himself*) Yes – in memory of a successful cure.

TEMPLE: What's worrying you, Dr Conrad?

CONRAD: You know perfectly well what's worrying me. (*A moment*) Was he really cured?

FADE.

FADE UP the sound of a door opening.
In the back the noise of water running into a bath can be heard.

STEVE: (*From the bathroom*) Is that you, Paul?

68

TEMPLE:	Yes.
STEVE:	I'll be with you in a minute, I'm just running my bath.
TEMPLE:	Yes, all right, darling.
STEVE:	(*Still calling from the bathroom*) Did you see Dr Conrad?
TEMPLE:	Yes …
STEVE:	How long is he staying here?
TEMPLE:	I don't know – not very long, I should think.
STEVE:	Has he seen Breckshaft?
TEMPLE:	Yes, he saw him in London. (*Curious*) Steve, what's this parcel on the bed?
STEVE:	(*Coming in from the bathroom*) Parcel? Oh, it's the blouse I bought this morning … You can unwrap it for me if you like. (*A moment*) Did you tell Conrad you knew about France?

TEMPLE starts to unwrap the parcel.

TEMPLE:	Yes …
STEVE:	What did he say?
TEMPLE:	(*His thoughts elsewhere*) He was pretty frank … with … me …
STEVE:	What's that you've got in your hand?
TEMPLE:	What does it look like?
STEVE:	It looks like one of those cocktail sticks. Why, it is! I can see the head – the Alsatian …
TEMPLE:	Yes …
STEVE:	Where on earth did you find that, Paul?
TEMPLE:	It was in the parcel, darling – with the blouse …

END OF EPISODE TWO

EPISODE THREE

HOTEL REUMER

OPEN TO:

STEVE: But who could have put a cocktail stick in the parcel with the blouse?

TEMPLE: Presumably someone at the shop.

STEVE: Madame Klein?

TEMPLE: Did she hand you the parcel personally?

STEVE: No, it was the other girl in the shop. The girl called Gerda.

TEMPLE: You said she understood English?

STEVE: Yes. She said she'd worked in England.

TEMPLE: Then presumably she could have overheard the little act you put on for Madame Klein's benefit?

STEVE: But even if she did why should she put that cocktail stick in the parcel?

TEMPLE: She may be one jump ahead of us, darling.

STEVE: What do you mean?

TEMPLE: Perhaps this stick is a pointer – a hint if you like – perhaps she wants us to go to the hotel where the cocktail sticks come from.

STEVE: Yes, I suppose that's possible. But we've got to be careful, Paul. This may be a trap …

TEMPLE: Yes, I know. All the same, I think we'll take a look at that place, later this evening.

STEVE: (*After a moment*) Paul, did you see Dr Conrad?

TEMPLE: Yes. He seems genuinely worried about his daughter's disappearance.

STEVE: Has he been to the school?

TEMPLE: Yes, he tried to find out what he could from Mrs Weldon. Naturally, she couldn't tell him any more than she's told us.

STEVE: Well, I'm glad he's showing some concern at last.

TEMPLE: Apparently he's very upset because Elliot France is involved. It seems that France was once a patient of his. He was desperately ill at the time.

STEVE: What was the matter with him?

TEMPLE: He had obsessional tendencies with regard to young women. He once tried to murder a girl who was a complete stranger to him.

STEVE: Good heavens! Did Conrad cure him?

TEMPLE: I should imagine so. Well, France gave him a cigarette case. It was most touchingly inscribed.

The telephone rings.

TEMPLE picks up the receiver.

TEMPLE: (*On the phone*) Hello? …

HARPER: (*On the other end of the phone*) Mr Temple?

TEMPLE: Yes … Who is that?

HARPER: It's Denis Harper. I'm downstairs – in the cocktail bar. You did ask me to drop in for a drink …

TEMPLE: Why, yes, of course, Harper! We'll be down in a few minutes …

TEMPLE replaces the receiver.

STEVE: Denis Harper?

TEMPLE: Yes.

STEVE: I wonder if this visit is the result of his little conference with Madame Klein. Remember I saw them in the café together this afternoon.

TEMPLE: Yes, I remember – but I did ask him to drop in, Steve. Anyhow, come along, dear – let's go down.

FADE.

FADE UP noises associated with a crowded cocktail bar.

HARPER: Good evening, Mrs Temple. And how are you feeling this evening? None the worse for your mishap?

STEVE: (*With a little laugh*) One or two bruises.

HARPER: That doesn't surprise me.

TEMPLE: Well, what will you drink, Harper?

HARPER: No, sir, this is on me. (*To STEVE*) Mrs Temple?

STEVE: May I have a sherry?

HARPER: Yes, of course. Mr Temple?

TEMPLE: I'll have a sherry, too, please.

HARPER: Two sherries, waiter, and another lager.

WAITER: Yes, sir.

HARPER: I seem to have quite a thirst this evening. I suppose it's because I missed my usual cup of tea. It's quite extraordinary, you know, even when you live on the Continent, you still can't get out of the habit of drinking tea in the middle of the afternoon.

STEVE: And you missed your tea this afternoon, Mr Harper?

HARPER: Yes, I'm afraid I did. I've been frantically busy ever since I got back to Garmisch.

TEMPLE: Things looks very prosperous in Bavaria. Is trade booming here?

HARPER: Yes, I think it is, on the whole. Of course there isn't a lot of industry just round Garmisch, but we have most of the tradespeople's accounts. You'd be surprised, one or two of the shops here are little goldmines.

TEMPLE: I can quite believe it.

HARPER: (*After a moment*) Did you find Schreidenstein all right, Mr Temple?

TEMPLE: Oh, yes, I found it.

HARPER: And the Countess?

75

TEMPLE: Yes, I saw Countess Dekker. But I'm afraid she couldn't throw much light on Betty Conrad's disappearance. Nor could Mr France.

HARPER: Oh, you saw Elliot France, too?

TEMPLE: Yes. But he wasn't particularly helpful, I'm afraid.

HARPER: This is certainly a strange case. I mean – why on earth should anyone want to abduct a kid like Betty Conrad?

STEVE: It could be for ransom, Mr Harper.

HARPER: Ransom? Yes, I suppose that's possible … (*To TEMPLE*) Has there been a demand then – for money, I mean?

TEMPLE: Not to my knowledge.

HARPER: I don't think it's a question of a ransom, Mr Temple. I don't even think she's been abducted. I think she just got tired of the school and her associates and decided to go away for four or five days.

TEMPLE: Did Betty give you the impression that she was tired of the school?

HARPER: No. I'm just – merely – expressing an opinion.

STEVE: What sort of a girl was Betty Conrad?

HARPER: You asked me that question this morning, Mrs Temple. She was intelligent, bright, well read, but not what you'd call a happy sort of girl – at least, she didn't appear to be happy.

STEVE: Would you say she – well – knew her way around?

HARPER: (*Laughing*) It depends what you mean by that.

STEVE: I think you know what I mean, Mr Harper.

HARPER: (*After a moment*) Betty was – no fool … Whether that comes under the heading of knowing your way around or not, I wouldn't know.

TEMPLE: Harper, will you leave me your address and telephone number, just in case I want to get in touch with you?

HARPER: Why, yes, certainly – I was going to suggest it in any case.

TEMPLE: Perhaps you'd write it down for me.

HARPER: Yes, of course. I've got a card here, somewhere.

HARPER feels in his pocket.

HARPER: Oh, here we are …

TEMPLE: You can borrow my pen …

HARPER: Thank you.

HARPER writes on the card.

HARPER: The telephone number is Munich 9-1984 … And this is the bank address – you can get me there in the daytime unless I'm away, of course, on one of those little trips.

TEMPLE: Thank you.

WAITER: A lager beer, sir – and two sherries.

HARPER: Thank you.

WAITER: I've brought you a medium sherry, sir – I hope that's all right …

TEMPLE: Yes, that's quite all right, thank you …

FADE.

FADE IN the sound of a car engine.

STEVE: … I like the way Harper said he missed his afternoon tea! I saw him come into the café … I saw him with my own eyes!

TEMPLE: Yes, I know you did, darling. But are you sure he didn't see you?

STEVE: Yes, I'm sure he didn't. I told you, I was sitting in an alcove …

77

TEMPLE:	Was there a mirror in the alcove?
STEVE:	(*Uncertain*) No, I don't think so …
TEMPLE:	I think there must have been, darling. At any rate, I'm quite sure that Harper saw you this afternoon.
STEVE:	Why do you say that?
TEMPLE:	(*Faintly amused*) Didn't you see the twinkle in his eye when he said he'd missed his afternoon tea?
STEVE:	No, I didn't. Paul, are you sure?
TEMPLE:	(*Amused*) Yes, darling. But don't let it get you down – it's not important. Let's concentrate on the Hotel Reumer – we'll be there in a minute or two.
STEVE:	(*Suddenly*) There's a signpost! Hotel Reumer – to the left …

FADE.

FADE IN a car travelling.
TEMPLE turns the car and drives down a private lane.
There is a pause.

TEMPLE:	Here we are …
STEVE:	It's quite a nice looking place … (*Suddenly*) Darling, look at the painting – on the wall, across the front of the hotel … Isn't it extraordinary?
TEMPLE:	Yes – it's awfully well done …
STEVE:	I think that's the park place over there.

FADE DOWN the noise of the car.

FADE UP the noise of the entrance hall of the hotel.

STEVE:	They're quite busy, by the look of things.
TEMPLE:	Yes. I ought to have telephoned and booked a table. Anyhow, we'll have a drink first …

STEVE:	This looks like the Head Waiter. Ask him about a table.
HEAD WAITER:	Good evening.
TEMPLE:	I want to reserve a table for two – for dinner.
HEAD WAITER:	Well, we're rather heavily booked at the moment, sir. Could you wait a little while?
TEMPLE:	Yes, we'll have a drink …
HEAD WAITER:	Yes, sir, the lounge is over on the right, past the reception desk. May I have your name, sir?
TEMPLE:	Temple.
HEAD WAITER:	(*A change of tone*) Oh, Mr Temple! Your table will be ready in about twenty minutes.
TEMPLE:	(*A little surprised at being recognised*) Thank you …
HEAD WAITER:	We've been expecting you, sir.
TEMPLE:	Expecting us?
HEAD WAITER:	Yes, sir. Come this way, please. I'll show you to the lounge …

FADE.

FADE UP the opening of a door.

TEMPLE:	What will you drink, Steve?
STEVE:	I'll have a sherry, please.
TEMPLE:	Yes, I'll have the same, too. No, on second thoughts I'll have a gin and Italian.
HEAD WAITER:	Very good, sir. I'll bring them over myself, Mr Temple.
TEMPLE:	Thank you.

The door closes.

STEVE:	Paul, he said he was expecting us …

79

TEMPLE:	Yes, I know. Someone must have telephoned and told him we were coming.
STEVE:	Do you think it was the girl – the girl who put the cocktail stick in the parcel?
TEMPLE:	I suppose it could have been ... (*Suddenly smiling*) Don't look so worried, darling! There's probably some perfectly simple explanation. This is rather a nice room, isn't it?
STEVE:	Yes ...
TEMPLE:	What are those pictures?
STEVE:	They look like photographs to me.
TEMPLE:	Yes, so they are.
STEVE:	(*After a moment*) This one looks as if it was taken on a film set. There's a lot of technicians and a camera and ...

TEMPLE crosses and joins STEVE.
They look at the photograph on the wall.

TEMPLE:	Yes, that's a film set all right, or a television studio.
STEVE:	Does that mean that the people who own this place have some connection with the film business?
TEMPLE:	Your guess is as good as mine, darling.

The door opens.

HEAD WAITER:	Your drinks, sir. And Herr Gunter will be along in a moment, Mr Temple.
TEMPLE:	Herr Gunter?
HEAD WAITER:	The proprietor, sir. He said he wanted to have a word with you and I told him that you were in the lounge.
TEMPLE:	Oh, I see. Well, thank you very much. Will you put the drinks on my bill?
HEAD WAITER:	Certainly, sir.

The door closes.

STEVE: Paul, have you heard of this man – Gunter?

TEMPLE: Yes, I think Breckshaft mentioned him.

STEVE: What did he say?

TEMPLE: Only that he was the proprietor …

STEVE: (*Suddenly*) Paul, look!

TEMPLE: M'm?

STEVE: Your cocktail stick …

TEMPLE: Oh yes – the dog's head. It's the same as the others, Steve. Well – cheerio, darling!

A slight pause.

TEMPLE: M'm – very good. How's the sherry?

JOYCE GUNTER enters and overhears TEMPLE's remark.

JOYCE: (*She is in her late twenties with a slight Scots accent*) Well, I hope it's satisfactory, Mrs Temple.

TEMPLE: Oh, good evening!

JOYCE: Good evening, Mr Temple. My husband sent me along – he won't be more than a few minutes.

STEVE: (*Slightly surprised*) You're Mrs Gunter?

JOYCE: That's right, Mrs Temple. You're thinking I'm a long way from home, no doubt?

TEMPLE: Would it be Perth?

JOYCE: (*Laughing*) Inverness.

TEMPLE: By Timothy, you are a long way from home, Mrs Gunter!

JOYCE: This is my home now, Mr Temple. You see, Fritz – that's my husband – came to England just before the war. He was an actor and I met him when he was on tour in Scotland. My father kept an hotel just outside Inverness. I was brought up in the hotel business. After the war we came back here and Fritz was in films for a time, but things were very difficult and the money was

81

uncertain. So when I heard this place was going I managed to persuade Fritz to let me buy it.

STEVE: I'm sure it's a great success.

JOYCE: Oh, we're paying our way, Mrs Temple, although I have to keep an eye on Fritz. He's a rare spender if he gets the chance.

TEMPLE: The hotel seems to be very busy this evening.

JOYCE: Well, we should be busy at this time of the year.

STEVE: Mrs Gunter, tell me something. The waiter said that you were expecting us this evening …

JOYCE: Yes, of course, Mrs Temple.

TEMPLE: But we didn't telephone for a table – we didn't even tell anyone we were coming here …

The door opens as TEMPLE finishes speaking.

JOYCE: Ah, here's Fritz! He'll explain everything.

FRITZ: (*He is in his thirties and has a slight German accent, with charm*) Good evening! I am so sorry to have kept you waiting.

TEMPLE: No, not at all, Herr Gunter. Your wife has been entertaining us.

FRITZ: Ah, yes – I'm sure she has. Joyce is always pleased to see visitors from England.

TEMPLE: Mrs Gunter said you could explain how you came to expect us this evening?

FRITZ: How we came to expect you? I do not understand.

JOYCE: Mr Temple is puzzled, Fritz. He never telephoned for a reservation so he can't understand why we expected him.

FRITZ: But haven't you told them about the phone call?

JOYCE: No, darling. I thought perhaps you ought to tell Mr Temple about it yourself.

FRITZ: There was a phone call from a lady, Mr Temple. I spoke to her myself. She sounded like an

82

	American. She said that a Mr and Mrs Paul Temple would be visiting us very soon – and she asked me to give you a message.
STEVE:	Who was this person?
FRITZ:	I don't know, Mrs Temple.
TEMPLE:	And the message?
FRITZ:	I wrote it down somewhere.

FRITZ feels in his pockets.

| FRITZ: | I have the paper in my pocket – Oh, here we are … The lady said it was urgent that you should go at once to this address. |

TEMPLE reads the piece of paper.

TEMPLE:	(*After a moment*) Briggenstraat 37, Innsbruck.
FRITZ:	Yes. Do you know the address, sir?
TEMPLE:	No, I'm afraid I don't. I don't know Innsbruck very well.
STEVE:	It's a pity you didn't get this woman's name, Herr Gunter.
FRITZ:	I asked for her name, Mrs Temple – I asked her twice if she would tell me who she was. I couldn't do more than that.
TEMPLE:	No, of course not.
FRITZ:	I did point out to the lady that there was no one staying here with the name of Temple, but she insisted that you would be coming. I mentioned your name to my wife and she recognised it at once.
JOYCE:	I've read several of your novels, Mr Temple, and … I know that you're associated with Scotland Yard.
TEMPLE:	Not officially, Mrs Gunter.
FRITZ:	We had a police inspector here called Breckshaft asking questions about a girl called Betty

Conrad. Are you concerned with the same investigations, Mr Temple?

TEMPLE: Yes, yes I am, Herr Gunter. I'll be quite frank with you. I'm investigating the disappearance of Betty Conrad. Indeed, that's why I'm staying here – in Bavaria.

FRITZ: So?

TEMPLE: I'm working in collaboration with the man you mentioned – Inspector Breckshaft.

FRITZ: This is interesting, Mr Temple, but I'm afraid I can't help you. I've already told the Inspector all I know.

TEMPLE: You told the Inspector that you never saw Betty Conrad, or any of the other girls from Mrs Weldon's school.

FRITZ: That is true. Neither my wife nor myself can recall seeing the missing girl. They showed us several photographs of her.

TEMPLE: Do you know Mrs Weldon – the owner of the school?

FRITZ: No.

TEMPLE: Do you know a young man called Denis Harper?

FRITZ: Harper? I cannot recall the name.

JOYCE: He'll be English, no doubt, with a name like that?

STEVE: Yes, he is English. Slim – fairly tall – very fair hair, and rather good looking.

FRITZ: There are many young men in these parts who would fit that description, Mrs Temple.

JOYCE: But he's English, Fritz. (*To STEVE*) Tall, very fair hair … (*Thoughtfully*) D'you know, I do remember an Englishman like that, Mrs Temple … He came here to dinner one night about a week ago – with a woman older than himself.

TEMPLE: Can you describe her?

JOYCE: I'm not very good at describing people. She was dark … good looking … about 42 or 43 … very smartly dressed. I'd a feeling I'd seen her before somewhere but I couldn't remember where.

STEVE: Could it have been in a dress shop – in Garmisch?

JOYCE: In Garmisch? (*Suddenly*) Why, yes, of course! That's it! I went there about a month ago … She didn't attend to me but I remember seeing her in the shop …

STEVE: It's Madame Klein, Paul.

FRITZ: Madame Klein?

TEMPLE: You've heard the name before, Herr Gunter?

FRITZ: (*Thoughtfully*) Klein … It's not an uncommon name around here, you know, Mr Temple.

JOYCE: Why are you interested in these people? Are they friends of Betty Conrad's?

TEMPLE: Well, Harper knew Betty Conrad – but just how well he knew her it's difficult to say. (*Suddenly, changing the subject*) Mrs Gunter, tell me – does Countess Dekker ever come here?

JOYCE: (*Obviously surprised by the question*) Why, yes …

FRITZ: She's a regular visitor. She dines or lunches here at least once a week. Usually with Mr France – the writer …

TEMPLE: Oh, I see. Well, thank you, Herr Gunter. By the way, my wife and I have been admiring your cocktail sticks.

FRITZ: Yes, they're rather unusual, aren't they, Mr Temple? They arouse a great deal of interest. (*Laughing*) It's what the Americans call a jimick …

85

JOYCE: (*Laughing*) Gimmick, Fritz!

TEMPLE: (*Also laughing*) Oh, gimmick …

The door opens.

HEAD WAITER: Excuse me. Your table is ready now, sir.

TEMPLE: Thank you.

FRITZ: If there's anything else we can tell you, Mr Temple, we'll be only too pleased. Naturally, we don't want any scandal – but on the other hand we would like to help you and the police if we can.

TEMPLE: Thank you. Well, you've been most helpful, Herr Gunter. We'll probably see you again before we go. Come along, darling …

STEVE: Goodnight, Mrs Gunter …

FADE SCENE.

FADE IN the sound of a car travelling along a country road.

STEVE: What did you make of the Gunters?

TEMPLE: A rather charming couple, I thought. An unusual combination. The Highlands of Scotland and the Bavarian Alps.

STEVE: I couldn't help feeling that somehow …

TEMPLE: Somehow what, darling?

STEVE: (*Vaguely*) Oh, I don't know …

TEMPLE: (*Laughing*) Don't tell me that good old intuition is beginning to work …

STEVE: If you ask me we could do with my good old intuition at the moment. We don't seem to be getting very far with this case.

A pause.

STEVE: (*Thoughtfully*) I wonder why that girl telephoned …

TEMPLE: Presumably because she wanted that message delivered about Innsbruck.

86

STEVE: Fritz Gunter said she had an American accent. I
            suppose it could have been June Jackson.

TEMPLE: Yes, I thought of that. She's certainly the only
            girl we know around here with an American
            accent. But why didn't she phone our hotel at
            Garmisch?

STEVE: I don't know …

TEMPLE: Well, we can easily find out. We can call at the
            school on our way back to the hotel. It's only
            five or six miles off our route.

STEVE: But it's nearly ten o'clock.

TEMPLE: Well, I doubt Mrs Weldon's young ladies go to
            bed much before ten.

STEVE: (*Thoughtfully*) Paul, if it was June Jackson who
            telephoned the hotel and left that message …

TEMPLE: Yes?

STEVE: D'you think it means that she's hand in glove
            with Gerda or Madame Klein?

TEMPLE: (*Faintly amused*) You mean – you think Gerda
            put the cocktail stick in your parcel to lead us to
            the Hotel Reumer, in order to get a message
            from June Jackson?

STEVE: Well, yes – that's what I mean. (*Vaguely*) Well,
            at least, that's what I think I mean …

TEMPLE: Wouldn't it have been simpler for June to have
            telephoned our hotel – or sent me a note?

STEVE: (*Grudgingly*) Yes, I suppose so. Well, anyway,
            someone telephoned Fritz Gunter. If it wasn't
            June, then who was it?

TEMPLE: That's one of the things we've got to find out,
            Steve … Just one of the things.

FADE.

FADE IN the sound of an electric doorbell ringing.

87

A heavy door is unlocked and opened.

TEMPLE: Good evening. Could we see Mrs Weldon, please?

MARIA: What name shall I say, sir?

TEMPLE: Mr and Mrs Temple.

MARIA: (*Hesitating*) Well – Mrs Weldon is entertaining some guests, sir. Would you wait a few moments?

TEMPLE: Yes, certainly.

MARIA: (*Still hesitant*) Well – perhaps you'd better come inside, sir, and wait in the hall.

TEMPLE: (*Pleasantly*) Thank you. Yes, I think it would be a little less draughty …

The door closes.

STEVE: (*Softly to TEMPLE*) Paul, this really is an imposition …

TEMPLE: Nonsense … She knows we're investigating the case … In any case the last time I saw her she asked me to call round whenever I felt like it.

STEVE: (*Quickly*) Look!

TEMPLE: What is it?

STEVE: I thought I saw someone on the landing …

TEMPLE: This light isn't very good – you probably imagined it.

A door opens.

MRS WELDON: (*Approaching*) Good evening, Mr Temple … Mrs Temple … How nice to see you both again!

TEMPLE: I'm sorry to trouble you at such a late hour, Mrs Weldon.

MRS WELDON: Not at all. You've met Countess Dekker and Mr France, of course?

TEMPLE:	Oh, good evening, Countess. I don't think you have met my wife?
MRS WELDON:	Oh, I beg your pardon …
TEMPLE:	(*Introductions*) Countess Dekker … Mr France … My wife …
STEVE:	Good evening …
ELSA:	Good evening, Mrs Temple.
FRANCE:	Delighted to meet you, Mrs Temple.
MRS WELDON:	I do hope you have some news for us, Mr Temple?
TEMPLE:	I'm sorry, Mrs Weldon.
MRS WELDON:	Oh … Oh, dear! When I saw you I felt sure you had …
TEMPLE:	Yes, of course …
ELSA:	You don't appear to be making much progress, Mr Temple. What on earth can have happened to the poor child?
TEMPLE:	I understand her father – Dr Conrad – has been to see you, Mrs Weldon – and you too, Mr France?
FRANCE:	Yes. A charming man, and quite brilliant. Did I tell you I was once a patient of his, Temple?
ELSA:	(*Softly, to FRANCE*) Elliot, please …
TEMPLE:	Yes, you did, France. (*To MRS WELDON*) Was Dr Conrad very upset, Mrs Weldon?
MRS WELDON:	Well, naturally a father _is_ upset if his daughter disappears, but he was very sensible about it. He seemed quite confident that either you or the police would find her in the next few days.
ELSA:	If you ask me, I think the man's a perfect monster!

MRS WELDON:	Now, Elsa, don't be stupid, darling.
ELSA:	Dashing back to London like that, without knowing if his child is dead or alive …
MRS WELDON:	He's a lot of important work to do. He realises he can't do anything by staying here in Garmisch.
ELSA:	Nevertheless, he should have stayed.
FRANCE:	Elsa, my dear, you're letting your emotions run away with you. In any case, the poor man hasn't gone yet …
ELSA:	If she were my daughter I should be mad with anxiety.
FRANCE:	(*Irritated by ELSA*) Elsa, this isn't getting us anywhere! I'm sure Mr and Mrs Temple called here with something definite in mind.
TEMPLE:	Well, yes, I wanted to take a look at Betty Conrad's room.
MRS WELDON:	It's rather late, Mr Temple, and June should be in bed by now.
TEMPLE:	Yes, I'm sorry, but …
MRS WELDON:	I thought you'd seen the room?
STEVE:	No, I went up there alone last time we called, if you remember.
MRS WELDON:	Oh yes! Yes, of course. But why do you want to see the room tonight, Mr Temple?
TEMPLE:	I rather expect to find something, Mrs Weldon.
STEVE:	(*Suddenly, catching her breath*) Oh!
TEMPLE:	(*Quickly*) What is it, Steve?
STEVE:	On the landing – look!
MRS WELDON:	Good gracious, it's June! (*Calling*) June – whatever are you doing up there at this time of the night?

JUNE:	(*From the balcony*) I couldn't sleep, Mrs Weldon. I thought I'd try and get a book from the library …
MRS WELDON:	I've told you before about reading in bed …
JUNE:	I'm sorry, Mrs Weldon.
MRS WELDON:	Go back to your room right away, June, and put the light out!
JUNE:	Yes, Mrs Weldon …
MRS WELDON:	(*Suddenly*) Oh, wait a moment! I was forgetting … Mr and Mrs Temple would like to take another look round your room.
JUNE:	(*Surprised, tense*) What – now – tonight?
TEMPLE:	Yes. It won't take five minutes, June.
JUNE:	I'm afraid the room's rather untidy, Mrs Weldon.
MRS WELDON:	That's all right, never mind. Take Mr and Mrs Temple up with you now. We'll wait down here, Mr Temple.
TEMPLE:	Thank you very much, Mrs Weldon.

FADE.

FADE UP the opening of a bedroom door.

JUNE:	Here we are … I'll just tidy up these magazines …

TEMPLE closes the door.

STEVE:	Let me help you, June.
JUNE:	(*Still a little tense*) No, it's all right, Mrs Temple.
TEMPLE:	I'm sorry you can't sleep, June. There's nothing on your mind? Nothing worrying you, I hope?
JUNE:	Why, no – no.

TEMPLE: Then you can answer a question I want to ask you with a clear conscience.

JUNE: Yes, of course. What is it?

TEMPLE: Why did you telephone the Hotel Reumer?

JUNE: (*Tensely*) I – I don't understand.

TEMPLE: Did you telephone the hotel?

JUNE: No.

TEMPLE: June, I want the truth. Didn't you telephone the Hotel Reumer and leave a message for me asking me to go to an address in Innsbruck? Briggenstraat 27 …

JUNE: No – no, I didn't. Of course I didn't, Mr Temple.

TEMPLE: You're quite sure?

JUNE: Yes – yes, I'm quite sure. (*Tensely*) Now, would you mind leaving me alone? I don't feel very well this evening …

STEVE: Paul … come along … I think you'd better see June some other time.

TEMPLE: No, wait a minute, Steve. June, I wish you'd tell me what's worrying you.

JUNE: There's nothing worrying me. I just don't feel very well, that's all.

TEMPLE: You were very fond of Betty, weren't you?

JUNE: Yes, of course I was.

TEMPLE: And you'd like us to find her?

JUNE: Naturally I'd like you to find her.

TEMPLE: Then it's a pity you don't try to help us. (*To STEVE*) All right, Steve …

JUNE: (*Suddenly*) Mr Temple!

TEMPLE: Yes?

JUNE: (*Changing her mind*) Nothing – nothing – it doesn't matter. (*A moment*) What are you looking at, Mr Temple?

TEMPLE:	You look very tired, June. I should go to bed. (*To STEVE*) Come along, Steve.
STEVE:	Goodnight, June.
JUNE:	Goodnight, Mrs Temple.

The door closes.

After a moment JUNE throws herself on the bed and starts to cry.

FADE SCENE on JUNE sobbing.

FADE IN the voice of MRS WELDON.

MRS WELDON:	(*Approaching*) Ah, here you are, Mr Temple. Can I get you some coffee before you leave? Mrs Temple?
STEVE:	No, thank you, Mrs Weldon.
TEMPLE:	I'm afraid it's rather late, and we've had rather a hectic day.
MRS WELDON:	I hope you didn't have any trouble with June?
TEMPLE:	No. Though she's rather a highly-strung type of girl, isn't she?
MRS WELDON:	Yes, I'm afraid she is. And of course she's been worse since Betty disappeared. They were awfully good friends, you know.
TEMPLE:	Yes.
ELSA:	Mr Temple …
TEMPLE:	Yes, Countess?
ELSA:	You weren't upstairs very long. You obviously found what you were looking for. Or perhaps it was just an excuse to have a private conversation with the girl?
TEMPLE:	No, Countess, I really was looking for something – and I found it.
FRANCE:	Elsa, you must let Mr Temple go to work in his own way.

ELSA: Don't be silly, Elliot, I'm just curious. I'm sure
           Mr Temple understands.
TEMPLE: Yes, of course! Would you like to see what it
           was I was looking for? What I found in Miss
           Jackson's room?
ELSA: (*Surprised by TEMPLE's frankness*) Yes, I
           would.
TEMPLE: (*After a moment*) Well, here it is …
ELSA: (*Surprised*) A cocktail stick!
TEMPLE: (*Pleasantly*) Yes – it's rather unusual, isn't it?
           You see the head? It's an Alsatian dog …

FADE IN incidental music.

FADE music.
FADE UP the sound of a car travelling along a country road.

STEVE: We're just coming to the bridge where the
           accident happened.
TEMPLE: Yes, that's right.
STEVE: It looks quite different at night.
TEMPLE: Yes. (*Yawning*) I'll be glad to get back to the
           hotel. I'm tired.
STEVE: Shall I drive, Paul?
TEMPLE: No, we haven't far to go, darling.

A pause.

STEVE: Paul … I didn't see you pick up that cocktail
           stick in June's room.
TEMPLE: (*Yawning*) Didn't you, Steve?
STEVE: I hope you're not trying to tell me the old story
           about the quickness of the hand deceiving the
           eye.
TEMPLE: I wouldn't dream of it!
STEVE: Then where did you get that cocktail stick from?
TEMPLE: From my drink at the Hotel Reumer.
STEVE: Well!

TEMPLE:	(*Amused*) Any objection?
STEVE:	Then why on earth did you tell Mrs Weldon and the others that you found it in the room?
TEMPLE:	I wanted to conceal the real reason for my visit – which was to question June Jackson.
STEVE:	Well, you didn't get very far, did you, darling? June didn't tell you anything.
TEMPLE:	On the contrary – she told me quite a lot.
STEVE:	Why, she hardly said anything!
TEMPLE:	It wasn't what she said, Steve – it was the way she looked …

FADE.

FADE UP noises associated with the entrance hall of the hotel.

TEMPLE:	I'll get the key, Steve.
STEVE:	Yes, all right.
TEMPLE:	(*Approaching the reception desk*) Can I have my key, please?
RECEPTIONIST:	Certainly, Mr Temple.
TEMPLE:	Thank you.
RECEPTIONIST:	Oh, Mr Temple, there's a gentleman waiting to see you. He's been here some time.
TEMPLE:	Oh?
RECEPTIONIST:	Yes, sir. A Dr Conrad. He's in the Residents' Lounge, over there.
TEMPLE:	Thank you very much. (*Turning to STEVE*) Will you go up, Steve? Dr Conrad wants a word with me.
STEVE:	Did you get the key?
TEMPLE:	Yes, here we are. I won't be long.

FADE DOWN the noises of the hotel lobby.

A door opens.

CONRAD: Ah, Mr Temple!

TEMPLE: Dr Conrad, I apologise. I'm sorry you've had such a long wait.

CONRAD: That's all right. I ought to have telephoned you first – but I'm flying back to London tomorrow night, and I thought I'd like a word with you before I left.

TEMPLE: Yes, of course. But I'm sorry, Dr Conrad, I've no news for you at the moment.

CONRAD: I hardly expected you would have. I'm sorry I have to leave Garmisch, but I've several patients in London I must see. It's important that I get back to London as soon as possible. I hope you understand.

TEMPLE: Yes, of course.

CONRAD: If there should be any development I'd be glad if you'd telephone me immediately.

TEMPLE: Yes, of course.

CONRAD: Here's my card. I've written down my private number as well as the one in Harley Street.

TEMPLE: Thank you, doctor.

CONRAD: There's just one other thing, Mr Temple …

TEMPLE: Yes?

CONRAD: I want you to forget what I told you about Elliot France. I had a long talk to him this afternoon and I'm quite convinced he's normal and perfectly fit. His cure was obviously of a permanent nature.

TEMPLE: What does that mean, exactly, Dr Conrad?

CONRAD: Well, it means – in my opinion – he's not involved in this affair in any way.

TEMPLE: And that's your professional opinion?

CONRAD: Yes, that's my professional opinion.

TEMPLE: Thank you, doctor. I'll bear it in mind.

FADE SCENE.

FADE IN incidental music.

FADE music.

FADE IN the opening of a door.

STEVE: Oh, there you are, Paul. What did Conrad want?

TEMPLE: Nothing very much. He's going back to London tomorrow and thought he'd have a word with me before he left.

STEVE: Nothing else?

TEMPLE: Apparently he's seen Elliot France again and he's convinced that he's cured – at least he says he is.

STEVE: Elliot France … M'm …

TEMPLE: What do you mean – "M'm"?

STEVE: I was just thinking about France, and that friend of his, Countess Dekker, or whatever she calls herself.

TEMPLE: It is Countess Dekker.

STEVE: Yes, well – she's a pretty smooth customer, if you ask me.

TEMPLE: (*Amused*) Yes, I rather thought that was your opinion of her.

STEVE: Oh dear – was it so obvious?

FADE.

FADE IN incidental music.

FADE music.

FADE IN a telephone ringing.

The receiver is quickly lifted by TEMPLE.

TEMPLE: (*On the telephone*) Hello?

JUNE: (*On the other end of the line*) Mr Temple?

97

TEMPLE: Yes – who is that?

JUNE: Briggenstraat 37 – not 27, Mr Temple.

JUNE replaces the receiver.

TEMPLE: Hello – hello …

TEMPLE puts down the receiver.

STEVE: (*Sleepily*) Who was it?

TEMPLE: (*Vaguely*) It's nothing, darling. Somebody wanted Room 256 … I expect the operator's a bit sleepy.

STEVE: The operator isn't the only one! Why, it's after three o'clock.

TEMPLE: Yes, I know. I'm sorry it woke you, Steve. I grabbed the thing just as soon as I could.

STEVE: Were you awake?

TEMPLE: Yes.

STEVE: So was I. What an extraordinary time for anyone to ring up … I can't get Elliot France out of my mind … You don't think France has got some kind of hold over Dr Conrad, do you?

TEMPLE: What do you mean – some kind of hold?

STEVE: Do you think he's blackmailing him? After all, Conrad seems to have changed his mind about France, doesn't he?

TEMPLE: I don't know whether you could say he's changed his mind exactly.

STEVE: Well, at one time he appeared to suspect him, and now, apparently, he doesn't.

TEMPLE: Go to sleep, darling.

STEVE: (*Almost asleep again*) M'm?

TEMPLE: I said go to sleep, darling.

STEVE: M'm? …

TEMPLE: I said … (*With a little laugh*) Goodnight, Steve.

FADE IN incidental music.

FADE music.

FADE in the sound of a clock.

After a moment there is a knock on the bedroom door.

The knock is repeated, and after a moment the door opens.

STEVE: Come in.

MAID: Good morning, madam. Your tea.

STEVE: (*Sleepily*) Oh, good morning. Would you draw the curtains, please?

MAID: Certainly.

The MAID draws the curtains across the window.

MAID: It's a lovely morning, Mrs Temple.

STEVE: (*Yawning*) Oh, yes, isn't it?

MAID: Herr Temple will not be wanting tea?

STEVE: I don't know, I should imagine he would. (*Calling*) Paul! Paul! Are you in the bathroom?

A pause.

STEVE: Paul! … My husband doesn't seem to be here.

MAID: It's such a lovely morning, madam. Perhaps he's gone for a walk.

STEVE: (*Thoughtfully*) Yes.

MAID: Is there anything you require?

STEVE: (*Her thoughts elsewhere*) M'm? Oh, no – no, thank you.

MAID: Thank you, madam.

The door closes.

As the door closes the telephone rings.

STEVE quickly picks up the receiver.

STEVE: (*On the phone*) Hello?

VOICE: (*On the other end of the line, exactly like TEMPLE's voice*) Is that you, Steve?

STEVE: Yes … Paul, what's happened? Where are you?

VOICE: (*With a little laugh*) You sound very worried, darling.

STEVE: I am worried! I wondered what on earth had happened to you.

VOICE: I got up early and drove over to Innsbruck.

STEVE: Are you in Innsbruck now?

VOICE: Yes … I've just been taking a look at that address – Briggenstraat 37. It's a barber's shop near the railway station.

STEVE: (*Surprised*) A barber's shop?

VOICE: Yes – now listen, Steve – this is what I want you to do. There's a train leaving Garmisch for Innsbruck at 9.24. Be on that train, darling, and I'll meet you at the station.

STEVE: Right!

VOICE: … And don't forget your passport, Steve!

STEVE: (*Laughing*) Of course, Innsbruck's in Austria … I should have forgotten it … All right, Paul!

VOICE: See you later …

STEVE: (*Suddenly*) Oh, Paul, wait a minute!

VOICE: Yes?

STEVE: Where's Charlie fishing?

VOICE: What did you say?

STEVE: I said "Where's Charlie fishing"?

A moment.

VOICE: Charlie?

STEVE: Yes.

VOICE: (*A moment, an uneasy little laugh*) I don't know what you mean, dear.

STEVE: (*Significantly*) Don't you, Mr Temple?

VOICE: (*Hesitantly, puzzled*) Who – who's Charlie?

STEVE suddenly replaces the receiver.

Quick FADE IN of incidental music.

FADE DOWN of music.

RECEPTIONIST: Good morning, Mrs Temple.

STEVE: Good morning.

RECEPTIONIST: There are two letters for you.

STEVE: Thank you. Have you seen my husband this morning?

RECEPTIONIST: Why no, Mrs Temple. But I've been busy sorting the mail, so I may have missed him, of course.

STEVE: Yes.

BRECKSHAFT: (*Approaching*) Good morning, Mrs Temple ...

STEVE: Oh, good morning, Herr Breckshaft.

BRECKSHAFT: I am so sorry to trouble you at this hour of the morning, but I wanted to see your husband.

STEVE: I'd rather like to see him myself at the moment.

BRECKSHAFT: Mr Temple is not here?

STEVE: No, I'm afraid he isn't. He must have gone out early for some reason or other.

BRECKSHAFT: You've no idea where he's gone?

STEVE: No, I'm afraid not. (*Suddenly*) Oh, here he is!

TEMPLE: (*Approaching, brightly*) Hello, darling! How are you? Good morning, Breckshaft!

BRECKSHAFT: Good morning.

STEVE: Paul, you went off without saying a word. I wondered where on earth you'd got to.

TEMPLE: I've only been to see about another car, Steve – I wasn't too happy about the first one, since that accident happened. I thought I'd get a better choice if I went out early.

STEVE: You don't know what a scare you gave me.

TEMPLE: (*Laughing at STEVE*) Did you think I'd run away with a synthetic blonde, or something! Come and have some breakfast with us, Breckshaft. I say, that sounds a bit off, doesn't it – come and have some breakfast with us, Breckshaft?

BRECKSHAFT: (*Unamused*) I have already had breakfast, thank you, Mr Temple. I called to see you because I happened to hear of your visit to the school last night.

TEMPLE: Now how did you get to hear about that?

BRECKSHAFT: I was speaking on the telephone to Mrs Weldon, checking one or two small routine matters. She mentioned it.

TEMPLE: I see.

BRECKSHAFT: She said you had found a cocktail stick from the Hotel Reumer in Betty Conrad's room.

TEMPLE: Well – that wasn't strictly true, Inspector.

BRECKSHAFT: (*Puzzled*) No?

TEMPLE: The cocktail stick certainly came from the Hotel Reumer, but I didn't find it in Betty Conrad's room.

BRECKSHAFT: Then why did you say …

TEMPLE: I simply wanted an excuse to visit the girl's room and ask one or two questions.

BRECKSHAFT: Of who did you ask the questions?

TEMPLE: June Jackson. But I didn't find out anything, Inspector. It was rather a wild goose chase, I'm afraid.

BRECKSHAFT: I see. Well, thank you, Mr Temple. I'm sorry to have disturbed you.

TEMPLE:	Just a moment, Breckshaft. Will you do something for me?
BRECKSHAFT:	Of course – if it's not too difficult.
TEMPLE:	Intensify the search for Betty Conrad. Put every man you can spare on the job.
BRECKSHAFT:	(*Sharply*) Why? Why do you say that? Has something happened, Mr Temple?
TEMPLE:	No, but …
BRECKSHAFT:	You must have a reason for saying a thing like that.
TEMPLE:	I have a reason, Breckshaft.
BRECKSHAFT:	Well, then?
TEMPLE:	(*Quite pleasantly*) You have a methodical mind, my friend – I don't really think my reason would impress you. (*With a little laugh, to STEVE*) Come along, darling, let's have some breakfast. (*To BRECKSHAFT*) Are you sure you won't join us, Inspector?
BRECKSHAFT:	No, thank you, Mr Temple. If you want to get in touch with me, I shall be at my office most of the day …
TEMPLE:	Thank you, Inspector.

FADE SCENE.

FADE IN STEVE: rather excited: she is at the end of a long story.

STEVE:	… And then I said – "Where's Charlie fishing?" – and he said, "I don't know what you mean, dear." Of course, as soon as he said that instead of "In the Thames", I realised it wasn't you.
TEMPLE:	Well, thank heavens you remembered that old trick, Steve …

103

STEVE:	Quite honestly, if I hadn't I'd have thought it was you, Paul.
TEMPLE:	You say, this man said that Briggenstraat 37 was a barber's shop?
STEVE:	Yes, near the railway station.
TEMPLE:	I wonder if he was telling the truth.
STEVE:	I don't know, darling. (*A moment*) Paul, you're awfully worried about this case, aren't you?
TEMPLE:	Yes. Yes, I am. I'm worried about it because I have an awful feeling I know what's going to happen.
STEVE:	How do you mean, Paul?
TEMPLE:	I think the police are going to find Betty Conrad.
STEVE:	(*Misunderstanding TEMPLE*) You do?
TEMPLE:	Yes.
STEVE:	When do you think they'll find her?
TEMPLE:	Tomorrow.
STEVE:	Why tomorrow, darling?
TEMPLE:	It's Friday the 18th. I think they'll find Betty Conrad tomorrow afternoon at four o'clock. I think she'll be dead and wearing a blue coat.

END OF EPISODE THREE

EPISODE FOUR

A VISIT TO
INNSBRUCK

OPEN TO:

TEMPLE: … I think they'll find Betty Conrad tomorrow
           afternoon at four o'clock. I think she'll be dead
           and wearing a blue coat.
STEVE: But why do you think that?
TEMPLE: It's just a feeling I've got – a sort of intuition.
STEVE: Darling, intuitions are my department – you
           thrive on facts.
TEMPLE: Yes, I know, but somehow –
WAITER: Croissants, sir?
TEMPLE: Thank you.
WAITER: Coffee, madame?
STEVE: Thank you.
WAITER: I'll put the coffee over here, madame.
STEVE: Yes – thank you very much.
A pause.
STEVE pours the coffee.
TEMPLE: Thank you, dear.
STEVE: Paul, if you feel so sure about this – about this
           intuition, I mean – don't you think you ought to
           do something about it?
TEMPLE: What do you suggest?
STEVE: Well – couldn't you … (*Lost for an explanation*)
TEMPLE: (*With a little laugh*) Exactly! There's nothing I
           can do other than what I've already done.
           Anyway, cheer up, Steve. My intuitions aren't
           always so hot. I should be more worried if you'd
           had this intuition instead of me.
STEVE: You're just saying that!
STEVE drinks her coffee.
STEVE: Paul, why did you get up so early?
TEMPLE: I told you – to arrange about another car.

STEVE: That wasn't the only thing you went out for – now was it?

TEMPLE: Of course not. You know how I enjoy a walk before breakfast.

STEVE: Yes, I know. Straight out of the house into the car. Well, as you've suddenly become so secretive about what happened before breakfast perhaps we'd better discuss our plans for the day.

TEMPLE starts eating his grapefruit.

TEMPLE: Jolly good idea …

STEVE: Do you intend to go over to Innsbruck this morning?

TEMPLE: No, we'll leave that for a little later on in the day.

STEVE: But why? I should have thought it would have been better to go this morning.

TEMPLE: (*Interrupting STEVE*) By Timothy, my beard's pretty rough this morning – I shall have to have another shave.

STEVE: Are you trying to change the subject?

TEMPLE: No, darling. Well, the fact of the matter is I don't want to leave the hotel just yet. I'm expecting a phone call.

STEVE: Oh? Who from?

TEMPLE: From the school.

STEVE: From Mrs Weldon?

TEMPLE: Yes.

STEVE: But you saw Mrs Weldon last night. Why should she telephone you this morning?

TEMPLE: I don't know why, until I get the phone call.

STEVE: But you said you were expecting the call?

TEMPLE: (*Unperturbed, eating his grapefruit*) That's right, darling, I am.

STEVE: Paul, you really are exasperating!

108

TEMPLE: (*Amused*) Steve, eat your breakfast.
FADE.
FADE IN incidental music.

Slow FADE DOWN of incidental music.
FADE IN background noises associated with a hotel vestibule.
TEMPLE: Are you going straight up to the room, Steve?
STEVE: Yes, darling. I left the key at the desk.
TEMPLE: Wait here, I'll get it.
KLEIN: (*Calling from the background*) Mrs Temple!
STEVE: Oh! Good morning, Madame Klein!
KLEIN: I'm delivering a parcel for an American lady who's staying at the hotel.
STEVE: Oh, I see.
KLEIN: I notice you're wearing the blouse, Mrs Temple. I hope you like it?
STEVE: The blouse? Oh yes – yes, it's very nice. My husband likes it, too, which is most unusual.
MADAME KLEIN laughs.
STEVE: Oh, here is my husband now. Paul, this is Madame Klein. You remember – where I bought my blouse …
TEMPLE: Yes, of course. How do you do?
KLEIN: Good morning, Mr Temple. I was just going to ask your wife about Betty Conrad. Is there any news of the poor girl?
TEMPLE: No, I'm afraid not.
KLEIN: Oh, dear!
TEMPLE: I believe Betty was a customer of yours?
KLEIN: Yes. Poor child. She was due to call tomorrow at four o'clock to pick up a coat we were making for her.
TEMPLE: So I understand.

KLEIN: But of course, she won't be there now, I'm afraid.

TEMPLE: Well, one never knows. A lot can happen in twenty-four hours. If you should hear anything – if by some extraordinary chance Betty Conrad did turn up for that appointment – I'd be most grateful if you'd telephone me, Madame Klein.

KLEIN: Why yes, of course, Mr Temple. I should be only too pleased.

TEMPLE: I understand a friend of yours is also very anxious about Betty Conrad?

KLEIN: Indeed? Who, may I ask?

TEMPLE: Denis Harper – the young man from Munich.

KLEIN: (*Apparently puzzled*) Harper? I'm afraid I know no one of that name, Mr Temple.

STEVE: But surely, Madame Klein, you …

TEMPLE: I'm sorry, I was under the impression that you were the lady who dined with Mr Harper at the Hotel Reumer. I must have been mistaken.

KLEIN: Hotel Reumer?

TEMPLE: At Oberammergau. It's run by two very nice people named Gunter. They have an unusual gimmick there, by the way … Wait a moment! … Ah, here we are …

KLEIN: (*Apparently surprised*) A cocktail stick?

TEMPLE: Yes – with the head of an Alsatian dog.

KLEIN: So I see.

TEMPLE: Have you seen a cocktail stick like this before?

KLEIN: (*After a moment*) Yes, I have.

TEMPLE: Where?

KLEIN: (*Hesitantly*) I can't remember where … Oh, yes! There's a shop in Munich, next to the Post Office. They sell bric a brac and imitation jewellery, and cocktail glasses and sticks. I think

110

I saw something like that in the window, Mr Temple. Now, if you'll excuse me, I must deliver this parcel.

TEMPLE: Goodbye, Madame Klein. Don't forget to telephone us if Miss Conrad turns up for the appointment …

COMPLETE FADE.

Slow FADE IN of the sound of an electric razor.
TEMPLE is shaving himself.

TEMPLE: There you are, Steve! It works beautifully …

STEVE: (*From the background*) What's that, darling?

TEMPLE: I said it works beautifully …

STEVE: I wish you'd switch that thing off. I can't hear a word you say!

The razor is switched off.

STEVE: Ah, that's better, darling …

TEMPLE: This is the best shave I've had for years.

STEVE: Well, I'm glad to hear it. That electric razor of yours has been behaving like a temperamental film star ever since we arrived here. (*A pause*) Paul, I've been thinking about Madame Klein …

TEMPLE: You do surprise me!

STEVE: Darling, I'm serious. Do you think she was lying?

TEMPLE: About the shop in Munich and the cocktail stick? Yes, I think she was. She's been to the Hotel Reumer all right – and with Denis Harper.

STEVE: What do you think of her?

TEMPLE: I was quite impressed. She's a very intelligent woman, I should imagine. Speaks awfully good English.

STEVE: Yes. Of course, she's years older than Denis Harper.

111

TEMPLE:	Yes, I suppose she is. But she's not entirely unattractive.
STEVE:	No, I suppose not, if you like that type.
TEMPLE:	Men usually do, darling. Dark, slender, seductive …
STEVE:	Well, I wouldn't exactly call her slender.

The telephone rings.

TEMPLE:	Will you answer that, Steve?
STEVE:	(*A little surprised*) Yes, of course – if you want me to.
TEMPLE:	Yes, I do, darling. And if it's Mrs Weldon, tell her we'll come down straight away.
STEVE:	(*Puzzled*) Yes, all right, dear.

STEVE picks up the telephone receiver.

STEVE:	(*On the phone*) Hello? …
MRS WELDON:	(*On the other end of the line*) Hello, is that you, Mrs Temple?
STEVE:	Yes …
MRS WELDON:	Could I speak to your husband, please?
STEVE:	I'm afraid he isn't here at the moment, Mrs Weldon. Can I take a message?
MRS WELDON:	Well, I'd like to see your husband this morning, Mrs Temple. It's frightfully urgent … Do you think he could come along to the school as soon as possible?
STEVE:	Yes, I think so, Mrs Weldon. Has something happened?
MRS WELDON:	Yes, but I can't tell you about it over the telephone. Tell your husband to come immediately … Please, Mrs Temple!
STEVE:	Yes, all right. Don't worry. I'll see he gets your message … Goodbye.

STEVE replaces the receiver.

TEMPLE:	Well?

STEVE:	She wants us to go down to the school straight away.
TEMPLE:	Yes, all right.
STEVE:	Paul, what is this? You were expecting that telephone call. What's happened, darling?
TEMPLE:	Didn't she tell you?
STEVE:	No, she didn't tell me anything – although she sounded desperately worried, poor woman.
TEMPLE:	One of her pupils has disappeared.
STEVE:	What! Another one?
TEMPLE:	Yes.
STEVE:	Well – who is it this time?
TEMPLE:	(*After a moment*) June Jackson …
STEVE:	Oh, no.

FADE.

FADE IN incidental music.

FADE music.

FADE IN the voice of MRS WELDON.

MRS WELDON:	… I just can't understand it, Mr Temple. It's a complete mystery.
TEMPLE:	When did you realise June was missing?
MRS WELDON:	At breakfast time. She wasn't in her place so I sent one of the girls up to her room. There was no sign of her.
STEVE:	Has anyone seen her this morning?
MRS WELDON:	Apparently not. I made enquiries at assembly after breakfast, but no one had seen her. It's most upsetting. I suppose I ought to cable her people.
TEMPLE:	I should wait a little while, Mrs Weldon. Let's hear a bit more about it first. Could

	you give me some idea of how she might have left the school without anyone seeing her?
MRS WELDON:	Her room is on the first floor ... I suppose she could easily have climbed down on to the terrace underneath and out on to the drive.
TEMPLE:	Wouldn't anyone have seen her?
MRS WELDON:	Well, it's doubtful, Mr Temple. After the first ten yards or so she would be screened by shrubs and bushes.
STEVE:	Supposing she just left her room by the door, and came out on to the landing – could she escape observation that way?
MRS WELDON:	Yes, I daresay she could, Mrs Temple, if she chose her time carefully.
TEMPLE:	That means she would simply walk down the stairs into the entrance hall and let herself out by the front door?
MRS WLDON:	Well yes, I suppose she could have done that, if there was no one about at that time.
STEVE:	On the other hand, I suppose, if there'd been a struggle and she'd screamed ...
MRS WELDON:	Oh, we should have heard her, Mrs Temple – I'm sure of that. No, I've come to the conclusion – the painful conclusion – that June must have walked out of her own free will.
TEMPLE:	Why?
MRS WELDON:	(*Surprised by the question*) I can't imagine why – I can't imagine why, unless, in some curious way, June is mixed up with the disappearance of Betty Conrad.

TEMPLE:	Have you told anyone else about this – outside the school, I mean?
MRS WELDON:	Yes, I told Elliot France. He happened to telephone me.
STEVE:	Had Mr France any idea why June might want to – well, walk out on you?
MRS WELDON:	No, of course he hadn't! He just couldn't understand it. He suggested I get in touch with your husband straight away, Mrs Temple.
TEMPLE:	(*Pleasant, but quite vague*) Well, I don't quite know what to suggest, Mrs Weldon.
STEVE:	Have you searched the girl's room?
MRS WELDON:	Yes, I took a quick look round, just after breakfast, but there didn't seem to be anything missing.
STEVE:	Perhaps if we went up there now, Paul …

STEVE is interrupted by the sound of a car drawing to a standstill on the drive outside the school.

MRS WELDON:	Oh, here's Mr France's car. Excuse me.

A pause.

STEVE:	(*Irritated*) Paul, what's the matter with you?
TEMPLE:	Nothing, Steve, nothing at all.
STEVE:	You're acting very strangely, darling! Aren't you interested in this new development?
TEMPLE:	Intensely interested.
STEVE:	Well, you don't sound it!
TEMPLE:	What would you like me to do, Steve – rush round the room taking fingerprints?
STEVE:	(*Exasperated*) I'd like you to ask a few intelligent questions and give poor Mrs

Weldon the impression that you are in the
least interested in the case.

*STEVE breaks off as ELLIOT FRANCE approaches with
MRS WELDON.*

FRANCE: (*Approaching*) Good morning, Temple …
               Mrs Temple. I can't tell you how relieved
               I am to see you.

TEMPLE: Good morning, France.

FRANCE: This is a dreadful business. You've no
               idea what could have become of June, I
               suppose.

TEMPLE: (*Quite pleasantly*) Well, she seems to
               have disappeared.

STEVE: (*Still exasperated with TEMPLE*)
               Darling, we know that.

FRANCE: I suppose she didn't leave a note or
               anything?

MRS WELDON: No, there's no message of any kind.

FRANCE: Have you searched her room, Temple?

TEMPLE: I haven't – but I believe Mrs Weldon has.

FRANCE: (*A little surprised*) Well, don't you think
               it might be a good idea if you did search
               it?

TEMPLE: (*Still pleasantly vague*) I don't really
               think so. (*To MRS WELDON*) You didn't
               find anything unusual in the room, did
               you, Mrs Weldon?

MRS WELDON: No – no, everything appeared to be
               perfectly normal.

FRANCE: (*Irritated*) Well, what do you suggest,
               Temple? Haven't you got any ideas?

TEMPLE: Yes, I have. I've got one rather good idea,
               Mr France.

FRANCE: Well – let's have it.

116

TEMPLE:	I suggest you get in touch with the police.
FRANCE:	Get in touch with the police?
TEMPLE:	Yes. It's the usual procedure in a case of this kind.
MRS WELDON:	But, Mr Temple, I was relying on you to …
TEMPLE:	You asked my advice, Mrs Weldon – I'm giving it to you. Get in touch with Inspector Breckshaft, straight away. Come along, darling, I think we'd better get back to Garmisch. There are one or two things I want to do this morning …

FADE.

FADE UP the sound of a car engine.
TEMPLE is driving the car.
FADE the noise of the car to the background.

STEVE:	Honestly, Paul, I'm surprised at you!
TEMPLE:	(*Innocently*) Surprised, dear? Why?
STEVE:	I should have thought you'd have made some effort to help that poor woman.
TEMPLE:	It so happened I realised there was nothing I could do.
STEVE:	Paul, have you really lost interest in this case? Because if you have we might just as well go back home.
TEMPLE:	What makes you think I've lost interest, Steve?
STEVE:	Well, you've been up in the clouds all morning, to say the least.
TEMPLE:	Are you complaining, Mrs Temple?
STEVE:	No, but – Paul, there's something very odd about this affair. I'm surprised you haven't noticed it.

TEMPLE: Perhaps I have noticed it, darling. (*A moment*) Seriously, Steve – I think I know what you mean.

STEVE: I doubt it …

TEMPLE: You mean that whoever we're up against – and notice I say whoever – not whatever – whoever we're up against chooses to remain discreetly in the background.

STEVE: Yes, that's it! In all the other cases we've investigated, the man behind it all – the person responsible – has always shown his hand in some way or other – a strange card, an anonymous note, a mysterious telephone call. But this person – whoever he is – remains in the background the whole time. We just don't know who we're up against.

TEMPLE: Don't we, darling? …

STEVE: (*After a moment*) Paul, what's your opinion of Breckshaft?

TEMPLE: Now why mention Breckshaft?

STEVE: What's your opinion of him?

TEMPLE: I think he's a very bright chap. Very bright.

STEVE: But –?

TEMPLE: But unfortunately he doesn't know who he's up against.

STEVE: Do you?

TEMPLE: Do I what?

STEVE: Do you know who he's up against?

TEMPLE: (*Quietly*) Yes, darling, I know. He's up against a person who isn't on any police file. A person who – as far as we are concerned – will be utterly and completely ruthless. I don't want you to forget that, Steve.

STEVE: I daresay we'll survive …

118

TEMPLE: Yes – but will Betty Conrad?
FADE IN incidental music.

FADE music.
TEMPLE: Enjoyed your lunch?
STEVE: Yes, very much. Did you?
TEMPLE: Would you like a liqueur?
STEVE: No, I don't think so, it'll only make me sleepy. What are we going to do this afternoon? I suppose you want to go to Innsbruck?
TEMPLE: Later, darling – probably this evening. So if you feel like taking a siesta this afternoon …
STEVE: I thought the trip to Innsbruck was urgent?
TEMPLE: It can wait. I'm not even sure that it's necessary …
STEVE: You mean it might be a trap?
TEMPLE: What's your opinion? You appear to have pretty definite opinions these days.
STEVE: Well, if it was a trap of some kind I don't see why anyone should … (*Breaking off her speech*) Is this man looking for you, Paul?
TEMPLE: Which man?
MAN: (*Approaching*) Herr Temple?
TEMPLE: Yes?
MAN: A telegram, sir …
TEMPLE: Oh, thank you!
TEMPLE takes the telegram and opens it.
There is a pause.
TEMPLE: Oh, good! … (*To the MAN*) That's all right.
MAN: No reply?
TEMPLE: (*Obviously pleased with himself*) No, thank you.
MAN: (*Taking the tip*) Oh, thank you, sir.
STEVE: (*Curious*) Who's that from, Paul?
TEMPLE: (*Vaguely*) Oh, just a friend of mine …

119

STEVE: The Inland Revenue, I presume?

TEMPLE: (*Laughing*) Would you like to see it?

STEVE: Yes, I would.

TEMPLE: Here you are.

STEVE: (*Reading the telegram*) "Munich ... 12.15 ...
            Parcel arrived safely ... Kindest regards. Sam."
            (*Looking up*) Who's Sam?

TEMPLE: Short for Samuel James Hinton. Esquire.

STEVE: Hinton?

TEMPLE: Do you remember the young American we met
            two years ago? We all had lunch together at the
            Waldorf in New York ...

STEVE: Yes, I remember – an awfully nice chap. He was
            with UNO.

TEMPLE: Yes. Well, he isn't any longer. He's working for
            the Americans now – in Munich.

STEVE: But what's all this about a parcel? Did you send
            him a parcel?

TEMPLE: (*Amused*) Sort of ...

STEVE: What do you mean – sort of?

TEMPLE: (*Amused*) Steve, you're asking far too many
            questions today.

STEVE: Well, they don't seem to get me anywhere – I
            get very poor answers!

TEMPLE laughs.

STEVE: Did you send him a parcel, Paul?

TEMPLE: (*Still amused*) Yes, darling – a lovely parcel ...
            all wrapped up in cellophane ...

TEMPLE continues laughing.

FADE on laughter.

FADE UP background noises of a busy thoroughfare.
TEMPLE and STEVE are walking along the pavement.

STEVE: (*Wearily*) It's a pity we didn't get here before the Post Office closed.

TEMPLE: Why?

STEVE: Well, at least they'd have been able to tell us if there is such a street as Briggenstraat, or whatever you call it …

TEMPLE: A lot of people seem to think there is …

STEVE: Well, it's a pity they can't tell us where it is! Gosh, I'm terribly thirsty, Paul!

TEMPLE: (*With a little laugh*) Steve, I don't think you like Innsbruck.

STEVE: Yes, darling, I do, but I'm awfully tired and terribly thirsty.

TEMPLE: Well, there's a café across the road – d'you think you could make it?

STEVE: I'll try – but no promises … (*Weakly*) Dry Martini – here I come!

TEMPLE laughs.

FADE STREET noises down to the distant background.

FADE SCENE.

FADE UP the noise of a small orchestra playing in a café.

WAITER: … Two dry Martinis.

TEMPLE: Thank you. And you can bring another two straight away.

WAITER: (*Surprised*) Two more, sir?

TEMPLE: Yes, two more.

WAITER: Very good, sir …

TEMPLE: Oh, and waiter – do you know a street called Briggenstraat?

WAITER: Briggenstraat?

TEMPLE: Yes.

WAITER: In Innsbruck, sir?

TEMPLE: Yes – in Innsbruck.

WAITER: No, sir. I've never heard of it. I've lived in Innsbruck all my life, but I've never heard of Briggenstraat …

STEVE: Would there be a district of that name, by any chance – or perhaps a village nearby?

WAITER: No, madam. (*Almost an afterthought*) Of course, there's a telephone exchange called Briggenstraat …

TEMPLE: A telephone exchange?

WAITER: Yes, sir …

TEMPLE: Thank you, waiter … (*To STEVE*) I ought to have thought of that, Steve … A telephone exchange. (*Suddenly*) Wait here, darling, there's a telephone box over there. I'll be back in a moment.

FADE the orchestra to the distant background.

The door of a telephone booth is opened.

We hear the lifting of a receiver and the dialling of a number. After a moment we hear the number ringing out and the receiver lifted at the other end of the line.

MAN: (*On the other end of the line: with a faint Austrian accent*) Hello?

TEMPLE: (*On the phone*) Is that Briggenstraat 37?

MAN: Yes – that's right. Who is that speaking?

TEMPLE: My name is Paul Temple …

MAN: Oh, yes, Mr Temple … I've been expecting to hear from you. Perhaps you would care to make a note of this address … Winterstrasse 16 … Winterstrasse 16, Mr Temple …

The MAN puts down the receiver.

TEMPLE: Hello? … Hello? … Hello – hello – hello.

TEMPLE taps the receiver, then after a moment he replaces it.

The door of the telephone box is opened.

FADE IN of the orchestra.
FADE IN of STEVE's voice.

STEVE: You certainly get around, Mr Harper. I didn't expect to see you in Innsbruck.

HARPER: Oh, I frequently visit other branches, Mrs Temple. That's part of my job.

STEVE: I see. When are you going back to Munich?

HARPER: This evening. I'm catching the 10.15.

STEVE: Oh – here's Paul!

TEMPLE: Hello, Harper! What brings you to Innsbruck?

HARPER: I'm here on business, just for a couple of hours. I'm having dinner with one of our accountants.

TEMPLE: I see.

HARPER: I was just asking Mrs Temple if there was any news of Betty Conrad.

TEMPLE: No, I'm afraid not. As a matter of fact the whole business seems to get more complicated.

HARPER: Indeed?

TEMPLE: Yes – I don't suppose you've heard, but June Jackson – Betty's room-mate – has disappeared.

HARPER: June Jackson? Good heavens, this is terrible! When did this happen?

TEMPLE: This morning.

HARPER: You know – really, Mr Temple, something should be done about this!

STEVE: Did you know June, Mr Harper?

HARPER: Yes, I knew her. Not very well, of course. A nice kid – American. But tell me, didn't she leave a note, or anything?

TEMPLE: Nothing.

HARPER: You've told the police about this, of course? You know, they really ought to do something about this, Temple. That poor woman who runs the school – Mrs Weldon – must be distracted.

123

TEMPLE: She's certainly very upset.

HARPER: Temple, tell me – what do you think is behind all this? Why were these girls abducted? Is it a question of money? Has anyone asked for a ransom?

TEMPLE: Not to my knowledge, and we can't be sure that the girls were abducted. They could easily have run away from school, of their own free will. Students do that sometimes, you know. As a matter of fact I believe you suggested that last time we met.

HARPER: Did I?

TEMPLE: Yes.

HARPER: But Betty liked the place. She adored it. Why should <u>she</u> run away?

STEVE: Perhaps she was lured away by someone?

HARPER: Yes, but why? What's the point? I just don't understand it.

TEMPLE: Don't you, Harper?

HARPER: No.

TEMPLE: (*Suddenly*) Well, if you'll excuse us …

HARPER: (*Relaxing*) Yes, of course. There's my man just coming in. Phone me if there's any news, Mr Temple.

TEMPLE: Yes, of course.

HARPER: Goodbye, Mrs Temple.

STEVE: Goodbye.

A pause.

STEVE: He certainly seemed upset about June Jackson, didn't he?

TEMPLE: Yes, he's a curious young man. Very highly strung.

STEVE: You don't often find a bank official with an artistic temperament.

124

TEMPLE: Is that what they call it? (*Calling*) Waiter!

WAITER: (*Approaching*) Yes, sir?

TEMPLE: Perhaps you'd be kind enough to give me a little more information. I'm now looking for a street called Winterstrasse.

WAITER: Ah, Winterstrasse!

TEMPLE: You know it?

WAITER: Yes – yes, of course. It's a little way out of the town sir – on the south side …

TEMPLE: How do I get there?

WAITER: Have you a car?

TEMPLE: Yes.

WAITER: Well, sir – the quickest way would be to keep down this main street to the crossroads. Then you turn left – and it's the …. now let me see … the fourth turning on the right.

FADE.

FADE UP the sound of a car engine.

STEVE: I think this is the fourth turning …

TEMPLE: Yes. This is it …

STEVE: There's a street sign on the corner by the lamp post.

The car slows down.

TEMPLE: Winterstrasse … Yes, that is it. It looks like a cul-de-sac … I think I'll leave the car here … What do you think, Steve?

STEVE: Yes, it's a good idea, Paul.

The car stops and the engine is switched off.

TEMPLE and STEVE get out of the car.

We hear the sound of their footsteps on the pavement.

A pause.

STEVE: It's a gloomy street, isn't it? These houses aren't very attractive …

125

TEMPLE: It's got rather a decayed look about it.

STEVE: Yes. I wonder why it's so deserted? I suppose the houses are occupied.

A moment.

TEMPLE: Can you see the number of this house?

STEVE: Ten ... Yes, this one's ten – the next is twelve – the next is fourteen, I believe.

TEMPLE: Sixteen ... Yes, this is it ...

The footsteps stop.

TEMPLE: Wait at the bottom of the steps, Steve, just in case ...

STEVE: All right.

TEMPLE walks up the stone steps.

TEMPLE: There's an old-fashioned bell.

TEMPLE pulls the bell and it can be heard ringing inside the house.

There is a pause.

STEVE: Is there anyone in?

TEMPLE: I can't hear anyone.

STEVE: Try the bell again.

TEMPLE: All right.

The bell can be heard ringing inside the house.

STEVE: (*Approaching TEMPLE*) But didn't the man on the phone say that they were expecting you?

TEMPLE: No, not exactly ...

STEVE: There's something I don't like about this road.

TEMPLE: I wonder if the house is empty?

As TEMPLE speaks there is the sound of a car in the distance.

STEVE: Oh, look, there's a car turned the corner at the bottom of the road! I thought this was a cul-de-sac?

TEMPLE: Yes, so did I ...

The car approaches.

STEVE: Paul – that light!

TEMPLE: What the devil is he doing? It's like a searchlight …

The car draws nearer.

STEVE: I can't see a thing … It's blinding me …

TEMPLE: (*Urgently*) Steve, get down! … Get down, darling!

The car races past and simultaneous with the noise of the car can be heard repeated revolver shots.

The car quickly disappears into the distance.

TEMPLE: Steve, are you hurt?

STEVE: (*Unhurt, but frightened*) Oh, Paul! …

TEMPLE: Steve, are you all right?

STEVE: Yes, I'm all right – but what about you?

TEMPLE: I'm all right, dear. Not a scratch … Did you see who it was, in the car?

STEVE: No, I couldn't see anything – the light was blinding …

TEMPLE: I can't understand it. I just can't understand it …

STEVE: What do you mean?

TEMPLE: What a minute, I'll get my torch out …

TEMPLE takes out his torch.

TEMPLE: I don't understand how they missed us, Steve … It's quite extraordinary – I just don't see how he could have missed us …

STEVE: Well, he did, darling …

A moment.

STEVE: What are you looking for?

TEMPLE: I'm just looking at the door and the stonework … There's no sign of a bullet mark anywhere …

STEVE: Well, what does that prove?

TEMPLE: It proves that the man in the car deliberately aimed very wide, or …

STEVE: Or what, darling?

TEMPLE: By Timothy, Steve! I've got it! He was using blanks!

FADE IN incidental music.

FADE DOWN music.
FADE UP noise of the hotel entrance hall.

TEMPLE: Good evening. My key, please …

RECEPTIONIST: Certainly, sir. (*After a moment*) Here's your key, Mr Temple – and have you seen Countess Dekker?

TEMPLE: Countess Dekker? No.

RECEPTIONIST: She was here a few moments ago, asking for you, sir. This is the second time she's called this evening. I think you'll probably find her in the lounge, Mr Temple.

TEMPLE: I see. Thank you very much.

FADE noises to the background.
FADE UP the orchestra in the hotel lounge.

TEMPLE: (*Approaching*) I'm so sorry to have kept you waiting, I'm afraid I wasn't expecting you …

ELSA: No, of course not, Mr Temple. I came on the off chance. Oh, good evening, Mrs Temple.

STEVE: Good evening.

ELSA: Mr Temple, I hate to trouble you, I know you're frightfully busy, but something rather unusual has happened this afternoon. I think you ought to know about it.

TEMPLE: Well – go on, Countess …

ELSA: This afternoon I went shopping in Garmisch. I parked my car in the usual

128

place. When I got back to the car I found this envelope on the driving seat.

TEMPLE takes the envelope.

TEMPLE: Thank you … No name on it, I see … I suppose it was intended for you?

ELSA: I really don't know.

STEVE: And what was inside it?

ELSA: This ring … And this cocktail stick – like the one Mr Temple found in June Jackson's room last night.

TEMPLE: M'm … Have you seen this ring before?

ELSA: No, but I was speaking to Mrs Weldon on the phone and I described the ring to her. She said it was June Jackson's.

STEVE: June Jackson's?

ELSA: Yes. But if it is June's, Mr Temple – why should anyone leave it in my car?

STEVE: Perhaps it was intended as a clue – or possibly a message of some kind.

ELSA: But why <u>my</u> car?

TEMPLE: It could have been a mistake, of course.

ELSA: Yes, but somehow I don't think it was.

TEMPLE: Have you told Mr France about this?

ELSA: Yes.

TEMPLE: And what did he say?

ELSA: He told me to get in touch with you …

TEMPLE: Did Mr France know that you were going into Garmisch this afternoon?

ELSA: Why, yes, of course. Why do you ask that?

TEMPLE: (*Ignoring her question*) Well, leave the ring and the cocktail stick with me. I'll have a word with Inspector Breckshaft

	about it. I shall probably be seeing him tomorrow morning.
ELSA:	(*Puzzled by TEMPLE's manner*) Yes, all right, Mr Temple. I'm sorry to have troubled you.
TEMPLE:	Not at all. Thank you very much for calling.
STEVE:	Can we offer you a drink, or some coffee, perhaps?
ELSA:	No – no thank you, Mrs Temple. I really must be going. Goodnight.
TEMPLE:	Goodnight.
STEVE:	Goodnight.
ELSA:	Goodnight, Mrs Temple.
FADE.	

FADE IN the sound of a lift gate opening.

STEVE:	The lift attendant doesn't seem to be here.
TEMPLE:	It's all right, Steve. We'll manage. In you go, darling.

TEMPLE and STEVE enter the lift.
The gates close.
We hear the sound of the lift ascending.

STEVE:	Do you think that ring really belongs to June?
TEMPLE:	I'm quite sure it does.
STEVE:	How can you be sure?
TEMPLE:	Because I saw it this morning.
STEVE:	This morning?
TEMPLE:	That's what I said, darling.
STEVE:	But how could you see it this morning? When we got to the school June had already gone.
TEMPLE:	I know.

130

STEVE: (*Puzzled*) And you never went into her room …
TEMPLE: Not this morning.
STEVE: Oh, so you saw it last night.
TEMPLE: (*Amused*) I didn't say that …
STEVE: (*A little exasperated*) Now, Paul, will you stop it
           and answer my question?

The lift stops.

TEMPLE: Here we are, Steve!

TEMPLE opens the gates.

TEMPLE: Come along, darling.

FADE ON the closing of the lift gates.

FADE IN the noise of an electric razor.

STEVE: (*Yawning*) What time is it, Paul?
TEMPLE: (*From the background*) It's nearly nine o'clock
           …
STEVE: Your beastly razor woke me …
TEMPLE: We should have been up hours ago …
STEVE: Why don't they fit those things with silencers?
TEMPLE: I can't imagine why. It's a lovely day, darling.
           Come along, get up!
STEVE: Has she brought the tea?
TEMPLE: Not yet. Any minute now, I should think.

The electric razor stops.

STEVE gets out of bed.

STEVE: What day is today, Paul?
TEMPLE: It's Friday … (*A moment*) The 18th.
STEVE: Friday, the 18th … Oh … What are we doing
           today?
TEMPLE: Well, I'd rather like to go over to
           Oberammergau again.
STEVE: What – to the hotel?
TEMPLE: Yes. I thought we might run over for lunch.
STEVE: Why? Do you want to see the Gunters?

131

TEMPLE: Well, actually I want to take another look at that photograph.

STEVE: Which photograph?

TEMPLE: The one in the small lounge. The photograph of Fritz Gunter that was taken on the film set.

STEVE: But why on earth should you want to see that?

STEVE is interrupted by knocking at the door.

TEMPLE: Here's some tea – come in.

The door opens.

STEVE: Good morning. Would you put the tray down by the dressing table, please?

FADE.

FADE IN voices and background noises of the Hotel Reumer lobby.

STEVE: They're certainly very busy today. Do you think we'll get a table?

TEMPLE: It looks a little doubtful.

STEVE: We should have telephoned.

TEMPLE: I particularly didn't want to do that.

STEVE: But surely the Gunters would never …

TEMPLE: Gunter's just caught sight of us. Steve, I want you to sneak into the small lounge and take a look at the photograph I told you about. There's a date on it. I want to know what it is.

STEVE: Yes, all right.

FRITZ: (*Approaching*) Why, Mr and Mrs Temple. This is a pleasant surprise. I am delighted you should honour us again so soon.

TEMPLE: It was such a pleasant morning, we were tempted to go out for a drive.

FRITZ: Of course.

STEVE: And finding ourselves in Oberammergau we instinctively started to think of food and drink

	(*With a little laugh*) – in fact we don't seem to have thought of anything else since we've been in Germany, Herr Gunter.
FRITZ:	(*Smiling*) I'm delighted to hear it, Mrs Temple. Shall we go into the cocktail bar?
STEVE:	Excuse me a moment, Paul …
TEMPLE:	Yes, of course, darling. We'll be in the cocktail bar.
FRITZ:	The cloakroom's on the first floor, Mrs Temple.
STEVE:	Thank you.

FADE noises to the background.

CROSS FADE to background noises of a crowded cocktail bar.

FADE voices to the background.

TEMPLE:	Your very good health, Herr Gunter.
FRITZ:	Thank you, Mr Temple. And yours too, sir.

They drink.

TEMPLE:	(*After drinking*) By Timothy, I needed that …
FRITZ:	Mr Temple, I've been meaning to ask you … that message I gave you – the one over the telephone – was it all right?
TEMPLE:	Well, not exactly. I'm afraid there was a little misunderstanding.
FRITZ:	Oh? I am so sorry. What was the trouble?
TEMPLE:	Well – it turned out that Briggenstraat wasn't a street after all. It was a telephone exchange.
FRITZ:	A telephone exchange! But of course! That was very stupid of me. I should have asked the caller to repeat the message. I'm sorry, Mr Temple.
TEMPLE:	Oh, that's all right. We managed to get it sorted out. Ah, here's my wife!
FRITZ:	Come and sit down, Mrs Temple. I've ordered you a dry Martini – is that all right?

STEVE: Yes. Perfect, thank you, Herr Gunter. Is Mrs Gunter here today?

FRITZ: Yes, we are rather – what do you say – short-handed?

TEMPLE: Yes, that's right – short-handed …

FRITZ: We're rather short-handed, so my wife's doing a little supervising in the kitchen. (*With a laugh*) Just to make matters worse. Which reminds me, I think perhaps I ought to go and have a word with her. Will you excuse me?

STEVE: Yes, of course.

FRITZ: I'll see about your table, Mr Temple.

TEMPLE: Thank you.

A pause.

TEMPLE: Well?

STEVE: It's gone, Paul …

TEMPLE: What do you mean – it's gone?

STEVE: The photograph – it's not in the room …

TEMPLE: Are you sure?

STEVE: Absolutely sure.

TEMPLE: It was in the far corner on the wall near the …

STEVE: Yes, I know, darling. It's gone, I tell you. It's been replaced by a very colourful photograph of the ski jump at Garmisch.

TEMPLE: Has it? … (*Obviously intrigued*) Has it, by Timothy?

FADE IN incidental music.

FADE music.

STEVE: Paul, have you seen those postcards I bought at Oberammergau? I seem to have lost them, darling …

TEMPLE: Didn't you put them inside the guide book?

STEVE:	Oh, yes. Here they are! I want to send one to Charlie. What time does the post go?
TEMPLE:	From the hotel? About six, I think.
STEVE:	What time is it now?
TEMPLE:	It's just about five-thirty.
STEVE:	Oh, good! What shall I say to Charlie, Paul?
TEMPLE:	Lovely weather … wonderful views … delightful country … back soon.
STEVE:	Back soon?
TEMPLE:	Keep him on his toes.
STEVE:	(*Amused*) Oh, yes. (*After a pause*) Paul …
TEMPLE:	Yes?
STEVE:	Why were you so interested in that photograph at the Hotel Reumer?
TEMPLE:	There was a date on it. Unfortunately I didn't make a note of it the first time I saw the photograph.
STEVE:	Yes, but why are you interested in the date?
TEMPLE:	Because I want to know exactly when the photograph was taken. Once I know that I can easily find out which studio it was – and the name of the film.
STEVE:	(*Puzzled*) Yes, but where will that get you, darling? After all, we know that Fritz Gunter was an actor, so I fail to see …

STEVE breaks off as someone knocks on the door.

TEMPLE:	There's someone at the door.
STEVE:	(*Surprised*) I'll go.

The door is opened.

STEVE:	Oh, good evening, Herr Breckshaft.
BRECKSHAFT:	(*Off*) May I come in, Mrs Temple?

STEVE:	Yes, of course. It's Herr Breckshaft, darling.
TEMPLE:	Come in, Breckshaft.
BRECKSHAFT:	Forgive me coming straight up to your room, Mr Temple, but I have some news for you.
TEMPLE:	You've found Betty Conrad?
BRECKSHAFT:	Yes. She's dead. We found her body in a field near Schreidenstein.
TEMPLE:	Schreidenstein? That's Countess Dekker's place.
BRECKSHAFT:	Yes … The body was in a dell about two miles from the house. It's not surprising we haven't found it before – it was covered in leaves and debris. Her face was battered – her coat has been pulled over her head… There'd obviously been a struggle.
TEMPLE:	Was it a blue coat, by any chance?
BRECKSHAFT:	(*Surprised*) Yes, it was a blue coat.
TEMPLE:	How did you come to find her?
BRECKSHAFT:	We had an anonymous telephone call about an hour ago. It was a man's voice. He told us exactly where to go.
TEMPLE:	I see. And what time was it when you found the body?
BRECKSHAFT:	Oh, about four-thirty – five o'clock.
TEMPLE:	You've no idea how long she'd been lying there?
BRECKSHAFT:	No. I haven't got the medical report yet. I shall get it as soon as I get back to the office.
TEMPLE:	I see. Well, thank you, Breckshaft, for letting me know about this.

BRECKSHAFT:	If only we had some idea of what this was all about, Mr Temple. If only we knew what the motive was …
STEVE:	You've telephoned the school?
BRECKSHAFT:	Not yet, Mrs Temple.
TEMPLE:	And Countess Dekker?
BRECKSHAFT:	No, I haven't seen the Countess, but I shall have to, of course, since the body was virtually found on her property.
TEMPLE:	I shall be interested to hear how she reacts when she does see you. Well, I'm sorry about this, Breckshaft. It's a pity it had to finish this way.
BRECKSHAFT:	Yes – a great pity. I'll telephone you later this evening, Mr Temple, if I have any more news.
TEMPLE:	Thank you, Breckshaft. I'll see you to the lift … I shan't be a moment, darling.
STEVE:	(*Obviously upset*) Goodbye, Herr Breckshaft.
BRECKSHAFT:	Goodnight, Mrs Temple.

The door closes.
STEVE pours herself a drink.
We hear the sound of liquid being poured into a glass.
There is a pause.
The door opens and TEMPLE returns.

STEVE:	I'm having a drink, Paul – do you want one?
TEMPLE:	What is it?
STEVE:	It's brandy – it was in the flask.
TEMPLE:	Yes, make it a pretty stiff one, dear.
STEVE:	Paul, couldn't this murder have been prevented?

137

TEMPLE: Steve, I tried! I did everything I could. I even
            … (*He hesitates*)
STEVE: Go on, darling.
TEMPLE: I don't think you realise it, Steve, but – I've
            been working like mad to prevent a second
            murder.
STEVE: A second murder?
The telephone rings.
TEMPLE: Yes, but please don't ask me for details.
TEMPLE breaks off hearing the telephone.
TEMPLE: It's all right, I'll take it.
TEMPLE lifts the receiver.
TEMPLE: (*On the phone*) Hello?
OPERATOR: (*On the other end of the line*) Herr Temple?
TEMPLE: Yes …
OPERATOR: I have a personal call for you from London –
            from Sir Graham Forbes.
TEMPLE: Thank you. Put him on, please. (*To STEVE*)
            It's Sir Graham …
There is a pause.
FORBES: (*On the other end of the line*) Hello –
            Temple?
TEMPLE: Hello, Sir Graham.
FORBES: Temple, can you hear me?
TEMPLE: Yes.
FORBES: I've got some news for you.
TEMPLE: Yes, I've got some news for you too, Sir
            Graham. Betty Conrad's dead.
FORBES: Dead?
TEMPLE: Yes – they found her body about an hour ago.
            She was murdered.
FORBES: Temple, are you all right?
TEMPLE: Of course I'm all right!

138

FORBES: Then what the devil are you talking about? Betty Conrad's alive. She's here now – in my office – sitting opposite me …!

END OF EPISODE FOUR

EPISODE FIVE

A DRY MARTINI

OPEN TO:

TEMPLE: They found her body about an hour ago. She was murdered.

FORBES: I tell you, Temple, Betty Conrad's here – now – in my office – sitting opposite me!

TEMPLE: But, Sir Graham, the body of a girl about Betty's age was found here this afternoon. Breckshaft thought it was Betty Conrad.

FORBES: But why should he?

TEMPLE: I suppose it was only natural. But tell me, is she all right?

FORBES: There's nothing wrong physically, but she isn't normal by any means. She either can't or won't tell us why she left the school and how she got to London …

TEMPLE: Has she been drugged, do you think?

FORBES: I don't think so, Temple. There are none of the usual symptoms, anyhow.

TEMPLE: Where did you find her?

FORBES: One of Vosper's men found her sitting on a seat in Hyde Park. She looked dazed and ill so he questioned the girl – to his astonishment he discovered she was Betty Conrad. He telephoned Harley Street at once and her stepmother came along and identified her.

TEMPLE: So there's no doubt that it is Betty Conrad?

FORBES: Not the slightest! By the way, you might let her father know – I understand he's still in Germany.

TEMPLE: Yes, he's here in Garmisch.

FORBES: And you might pass the word to Breckshaft as well. It'll save me phoning him direct.

TEMPLE: Yes, of course. Sir Graham, what line are you taking about Betty Conrad now?

FORBES: What do you mean?

TEMPLE: Well – what's the next step?

FORBES: So far as we're concerned, there isn't a next step. Betty Conrad's safe so …

TEMPLE: Yes, but there's this other girl …

FORBES: That's Breckshaft's pigeon. In any case, I doubt whether that's tied up with the Conrad affair.

TEMPLE: We shall see. Anyway, I'll be in touch, Sir Graham.

FORBES: Yes, all right. My love to Steve.

TEMPLE: Thanks for telephoning. Goodbye.

TEMPLE replaces the receiver.

STEVE: Paul, what was all that about?

TEMPLE: Betty Conrad's alive. She's in London.

STEVE: What! Paul, are you sure?

TEMPLE: There's no doubt about it, Steve – she's in London. Her stepmother's identified her.

STEVE: Is she all right?

TEMPLE: Yes – except that she won't talk …

STEVE: Then what about this other girl – the one that Breckshaft found?

TEMPLE: That's obviously someone else …

A slight pause.

STEVE: Paul, how could Betty Conrad possibly have got back to England without remembering anything?

TEMPLE: Sir Graham didn't say she can't remember anything – he simply said she won't talk.

STEVE: Do you think she may be frightened to talk?

TEMPLE: Well, that's possible, of course. Sir Graham doesn't think she's been drugged.

STEVE: Perhaps her father will persuade her to talk when he gets back to London.

144

TEMPLE:	Yes – and that reminds me, I promised to get in touch with Dr Conrad.
STEVE:	He's at the Park Hotel.
TEMPLE:	Yes …
STEVE:	Unless he's already left. He did say he was returning to England.
TEMPLE:	Yes, but he's not going until tomorrow.
STEVE:	Oh!
TEMPLE:	What is it?
STEVE:	Oh dear, it just occurred to me – if he hasn't gone, the Inspector might have told him that that other girl …
TEMPLE:	… that the dead girl was his daughter! Yes, I'd better get in touch with Breckshaft straight away …

TEMPLE picks up the telephone receiver.
FADE.

FADE IN the opening of a door.
The door closes.

BRECKSHAFT:	(*Approaching*) Please come in. Take this chair, Mrs Temple, I think you'll find it more comfortable …
STEVE:	Thank you, Herr Breckshaft.
BRECKSHAFT:	I'm glad you were able to come round so quickly, Temple.
TEMPLE:	Well, events seem to be moving so fast – the least we can do is try to keep up with them.
BRECKSHAFT:	Yes. I'm still bewildered by the news you gave me on the telephone. It seems so strange that this girl – Betty Conrad – should have found her way to England … A great many people have been looking

for the young lady during the past few days.

TEMPLE: Yes. But tell me – what made you think that this other girl – the murdered girl – was Betty Conrad?

BRECKSHAFT: Well, the dead girl was approximately the same height, Temple, and had the same coloured hair as Betty Conrad. Also she was wearing a dress and shoes which had been bought in Bond Street, London.

STEVE: Yes, of course that would make you think it was Betty.

TEMPLE: Did you manage to get hold of Dr Conrad?

BRECKSHAFT: No, he was out when I telephoned his hotel. I left a message for him to get in touch with us as soon as he got back.

The door opens.

TEMPLE: Good. Now, Inspector, I'd like to take the coat that the dead girl was wearing and …

TEMPLE breaks off.

CLERK: Excuse me, sir …

BRECKSHAFT: Yes – what is it?

CLERK: Dr Conrad is here, sir, and would like to see you …

TEMPLE: He hasn't lost much time. When did you telephone him?

BRECKSHAFT: About an hour ago.

TEMPLE: Inspector, I suggest we don't tell him about the murdered girl – just that his daughter is safe.

BRECKSHAFT: Why?

TEMPLE:	Because the murdered girl is hardly any concern of Dr Conrad's. Or perhaps you don't agree with me?
BRECKSHAFT:	I don't see why we shouldn't tell Dr Conrad about … (*He hesitates*) No, on second thoughts, perhaps you're right. (*To the CLERK*) Ask him to come in.
CLERK:	Will you please come in?
CONRAD:	Thank you.
There is a pause.	
BRECKSHAFT:	Good evening, Dr Conrad. I think you know Mr and Mrs Temple?
CONRAD:	Yes … There was a message at the hotel, Herr Breckshaft.
BRECKSHAFT:	That's right. I telephoned you about an hour ago.
CONRAD:	Is it bad news?
BRECKSHAFT:	On the contrary, sir – it's very good news so far as you're concerned. Your daughter's in London and apparently quite safe …
CONRAD:	(*Surprised*) In London?
TEMPLE:	Sir Graham Forbes telephoned me. Betty was actually in his office at the time.
CONRAD:	And she's all right?
TEMPLE:	Yes, I understand so. Except that she refuses to talk …
CONRAD:	You mean she refuses to give an explanation of her disappearance?
TEMPLE:	Yes. According to Sir Graham she won't say anything.
STEVE:	Dr Conrad, has your daughter ever suffered from amnesia?

147

CONRAD: No, never. If she had I should have told the police about it a long time ago.

TEMPLE: Well, no doubt you'll talk to her when you get back to London.

CONRAD: I most certainly will.

TEMPLE: And if you feel she's deliberately concealing anything, either from fear or any other reason, let Sir Graham know.

CONRAD: Of course. In any case I'll probably keep her at home for a few weeks, until the end of term.

STEVE: Will you be sending her back to Mrs Weldon's next term?

CONRAD: I don't know. She's due to leave school fairly soon anyway. I'll talk to my wife about it. Meanwhile, I'm very grateful to you, Mr Temple – and Herr Breckshaft, of course.

BRECKSHAFT: I'm only sorry we could not be of more help.

CONRAD: You've been most helpful, and more than kind. Betty's safe, thank God; that's the main thing. Give me a ring when you get back to London, Mr Temple, and I'll let you know how Betty's getting along.

TEMPLE: Thank you. Yes, I'll do that.

CONRAD: Goodbye, Mrs Temple.

STEVE: Goodbye, Dr Conrad.

BRECKSHAFT: I'll see you out, doctor.

The door opens.

There is a slight pause.

STEVE: Well? What now, Paul?

TEMPLE: I want to have another word with Breckshaft, then we'll go over to the

148

	school and break the news to Mrs Weldon.
STEVE:	I was forgetting Mrs Weldon. I expect she'll be delighted …

FADE.

FADE IN the voice of MRS WELDON.

MRS WELDON:	Well, of course I'm delighted the silly girl's alright.
TEMPLE:	But?
MRS WELDON:	Well, it's not very satisfactory, is it? I mean, it's all rather vague – Betty's suddenly turning up in London without accounting for her movements.
TEMPLE:	Well, that's all I can tell you, Mrs Weldon.
MRS WELDON:	Hasn't she offered any explanation?
TEMPLE:	Apparently not.
MRS WELDON:	Well, what exactly happened? How was she found? Presumably she wasn't just conjured out of the air!
TEMPLE:	A policeman found her sitting on a bench in Hyde Park.
MRS WELDON:	In Hyde Park?
TEMPLE:	Yes. But I'm sure you'll be getting a letter from Dr Conrad in a day or two, Mrs Weldon. He'll probably write to you after he's seen Betty himself.
MRS WELDON:	Yes. Well, I'm delighted the silly girl's all right, of course – not that I had any fears on that score – but I should have thought Herr Breckshaft would have been in touch with me personally by now.

TEMPLE:	I told him I was seeing you, Mrs Weldon. He probably considers that quite sufficient.
MRS WELDON:	Well, I don't. It was his duty to get in touch with me personally, straight away.
TEMPLE:	But Herr Breckshaft didn't actually get the message, Mrs Weldon. I got it.
STEVE:	I don't think you quite understand, Mrs Weldon. It was my husband that Sir Graham telephoned …
MRS WELDON:	I fully appreciate that, Mrs Temple, but nevertheless, there's a certain etiquette in these matters. Incidentally, does Elliot – Mr France – know that the girl's all right?
TEMPLE:	I haven't told him. I trust that's not a breach of etiquette, Mrs Weldon?
MRS WELDON:	(*Ignoring the sarcasm*) No, but I think the poor man ought to know. He's been so terribly worried, although I can't imagine why …
STEVE:	Mr France was a suspect – that's why.
MRS WELDON:	A suspect? What on earth are you talking about?
STEVE:	You forget he was supposed to have invited Betty to tea on the day she disappeared.

The door opens.

MRS WELDON:	Yes, but surely no one in their right senses would have considered Elliot … What is it, Maria?
MARIA:	Countess Dekker and Mr France are here, madam, and would like to see you.
MRS WELDON:	Oh, come in, Elliot! We were just talking about you …

150

ELSA:	Have you heard the news, Elizabeth?
MRS WELDON:	Yes, Elsa, I've just been talking to Mr Temple about it. But how did you know that …
FRANCE:	This must have been a great shock to you, my dear. I can't tell you how sorry we are. Mr Temple, there's something I'd like you to know. When the body was found …
MRS WELDON:	Body? What body? Elliot, what are you talking about?
FRANCE:	I'm talking about Betty Conrad! I thought you said you knew?
ELSA:	Elizabeth, haven't you heard? Betty's dead! They found her body in a field near …
MRS WELDON:	Mr Temple, what is this? I thought you said Betty was in London.
TEMPLE:	Betty Conrad isn't dead. She is in London. I had a telephone message from Sir Graham Forbes about an hour ago.
FRANCE:	But that's impossible!
ELSA:	They found the poor girl this afternoon – dead …
TEMPLE:	That wasn't Betty Conrad!
ELSA:	It wasn't?
TEMPLE:	No.
FRANCE:	Are you sure, Mr Temple?
TEMPLE:	Quite sure. I've told you – Betty Conrad's in London.
ELSA:	Then if it wasn't Betty Conrad they found – who was it?
TEMPLE:	We don't know – not yet. The police haven't identified the body.

MRS WELDON:	Oh, heavens!
STEVE:	What is it, Mrs Weldon?
ELSA:	Elizabeth, what is it?
FRANCE:	What's the matter, Elizabeth?
MRS WELDON:	It's just occurred to me that if it isn't Betty …
TEMPLE:	The dead girl isn't June Jackson, Mrs Weldon – if that's what you're thinking.
MRS WELDON:	That's exactly what I was thinking. You're sure it isn't June?
TEMPLE:	I'm quite sure. In the first place June and Betty Conrad are quite different in appearance. There could be no question of confusion. And in the second place … (*He hesitates*)

A tiny pause.

FRANCE:	Well, go on, Mr Temple. In the second place …?
TEMPLE:	In the second place I have my own reasons for knowing that the dead girl could not possibly be June Jackson.

FADE IN incidental music.

FADE music.
FADE UP the noise of a car engine.
A pause.

STEVE:	Paul, what made you shut up like a clam about June Jackson?
TEMPLE:	Did I shut up like a clam?
STEVE:	Yes. You got all mysterious and refused to explain anything. To put it mildly, you circumnavigated. Yet you were so arbitrary.

152

TEMPLE: My! Those are mighty big words, Mrs Temple!

STEVE: How can you be so sure that the dead girl isn't June Jackson?

TEMPLE: Because I happen to know that June's back in America by now with her parents.

STEVE: In America? Are you sure?

TEMPLE: Quite sure. Because I planned the whole thing. That was the point of the telegram from Sam Hinton. June Jackson was the parcel he referred to.

STEVE: You mean Sam met her at Munich and put her on board the plane?

TEMPLE: That's right, darling.

STEVE: Why didn't you tell me about this before?

TEMPLE: Because I had no time for explanations, my sweet, that's why. I had to act quickly.

STEVE: Paul, was June is some kind of danger?

TEMPLE: She certainly was.

STEVE: How did you find out about it?

TEMPLE: About what?

STEVE: How did you find out that she was in danger?

TEMPLE: I looked into her eyes.

STEVE: You what?

TEMPLE: I looked into her eyes.

STEVE: You looked into …

TEMPLE: (*Changing the subject*) Steve, as soon as we get back to the hotel, I want you to start packing.

STEVE: Then we're leaving Garmisch?

TEMPLE: That's right.

STEVE: Are we going back to London?

TEMPLE: We are.

STEVE: When?

TEMPLE: Perhaps tomorrow – perhaps the next day – maybe next week …

STEVE: (*After a moment*) Paul, does this mean you're giving up the case?

TEMPLE: Darling, have you ever known me give up anything?

STEVE: You gave up that diet you started …

TEMPLE: Diets are different, darling. They don't count.

FADE IN incidental music.

FADE music.

FADE UP background noises of a hotel vestibule.

STEVE: Look, Paul! There's Madame Klein …

TEMPLE: So it is.

STEVE: She's coming over.

KLEIN: (*Approaching*) I would like to speak to you, Mr Temple. Could you spare me a moment?

TEMPLE: Yes, of course. Shall we go into the lounge?

KLEIN: Thank you …

A pause.

FADE IN the sound of a light orchestra playing in the lounge.

TEMPLE: Now, Madame Klein – what is it? What's worrying you?

KLEIN: It's Gerda, Mr Temple …

TEMPLE: Gerda? …

KLEIN: … She's my assistant, at the shop … You probably remember her, Mrs Temple – a tall, fair haired, rather good-looking girl. I believe she attended to you when you bought the blouse.

STEVE: Oh yes, of course. I remember her very well.

TEMPLE: What's happened to Gerda?

KLEIN: Well, she seems to have disappeared, Mr Temple. She went out to lunch yesterday and did not return to the shop. No one has seen her since midday yesterday.

STEVE: Have you told the police about this?

KLEIN: No, not yet, Mrs Temple. But I'm very worried – terribly worried. I thought your husband might be able to advise me.

TEMPLE: Well, I advise you to go to the police, Madame Klein, and then get in touch with the girl's parents.

STEVE: D'you know her parents?

KLEIN: Yes, I do, Mrs Temple. And I must confess I'm rather frightened of getting in touch with them.

STEVE: Frightened?

KLEIN: Yes; you see Gerda's father is a wealthy publisher – one of the biggest in Germany. Gerda was not attracted by the book business, she was mad on fashions, like so many girls of her age. Her father paid a premium for her to join our shop in Munich. When I came to Garmisch they asked me to bring her with me and keep an eye on the girl.

TEMPLE: Then she lives in Garmisch?

KLEIN: Oh yes, she has a small apartment in the Baumerstrasse. I've seen her landlady, who said that Gerda left the flat just after lunch yesterday – presumably to return to the shop. But she didn't return.

TEMPLE: And she didn't return to the flat last night?

KLEIN: No.

STEVE: You don't think there's a young man …

KLEIN: No, I'm sure it's nothing like that, Mrs Temple …

TEMPLE: Madame Klein, tell me – did Gerda have a distinguishing mark of any kind?

KLEIN: No – no, I don't think so. Why do you ask?

TEMPLE: Well, do you know of anything that would help to identify her?

KLEIN:	Nothing … Oh yes – there's one little thing that might help, Mr Temple.
TEMPLE:	What's that?
KLEIN:	She had two teeth missing at the side – here … and she wore a – what do you call it – a plate?
STEVE:	A denture …
KLEIN:	That is it. I remember only this weekend, she said one of the teeth was loose and she must see her dentist about it.
TEMPLE:	Thank you. Now don't worry. Leave this with me. I'll contact the police for you. Steve, take Madame Klein to the small bar and give her a brandy. I'm going to make a telephone call, darling.
STEVE:	Yes, all right, Paul.
FADE.	

FADE IN of TEMPLE on the telephone.

TEMPLE:	(*On the phone*) Hello? … Hello? …
CLERK:	(*On the other end of the line*) One moment, Mr Temple … Herr Breckshaft is coming …

A pause.

BRECKSHAFT:	(*On the other end of the line*) Temple?
TEMPLE:	Breckshaft, I've just had a visit from a woman called Madame Klein …
BRECKSHAFT:	I know the lady – she is from the dress shop – Brenner's.
TEMPLE:	That's right. It seems her assistant – a girl named Gerda Holman – has been missing since midday yesterday. My wife knows this girl by sight and says that her

description would tally roughly with that of Betty Conrad.

BRECKSHAFT: Indeed?

TEMPLE: The girl from the shop has one distinguishing feature – a denture with two teeth on it. One of them, apparently, is loose …

BRECKSHAFT: All right. I'll look into this. I think I know what's in your mind.

TEMPLE: Thank you, Breckshaft.

BRECKSHAFT: I'll ring you back if there's any news.

TEMPLE: All right, thank you again. Goodbye.

TEMPLE puts down the receiver.

The door of the telephone box opens and TEMPLE enters the vestibule.

FADE UP background noises of the vestibule.

PAGE BOY: Mr Temple, please?

TEMPLE: Yes, what is it?

PAGE BOY: A lady asked me to give you this note, sir.

TEMPLE: Oh, thank you. Just a minute.

TEMPLE opens the note and reads it.

TEMPLE: That's all right. I'll see to it.

PAGE BOY: Thank you, sir.

FADE.

FADE IN the opening and closing of a door.

STEVE: Hello, dear.

TEMPLE: I've been looking for you in the lounge.

STEVE: Madame Klein decided she didn't want the drink, after all.

TEMPLE: Did she say anything else after I left?

STEVE: No, nothing of importance. I think she was quite genuinely distressed, don't you?

TEMPLE: I don't know. It's very difficult to tell with some women. I shouldn't be surprised if she isn't a pretty good actress. Steve, you remember the morning you bought the blouse …?

STEVE: Yes?

TEMPLE: Can you remember whether …?

TEMPLE is interrupted by the ringing of the telephone.

STEVE: Are you expecting a call?

TEMPLE: It could be the Inspector, I suppose – but he's been pretty quick, if it is.

TEMPLE lifts the receiver.

TEMPLE: (*On the phone*) Hello?

HARPER: (*On the other end of the line*) Good evening, Mr Temple. This is Denis Harper.

TEMPLE: Oh, hello, Harper.

HARPER: I thought I'd give you a ring, just in case I don't see you before I go back to England.

TEMPLE: Back to England? Are you leaving Germany, then?

HARPER: Yes. This Conrad case has had some repercussions on my career. I thought it would – eventually. It's all these confounded police enquiries. You know how they've checked up on me during the past week or two.

TEMPLE: It was just routine, I told you that.

HARPER: I'm afraid the bank directors don't look at it that way. They've transferred me to our Kensington Branch.

TEMPLE: Well, that sounds pleasant enough. Won't you be glad to get back to London?

HARPER: No jolly fear. I'm just a cog in the machine over there. Daren't even dash out for a cup of coffee when I feel like it. It's too frightfully depressing

158

	to even think about. (*Pause*) There's no news of Betty, I suppose?
TEMPLE:	Yes, as a matter of fact there is.
HARPER:	Oh?
TEMPLE:	She's been found.
HARPER:	(*After a moment*) Oh, has she? Well, we've been expecting it, haven't we?
TEMPLE:	Well, that rather depends. She's alive and apparently quite well, if that's what you mean.
HARPER:	(*Almost tonelessly*) Alive, did you say?
TEMPLE:	Yes, that's right, Harper – she's alive.
HARPER:	Well, I … I … I don't know what to say.
TEMPLE:	You sound surprised?
HARPER:	I am.
TEMPLE:	It's never wise to jump to conclusions, Harper.
HARPER:	No, I suppose it isn't. (*Regaining a little of his self-confidence*) Although everyone tends to do it – even the directors of my bank.
TEMPLE:	When do you go back to London?
HARPER:	Tomorrow.
TEMPLE:	As soon as that? Well, I expect to be back there myself quite soon. You know where to get in touch with me if you want me.
HARPER:	Yes, thank you. (*After a moment*) This is on the level, isn't it? I mean Betty is – she is all right?
TEMPLE:	Yes, it's on the level, Harper. She's quite all right.
HARPER:	Well – it's very good news, I must say.
TEMPLE:	I'm glad you think so.
HARPER:	Well, goodbye. Give my regards to Mrs Temple.
TEMPLE:	Thank you, I'll do that. Goodbye, Harper.

TEMPLE replaces the receiver.

| STEVE: | Was he pleased to hear about Betty Conrad? |

TEMPLE: I don't know if pleased is quite the right word. He appears to be more concerned about himself at the moment. The bank have transferred him to Kensington, apparently under the impression that he's mixed up in this Conrad affair. So I suppose from his point of view it's a bit ironic that Betty Conrad should have turned up after all.

STEVE: Still, he was on familiar terms with the girl. If she'd been murdered he would have been a suspect, along with Elliot France and Countess Dekker.

TEMPLE: Yes. You know, it's rather curious, Steve – when I told him that Betty had been found he immediately jumped to the conclusion that she'd been found murdered.

STEVE: Perhaps he's heard about this other girl – the one that Breckshaft told you about.

TEMPLE: He didn't say so.

STEVE: Of course, it isn't easy to judge a person's reaction on the telephone.

TEMPLE: It isn't easy to judge Mr Harper's reactions at any time.

FADE.

FADE IN the orchestra playing in the lounge.

STEVE: It's rather quiet in here tonight, Paul.

TEMPLE: Yes. Would you like another drink, darling? You must be tired after all that packing …

STEVE: No, I won't have another one, thank you.

TEMPLE: I'm surprised I haven't heard from Breckshaft. He said he was going to telephone.

160

STEVE:	I expect the poor man's rather bewildered at the moment. I'm sure he was convinced that … Here he <u>is</u>, darling!

A slight pause.

TEMPLE:	Hello, Inspector!
BRECKSHAFT:	I was passing the hotel, so I thought I might just as well drop in and see you instead of telephoning.
TEMPLE:	Yes, of course. Would you like a drink?
BRECKSHAFT:	No, thank you. I'm afraid I'm in rather a hurry. (*With a little laugh*) I'm meeting my wife, Mrs Temple. She phoned me this afternoon and said she couldn't remember what I looked like …

STEVE laughs.

TEMPLE:	Is there any news?
BRECKSHAFT:	Yes – you were right. There's no doubt that the girl we found is the one who was missing from the dress shop.
STEVE:	Gerda!
TEMPLE:	Well, that's one step forward, anyway. Have you any idea of the motive?
BRECKSHAFT:	No – not at the moment. I've interviewed Madame Klein, but apparently she knows very little.
TEMPLE:	You can't trace any association with the people we've questioned? Harper, for instance – Elliot France – Countess Dekker …?
BRECKSHAFT:	No. It looks as if this is a completely new case, Mr Temple. I think we have no alternative but to treat it as such.
TEMPLE:	You think so?

161

BRECKSHAFT:	Yes, I do. From your knowledge of police routine, you'll appreciate that side issues can be most distracting, especially in a murder investigation.
TEMPLE:	Surely that rather depends on the side issue? However, I see your point, Breckshaft, and, of course, I wouldn't dream of intruding. In any case, we were thinking of going back to London tomorrow.
BRECKSHAFT:	So soon?
TEMPLE:	Yes.
BRECKSHAFT:	Why don't you stay and enjoy yourself? It's a very pleasant countryside.
TEMPLE:	It is indeed, but we must get back to London.
BRECKSHAFT:	Well, there's very little point in staying, I suppose, now the case is over.
TEMPLE:	I didn't say the case was over.
BRECKSHAFT:	But the girl's been found – according to Sir Graham she's perfectly all right.
TEMPLE:	Yes, but in my opinion there's more to this case than just the disappearance of Betty Conrad.
BRECKSHAFT:	Yes?
TEMPLE:	Yes. However, if there are any new developments, no doubt you'll be getting in touch with Sir Graham?
BRECKSHAFT:	Of course, immediately. Goodnight, Mrs Temple …
STEVE:	Goodnight, Herr Breckshaft. I hope we shall see you in London very soon.
BRECKSHAFT:	Thank you.
TEMPLE:	Goodnight, Breckshaft.

BRECKSHAFT:	Goodbye, and I'm greatly obliged to you for all the help you've given us. I hope you have a pleasant journey.
TEMPLE:	Thank you very much.

BRECKSHAFT goes.

A slight pause.

STEVE:	So you've made your mind up, Paul?
TEMPLE:	What do you mean?
STEVE:	About returning home.
TEMPLE:	Er – yes.
STEVE:	Well, I shan't be sorry. I like it here, but it's always nice to get back home. When do we leave, darling?
TEMPLE:	Well – that rather depends.
STEVE:	On what?
TEMPLE:	On whether I get a cherry with my dry Martini …
STEVE:	Darling, you never get a cherry with a dry Martini!
TEMPLE:	We shall see …

FADE.

FADE IN the sound of a car engine.

FADE the engine to the background.

STEVE:	Paul, this is the road to Oberammergau, isn't it?
TEMPLE:	I think it is.
STEVE:	Are we going to the Hotel Reumer again?
TEMPLE:	Yes, darling, I thought we might have dinner there. The food's awfully good.
STEVE:	Paul! We're not dashing out to Oberammergau just because the food's good! Now what's this all about?
TEMPLE:	(*Amused*) I'll explain later, Steve.

FADE UP the sound of a car gradually slowing down.
The car stops.

STEVE: Why are we stopping here? This isn't the Hotel
          Reumer parking place.

TEMPLE: I didn't want to drive into the hotel courtyard.

STEVE: But we're going there for dinner, aren't we?

TEMPLE: Yes.

STEVE: Then I don't see why we shouldn't park the car.

TEMPLE: Yes, darling, but wait a minute, and I'll explain.

TEMPLE switches off the car engine.

TEMPLE: … Now listen, Steve. After I telephoned
          Breckshaft this evening, I was handed a note. It
          was from Mrs Gunter.

STEVE: Mrs Gunter! What did she want?

TEMPLE: The note said she wanted to have a word with
          me about Betty Conrad. She said she knew Betty
          was alive but there was something I ought to
          know …

STEVE: Then it looks as if Joyce Gunter is involved in
          some way?

TEMPLE: That's what we have to find out. Anyhow she
          suggested we should dine at the hotel this
          evening, and she told me to leave the car here
          under this tree, just out of sight of the hotel.

STEVE: Why?

TEMPLE: Well, apparently I'm to order a drink – a dry
          Martini. If there's a cherry in it by mistake, that
          means she'll slip out and meet me by the car.

STEVE: And supposing there isn't?

TEMPLE: Then we'll try again tomorrow.

STEVE: But we can't keep calling here and ordering dry
          Martinis! Besides, I thought you wanted to get
          back to London?

TEMPLE: I do. But I think this is pretty important, Steve.

STEVE: (*After a moment*) She obviously wants to talk to you privately, without someone else at the hotel seeing her.

TEMPLE: Yes, that's the obvious assumption.

STEVE: Who do you think she's frightened of – her husband?

TEMPLE: Yes, that's my guess. Now, the point is, Steve, I've got to have some excuse for coming back to the car …

STEVE: Yes.

A slight pause.

STEVE: Paul, I'll tell you what we'll do. I'll leave my handbag here – and then if the cherry turns up, I'll ask you to fetch it from the car.

TEMPLE: Jolly good idea, darling. Come along, let's get moving …

TEMPLE opens the car door.

FADE SCENE.

FADE IN background voices and noises of a cocktail bar.

FADE noises and voices to the background.

FRITZ: (*Approaching*) Why, Mr and Mrs Temple! How very nice to see you again.

TEMPLE: Good evening, Herr Gunter. We thought we'd like to have dinner here again – this may be our last visit to Oberammergau.

FRITZ: So you are returning to London?

TEMPLE: Yes, I think so.

FRITZ: I wish I were coming with you, Mr Temple. It would be good to meet some of my old friends.

JOYCE: (*Approaching*) Good evening, Mr Temple – Mrs Temple.

STEVE: Hello, Mrs Gunter …

TEMPLE: Good evening.

165

FRITZ: Mr Temple tells me he is leaving us, Joyce.

JOYCE: Oh, I'm sorry to hear that. Well, I think this calls for a farewell drink.

FRITZ: Yes – yes, of course! Mrs Temple, what can I get you?

STEVE: May I have a sherry?

FRITZ: Yes, of course. And your husband?

TEMPLE: I think I'll have a dry Martini, if I may.

JOYCE: I'll get them, darling. Kurt is rather busy at the moment.

FRITZ: I hope this will not be your last visit to Oberammergau, Mr Temple?

TEMPLE: I sincerely hope not. We like the country very much, don't we, darling? We had a lovely ride this afternoon out to Schongau.

FRITZ: Yes, it's very beautiful, this time of the year.

STEVE: If ever you find yourself in London, Herr Gunter, I hope you'll call round and see us. We're in the telephone book.

FRITZ: Thank you, Mrs Temple. I would be delighted. But I see no prospect at the moment. There's nothing I would enjoy more than seeing some of my old haunts.

TEMPLE: You know, Herr Gunter, I've a vague idea we met once before – a long time ago at a film studio?

FRITZ: Yes?

TEMPLE: Were you ever in a film called The Man with a Thousand Voices?

FRITZ: The Man with … No, I don't think so, although I made several films, of course. (*Laughing*) You know, I can never remember the titles.

TEMPLE: This film was made at Elstree.

166

FRITZ: Yes, it's possible, I suppose. We may have met, Mr Temple. I had small parts in two or three very important films that were made at Elstree. But most of my acting was on the stage, you know. I much preferred it.

STEVE: Yes, I can understand that.

FRITZ: I remember I toured for many months with a play called Autumn Crocus. You remember the play, Mr Temple?

TEMPLE: Yes, I do indeed.

JOYCE: (*Approaching with a tray*) Here are the drinks; Mrs Temple – your sherry.

STEVE: Thank you.

JOYCE: Mr Temple – dry Martini.

STEVE: Paul, there's a cherry in your drink …

JOYCE: Oh, dear! Shouldn't I have put a cherry in a dry Martini?

TEMPLE: (*Laughing*) It's all right, Mrs Gunter. I'll have it. I love cherries!

FRITZ: It's a good job Mr Temple isn't an American, or you'd be for the high jump, my darling.

They all laugh.

TEMPLE: Skoal!

JOYCE: Here's to a pleasant journey, Mrs Temple!

STEVE: Thank you very much, Mrs Gunter.

FRITZ: Give my love to Piccadilly Circus …

JOYCE: Have you reserved a table for Mr Temple?

FRITZ: No, I haven't. I'll see about it straight away. Will you excuse me, Mrs Temple – Mr Temple? We're rather busy this evening.

TEMPLE: Yes, of course. We'll see you later.

STEVE: (*Casually*) Oh, Paul, I think I left my handbag in the car.

167

TEMPLE: Did you, darling? All right, I'll get it for you. I shan't be a minute.

FADE noises to the background.

FADE UP the opening of a car door.

TEMPLE: (*Quietly*) You'd better get in the back seat, Mrs Gunter – there's less chance of your being seen.

JOYCE: Thank you.

JOYCE gets into the car.

The car door closes.

JOYCE: I can't stay long, Mr Temple, otherwise he'll get suspicious. But I had to see you – I had to warn you …

TEMPLE: Warn me about what, exactly?

JOYCE: Although they've found Betty Conrad, this affair isn't over, Mr Temple. Don't run away with that idea. Don't think that just because Betty is safe … (*She hesitates*)

TEMPLE: Go on …

JOYCE: (*Tensely*) You've got to go back to London. You've got to drop your investigations – now, tonight …

TEMPLE: And if I don't?

JOYCE: You're not taking me seriously!

TEMPLE: I am taking you seriously, Mrs Gunter. But so far, you haven't told me anything. Now, what exactly is it you're warning me against?

JOYCE: If you continue to make enquiries about Betty Conrad – about why she disappeared – you or Mrs Temple will be murdered. There's no doubt about that. Please believe me, Mr Temple, there's no doubt …

TEMPLE: Mrs Gunter, I realise you're trying to help me. I realise you're warning me against something,

168

	but unless you can be just a little bit more specific …
JOYCE:	I can't go into details …
TEMPLE:	Can't – or won't?
JOYCE:	You know I'm taking a risk by talking to you like this – a greater risk than you'll ever realise. Now I'm going to give you a piece of advice, Mr Temple. I hope for your own sake – and for Mrs Temple's – you won't forget it.
TEMPLE:	I'm always prepared to take good advice.
JOYCE:	When you get back to London, someone will try to get in touch with you …
TEMPLE:	Someone?
JOYCE:	A man – a man called Smith. Have nothing to do with him. Do you hear me? Whatever happens, have nothing to do with him, Mr Temple.
TEMPLE:	Smith? London's full of people called Smith, you know.
JOYCE:	This man calls himself Captain Smith. Now remember what I'm telling you, Mr Temple. Whatever happens, have nothing to do with him.

FADE.

CROSSFADE to noise associated with airport activity: loudspeaker announcements of arrivals and departures of aircraft.

STEVE:	Everything all right, darling?
TEMPLE:	Yes, I gather we'll be boarding the plane in about five minutes. I've sent Charlie a wire.
STEVE:	Let's hope he's in and not at the Palais de Danse. What did you tell him?
TEMPLE:	I wired the time of arrival and asked him to meet us at the airport.

STEVE:	Oh, he'll adore that. Nosing around the airport's one of his greatest joys these days.
TEMPLE:	There's time for a drink, if you feel like it.
STEVE:	No, I don't think so. (*A moment*) Paul … if you hadn't talked to Joyce Gunter last night, would we be going back so soon?
TEMPLE:	Yes – to be honest, she didn't influence me one way or the other. No, what I'm really interested in, Steve, is having a talk to Betty Conrad.
STEVE:	Yes, well, it doesn't sound as if you'll get much out of her, according to Sir Graham.
TEMPLE:	We shall see.
STEVE:	(*After a moment*) Paul, do you think Joyce Gunter was sincere last night, or do you think she was just putting on an act?
TEMPLE:	No, I think she was sincere. But she was also frightened. And when a person's frightened, they tend to exaggerate.
STEVE:	In other words you don't think we are in danger?
TEMPLE:	I wouldn't say that – but I think it's the sort of danger we can cope with. (*A laugh*) At least I hope so.
STEVE:	(*Laughing*) I was just going to say – Famous Last Words!
TEMPLE:	Anyway, it'll be good to be home again. There are a hundred and one things I want to do.
STEVE:	Yes, and I'll bet I know what one of them is.
TEMPLE:	What?

170

STEVE:	You want to make enquiries about Captain Smith?
TEMPLE:	(*Laughing*) Steve, you can read me like a book! Well, I did intend to have a word with Vosper about it. If the man's got a record there's an outside chance that …
STEWARDESS:	Excuse me, sir …
TEMPLE:	Yes?
STEWARDESS:	These flowers are for Mrs Temple …
STEVE:	Oh, Paul! Aren't they heavenly!

STEVE takes the flowers.

STEVE:	Thank you very much …
TEMPLE:	Who sent them, do you know?
STEWARDESS:	Yes, the lady at the kiosk told me that a Herr Breckshaft telephoned first thing this morning and ordered them specially for Mrs Temple.
STEVE:	Oh, darling, how very kind! And they say <u>our</u> policemen are wonderful!
STEWARDESS:	(*Laughing*) We're ready to board now, sir. If you'll come this way …
TEMPLE:	Oh, thank you. Come along, Steve. (*Laughing*) You look exactly like a film star, darling …
STEVE:	Don't be silly, sweetie – you're my husband!

TEMPLE and the STEWARDESS laugh.
FADE.
FADE IN incidental music.

FADE music.
CROSSFADE to the noise of an aircraft in flight.

TEMPLE:	You can unfasten your seat belt now, Steve.

STEVE:	Oh, good. It was a pretty smooth take-off, wasn't it?
TEMPLE:	Yes.
STEVE:	(*Yawning*) Oh dear, I'm terribly tired ... I think I'll have a sleep.
TEMPLE:	You get more like Napoleon every day, darling ...
STEVE:	(*Sleepily*) Napoleon? Why Napoleon?
TEMPLE:	He could sleep anywhere – even on horseback.
STEVE:	(*Yawning*) Maybe I'll try it sometime ... if I can find a nice quiet horse ...

FADE.

A long pause.

STEWARDESS:	Excuse me, sir ...
TEMPLE:	Yes, what is it?
STEWARDESS:	I think this note must have fallen out of Mrs Temple's bouquet.
STEVE:	(*Waking up, very sleepy*) How long have I been asleep, darling?
TEMPLE:	Only about twenty minutes.
STEVE:	What was the stewardess saying?
TEMPLE:	She brought this note. She said it must have fallen out of the bouquet.
STEVE:	Oh – that explains why there was no card.

A pause.

| TEMPLE: | What does it say, darling? (*A moment: alarmed*) Steve! What is it? |
| STEVE: | (*Tensely; frightened*) Paul, listen to this! (*Reading the note*) "There is a bomb on the plane. Tell the Captain to turn back." |

END OF EPISODE FIVE

EPISODE SIX

CONCERNING
CAPTAIN SMITH

OPEN TO: *The noise of an aircraft in flight.*
FADE the noise of the aircraft to the background.

STEVE: … (*Tensely, reading a note*) "There is a
                     bomb on the plane. Tell the Captain to
                     turn back."

TEMPLE: Let me see the note, Steve … (*After a
                     moment*) It looks like a woman's
                     handwriting.

STEVE: (*Nervously*) I suppose it could be some
                     sort of a joke, though surely Breckshaft
                     would never do a thing like that.

TEMPLE: It's nothing to do with Breckshaft, I'm
                     sure of that.

STEVE: What are we going to do?

TEMPLE: The first thing is not to panic. If there is a
                     bomb on board then obviously …

TEMPLE breaks off as the STEWARDESS approaches.

STEWARDESS: Can I get you anything, sir?

TEMPLE: Not at the moment, thank you – but I'd be
                     glad of some information.

STEWARDESS: Yes, of course, sir.

TEMPLE: Can you tell me the name of the captain?

STEWARDESS: Captain Williams, sir.

TEMPLE: Would it be possible for me to have a
                     word with him? My name is Temple.

STEWARDESS: Would you like to see him now, Mr
                     Temple – immediately?

TEMPLE: Yes, I would. It's rather urgent.

STEWARDESS: I'll ask Captain Williams if he can see
                     you, sir.

TEMPLE: Thank you.

FADE.

177

FADE UP.

FADE IN the noise of the aircraft in flight in the background.

STEVE: (*Nervously*) I wish to goodness she'd hurry.

TEMPLE: Don't worry, Steve – everything will be all right, I'm sure.

STEVE: I hope so. (*A pause*) Paul, I really am frightened – I really am, darling.

TEMPLE: Steve, don't worry …

STEVE: Do you think if there is a bomb on board it'll explode?

TEMPLE: Now, take it easy … relax.

STEVE: Relax!

STEWARDESS: (*Approaching*) Captain Williams will see you, Mr Temple. Will you come through?

TEMPLE: Thank you. (*To STEVE*) Don't worry, Steve, I'll be back in a minute or two …

Hold the noise of the aircraft for a little while.

FADE the noise to the background.

STEVE: (*Anxiously, as TEMPLE approaches*) Paul, what did he say?

TEMPLE: Not so loud, darling. This chap knows his business – we're in very good hands.

STEVE: What did he say?

TEMPLE: He thinks it's a hoax. Apparently there have been one or two in the last six months. But he's not taking any chances.

The voice of CAPTAIN WILLIAMS can be heard through the internal speaker in the aircraft.

WILLIAMS: (*On the speaker*) Good afternoon, ladies and gentlemen. This is Captain Williams speaking. If I may have your attention for a moment, please. I am sorry to tell you that, acting under instructions, we have to return to Munich. I should like to reassure you, however, that this is not in any way connected with …

FADE.

FADE UP noises of an aircraft.
CROSS FADE to background noises of Munich Airport.

WILLIAMS: Well, we made it, Mr Temple.

TEMPLE: I'm very sorry to have given you this trouble, Captain Williams.

WILLIAMS: Not at all – can't take any chances. Damned frustrating, of course, but there you are – it's all part of the day's work. They should have another plane ready in about an hour.

TEMPLE: Good.

WILLIAMS: If you'll excuse me, Mr Temple. I'll see how the search is getting on.

TEMPLE: Yes, of course.

WILLIAMS: I expect the Controller will want a statement from you – to confirm my radio message. You'd better take that note along with you, Mrs Temple.

STEVE: Yes, of course …

WILLIAMS: (*Calling*) Stewardess! Take Mr Temple to the Controller's office, will you?

STEWARDESS: Yes, of course, Captain. (*To TEMPLE and STEVE*) This way, please …

WILLIAMS: See you presently, Mr Temple. I'll be in to report.

FADE noises of the airport.
FADE IN of TEMPLE dialling a number on a telephone.

179

After a moment we hear the number ringing out and the receiver being lifted at the other end of the line.

OFFICER: (*On the other end of the line*) … Police Headquarters, Garmisch …

TEMPLE: Paul Temple here. I want to speak to Herr Breckshaft, please, it's urgent.

OFFICER: Herr Breckshaft is in conference at the moment and can't be disturbed.

TEMPLE: Would you please tell him that Paul Temple is on the line and the matter is extremely urgent?

OFFICER: One moment, Mr Temple.

There is a pause, then a click as TEMPLE is put through on an extension.

BRECKSHAFT: This is a surprise, Temple! Where are you speaking from?

TEMPLE: I'm at the airport. We had to turn back. Breckshaft, forgive my asking, but did you send my wife some flowers?

BRECKSHAFT: Flowers?

TEMPLE: Yes – a bouquet. There was a note inside.

BRECKSHAFT: Why, no – I'm afraid I didn't.

TEMPLE: That's all right, Breckshaft. It just happened that Steve had a bouquet delivered in your name – inside was a note warning us that there was a bomb on the plane.

BRECKSHAFT: But I know nothing about this, I assure you.

TEMPLE: No, I didn't think you did.

BRECKSHAFT: But was there a bomb on the plane?

TEMPLE: We don't know. They're still searching it. I've left the note with the Controller of the

	airport – he'll be getting in touch with you.
BRECKSHAFT:	Thank you, Temple. How's your wife?
TEMPLE:	She's all right, but she's a bit shaky, of course.
BRECKSHAFT:	I'm sure she's shaky! What an experience!
TEMPLE:	Breckshaft, tell me – is there any more news about that girl – Gerda Holman?
BRECKSHAFT:	No, there's no news – although curiously enough we found something in her handbag which might interest you.
TEMPLE:	Oh – what was that?
BRECKSHAFT:	We found a membership card for the Groove Club, Soho, London. It was dated about three weeks ago.
TEMPLE:	(*Reflectively*) The Groove Club … That's interesting. So Gerda was in London just before Betty Conrad disappeared.
BRECKSHAFT:	Yes, yes. Madame Klein tells me she was there on holiday. It seems that she'd been there three times in the past eighteen months. Madame Klein has given me quite a lot of information about her. Her father owns the House of Holman – the book publishers – but Gerda insisted on going into the dress business.
TEMPLE:	Yes, I know. Well, I'll be interested to hear of any further developments.
BRECKSHAFT:	I shall be telephoning Sir Graham. I may even be in London myself very soon.
TEMPLE:	Really? Well, I shall look forward to seeing you. Goodbye.

181

BRECKSHAFT:	Goodbye. And I hope you have a pleasant journey.
TEMPLE:	Thank you. (*A sudden thought*) Oh, Breckshaft, just a moment … About that publishing firm, the House of Holman …
BRECKSHAFT:	Yes?
TEMPLE:	What sort of books do they publish, do you know?
BRECKSHAFT:	I think they are just general publishers. Why do you ask?
TEMPLE:	I wondered, that's all. Excuse me, here's the captain of our plane. I think he wants to have a word with me.
BRECKSHAFT:	Goodbye, Mr Temple.
TEMPLE:	Goodbye.

TEMPLE replaces the receiver.
The door of the telephone box is opened, and TEMPLE joins CAPTAIN WILLIAMS.

TEMPLE:	Any news, Captain?
WILLIAMS:	Good news, I'm glad to say. We haven't found anything.
TEMPLE:	No bombs?
WILLIAMS:	Not even a Japanese Cracker, Mr Temple. But they're holding the plane in dock till tomorrow morning – just in case.
TEMPLE:	I see.
WILLIAMS:	The other plane should be ready in about half an hour. The stewardess will let you know.
TEMPLE:	Thank you.

FADE.

FADE UP background noise of the airport.
A pause.

STEVE: (*Approaching*) I thought you were never coming, darling. Did you speak to the Inspector?

TEMPLE: I did. And I saw Captain Williams – he said we'll be off in about half an hour.

STEVE: Then there wasn't a bomb on the plane?

TEMPLE: No, darling – it was a false alarm.

STEVE: Do you think it was a hoax about the bomb on the plane?

TEMPLE: No, I don't. I think the warning was quite genuine. Whoever sent it – and by the way, they weren't Breckshaft's flowers – whoever sent it really believed there would be a bomb on the plane.

FADE.

FADE UP the noise of an aircraft in flight.

TEMPLE: Fasten your belt, Steve – we're coming in to land.

STEVE: It's never been unfastened.

TEMPLE: (*Laughing*) Steve!

STEVE: I expect Charlie's getting tired of waiting.

TEMPLE: I daresay he's managed to amuse himself. Look, darling – there's the airport over there.

STEVE: You look – I'll take it as read.

TEMPLE laughs.

FADE.

FADE UP noises of the exterior of London Airport.

TEMPLE: All the luggage stowed away, Charlie?

CHARLIE: Yes, Mr Temple.

TEMPLE: All right, then let's go.

The car starts.

The sound of door closing.

The car drives away.

CHARLIE is driving.

STEVE: Everything all right at home, Charlie?

CHARLIE: Oh, yes, Mrs Temple – everything's okay – neat as a new pin.

STEVE: Sorry you've been kept waiting.

CHARLIE: That's all right, Mrs Temple. I had a cup of tea.

STEVE: Have you been dancing at all while we've been away?

CHARLIE: Well – once or twice. Went to the Palais one night; but Beryl hasn't been too good. Hay fever. She gets it something shocking this time of the year.

TEMPLE: Charlie, have you ever been to a place called The Groove Club?

CHARLIE: Why, yes. We've been there several times. It's in Soho. It's a real cool joint – groovy, if you know what I mean.

TEMPLE: All the latest skiffle?

CHARLIE: (*Scornfully*) Skiffle! That went out with the polka, Mr Temple. No, they get all the latest stuff at the Groove.

STEVE: Is it well run? No rough stuff?

CHARLIE: Oh, I wouldn't say that. Gets a bit dicey at times. I don't think it's your cup of tea, Mrs Temple. It's more for young people …

STEVE: Thank you for those kind words. (*To TEMPLE*) We're home, darling!

FADE.

FADE IN incidental music.

Slow FADE DOWN of music.

FADE UP of a syphon splashing soda into glasses.

FORBES: Well, you've had an interesting trip, Temple, if nothing else.

184

TEMPLE: Yes, Sir Graham.

STEVE: We've been thoroughly scared on several occasions without achieving very much.

FORBES: Oh, I wouldn't say that, Steve. I think you've both done very well.

TEMPLE: Your drink, Sir Graham.

FORBES: Thank you, Temple. Well, here's to a quick solution to our problems.

They drink.

FORBES: I must say I'm surprised that Breckshaft takes that attitude about the Holman murder.

STEVE: Then you think it is connected with the Conrad affair?

FORBES: There's no doubt at all in my mind, Steve. Of course, I didn't contradict him on the phone …

TEMPLE: Then he's telephoned you?

FORBES: Oh yes, earlier this evening. He was anxious to know if you were back safely – he told me all about the bomb affair. Breckshaft's a very nice chap but there are times when he lacks perspective.

TEMPLE: Yes, I agree with you. Did he tell you about the card that was found on the murdered girl?

FORBES: Yes, he did. I put Vosper on to that straight away. Incidentally, I asked Vosper to drop in on us – I hope you don't mind.

TEMPLE: Not at all.

FORBES: Of course, the odds are that this club's pretty harmless. I expect some young blood took Gerda Holman to it while she was over here.

STEVE: Yes, I should think that's the most likely explanation.

TEMPLE: Well, we'll see what Vosper digs up. You say he's taking a look at the place this evening?

185

FORBES: Yes.

STEVE: Is there any more news about Betty Conrad? Is she back home with her stepmother?

FORBES: Yes. You know, there's something very odd about that girl, Steve. I can't help feeling she's had a terrible shock of some kind.

TEMPLE: She still won't talk?

FORBES: No, she won't say a word. By the way, I've made an appointment for you to see her tomorrow morning at my office. Is 11 o'clock all right?

TEMPLE: Yes, that's fine.

FORBES: Well, maybe you'll have better luck, Temple.

TEMPLE: Did you get a medical report on her?

FORBES: Yes. Physically she's perfectly all right.

TEMPLE: No sign of drugs?

FORBES: None whatsoever.

TEMPLE: Have you told Betty about the murder of Gerda Holman?

FORBES: No, I thought I'd leave that to you, Temple. It might give you some kind of lead.

TEMPLE: Yes, I agree, Sir Graham.

The door opens.

CHARLIE: Inspector Vosper says you're expecting him?

TEMPLE: Oh, yes, show him in, Charlie.

CHARLIE: This way, sir.

VOSPER: (*Approaching*) Good evening, Mrs Temple.

STEVE: Good evening, Inspector.

VOSPER: Hello, Temple! Nice to have you back …

TEMPLE: Thank you, Vosper.

VOSPER: Evening, Sir Graham.

FORBES: Hello, Vosper …

TEMPLE: What can I get you to drink, Inspector?

VOSPER: Nothing at the moment, thank you. I've been drinking cocktails for the last half hour at the

Groove Club. Wretched concoctions! Oh, before I forget, Sir Graham, another call came through for you from Breckshaft, just after you left the office.

FORBES: Oh – what is it this time?

VOSPER: He says he'll be in London tomorrow and will be getting in touch with you. And when I said I was seeing Temple this evening, he asked me to deliver a message.

FORBES: Well, what was it?

VOSPER: It was about a firm of publishers, sir. He said the name was Holman …

TEMPLE: That's right – the House of Holman. What about them?

VOSPER: He said I was to tell you that they specialised in medical books, particularly on neurology and psychiatry. Does that make any sense to you?

TEMPLE: Yes, it's an answer to a question I asked him over the telephone. Thank you, Inspector.

FORBES: (*Curious*) Holman – that's the same name as the murdered girl …

TEMPLE: Yes, it's the family firm I mentioned to you, Sir Graham. It's just an idea that occurred to me. Well, how did you get on at the Groove Club, Vosper?

VOSPER: It's not much of a place to look at. Typical Soho … A bit on the shabby side but seems harmless enough.

STEVE: Perhaps the fun starts later on in the evening.

VOSPER: That could be, Mrs Temple – but I didn't see much sign of fun.

FORBES: You've checked our reports on the place?

VOSPER: Yes, it's been going about two years, sir. No real trouble so far as we're concerned. But the Narcotics Squad have had their eye on it.

FORBES: Have they? That's interesting. Who told you that?

VOSPER: Colonel Webster, sir, he's in charge of the N.S.

FORBES: M'm … Well, I expect you're very tired after your journey, Steve. You'll both want to turn in pretty soon. Come along, Vosper.

TEMPLE: See you tomorrow, Sir Graham. Are you sure you won't have that drink, Inspector?

VOSPER: Quite sure, thank you, Mr Temple.

FORBES: Good night, Steve … Good night, Temple …

STEVE: Good night, Sir Graham.

VOSPER: Goodbye, Mrs Temple.

STEVE: Good night, Inspector.

The door opens and closes.

There is a pause.

STEVE: Gosh, I'm tired! I don't think I'll have any difficulty in sleeping tonight. (*A moment*) Paul, why do you think Breckshaft's coming to London?

TEMPLE: I don't know. He said he might be coming over here, you know.

STEVE: I should have thought he was up to his eyes with the Gerda Holman case.

TEMPLE: So he is.

STEVE: Then you think he may have found some connection between this Holman affair and Betty Conrad?

TEMPLE: Yes, I do.

In the background the doorbell is ringing.

STEVE: Oh, Lord! Not more visitors …

TEMPLE: Charlie will go.

STEVE: You're not expecting anyone, are you?

TEMPLE: No, darling.

The door opens.

CHARLIE: Telegram, Mr Temple. They're waiting for an answer.

TEMPLE: Thank you, Charlie.

TEMPLE takes the telegram and opens it.

TEMPLE: M'm … That's all right, Charlie – there's no reply.

CHARLIE: Okey-dokey, sir.

The door closes.

STEVE: Who's it from?

TEMPLE: It doesn't say – but I know who it's from. It's from Joyce Gunter. It says … "Don't forget my warning about Captain Smith. I was serious, Mr Temple."

STEVE: Captain Smith? What was her warning, exactly? You know, you told me about Smith, Paul – but you didn't tell me exactly what Joyce Gunter said.

TEMPLE: She simply said that Smith would try to contact me, and she told me to stay clear of him.

STEVE: But who is this man Smith?

TEMPLE: (*Thoughtfully*) I don't know, darling. But it's pretty obvious that Joyce Gunter thinks …

TEMPLE is interrupted by the telephone.

He lifts the receiver.

TEMPLE: (*On the phone*) Hello?

ELSA: (*On the other end of the line: obviously agitated*) Mr Temple?

TEMPLE: Yes, who is that?

ELSA: (*Tensely*) This is Elsa – Countess Dekker.

TEMPLE: (*Surprised*) Oh, good evening! Where are you speaking from?

ELSA:	I'm in London, staying at the Coronet Hotel …
TEMPLE:	The Coronet – in Bloomsbury?
ELSA:	Yes. I must see you, Mr Temple. It's urgent- very urgent.
TEMPLE:	Yes, of course. Sometime tomorrow?
ELSA:	No, please – tonight, if it's possible. I've got a lot to tell you about this affair and I don't want …
TEMPLE:	Which affair?
ELSA:	The disappearance of Betty Conrad – the murder of Gerda Holman. There's so much you do not know, Mr Temple. So much I've got to tell you – not only about Betty Conrad, but about – (*Hesitating*) – Elliot France …
TEMPLE:	Is Mr France with you?
ELSA:	No – no, he's not with me … I've left him behind in Garmisch. We – we've had a disagreement.
TEMPLE:	I see …
ELSA:	It's very important that I see you. Please believe me …
TEMPLE:	Very well. Where shall we meet?
ELSA:	Could you come round here? I am in room 14, on the first floor. Ask for Mrs Dekker.
TEMPLE:	Mrs Dekker?
ELSA:	Yes …
TEMPLE:	I'll be with you in about half an hour.
ELSA:	(*Obviously relieved*) Thank you. I'm most grateful.
TEMPLE:	Oh, just a moment, Countess.
ELSA:	Yes?
TEMPLE:	Do you know a man called Captain Smith – by any chance?
ELSA:	Captain Smith? Why – no …
TEMPLE:	You've never heard of him?

ELSA: No, I'm afraid I haven't. Who is he?

TEMPLE: (*Ignoring her question*) I'll see you in about half
           an hour. Goodbye.

TEMPLE puts down the receiver.

STEVE: Well, she's certainly upset about something …

TEMPLE: You heard?

STEVE: Almost every word. She's certainly in a tizzy.

TEMPLE: I wonder what she's doing in London?

STEVE: It sounds to me as if she's had a row with Elliot
           France …

TEMPLE: Yes – that's what I thought. There may be
           nothing to this, of course – it may be just a lot of
           silly tantrums. Still, I'd better look into it. You
           go to bed, Steve. I won't be very long …

STEVE: I feel quite wide awake now.

TEMPLE: You don't want to come careering round
           Bloomsbury at this time of night.

STEVE: Well, if she's in a nervous state, and she
           certainly sounded like it, don't you think it might
           be a very good idea if I …

STEVE is interrupted by the opening of the door.

CHARLIE: There's a Dr Conrad here – he wants to see Mr
           Temple.

STEVE: Dr Conrad!

TEMPLE: Ask him to come in, Charlie.

A pause.

STEVE: (*Quietly*) I wonder what he wants?

CONRAD: (*Approaching*) It's very good of you to see me
           at this time of night. I do apologise for disturbing
           you …

TEMPLE: (*Pleasantly*) Come in, Doctor … That's all right,
           Charlie.

The door closes.

TEMPLE: You know my wife, of course.

191

CONRAD: Yes, indeed. Good evening, Mrs Temple. Please accept my apologies for bursting in on you like this.

STEVE: Can we get you a drink, Dr Conrad?

CONRAD: No, thank you, Mrs Temple. It's very kind of you …

TEMPLE: You look upset, Doctor. Has something happened?

CONRAD: I'm very worried about Betty, Mr Temple – desperately worried. Something's happened. She's a completely different girl … She sits around, brooding all day, never speaking to anyone unless she's spoken to …

TEMPLE: Sir Graham thinks she's had a severe shock of some kind.

CONRAD: Well, if she has I wish she'd tell me about it. I tried to get her to see a colleague of mine, but she wouldn't hear of it. She won't say a word, Mr Temple – she won't tell us anything about what's happened during the past week or so.

TEMPLE: I asked Sir Graham whether he thought she'd been drugged or not?

CONRAD: No, she hasn't, I'm sure of that – if she had have been I'd have noticed it. I can't tell you how depressing it is, Mrs Temple, just to see her sitting – not talking – jumping like a scared rabbit every time the telephone rings.

TEMPLE: Do you think she's expecting a phone call from anyone?

CONRAD: She had one this evening. In fact, that's why I came to see you.

TEMPLE: Who was it from – do you know?

CONRAD: I haven't the slightest idea. All I know is, immediately after she received the call she put on her hat and coat and went out of the house.

TEMPLE: Did you ask her where she was going?

CONRAD: She refused to tell me – all she said was, she'd be back later this evening. Mr Temple, I'm frightfully worried – I have an awful premonition that something might happen to Betty.

TEMPLE: When your daughter answered the phone did she speak in English, or German?

CONRAD: English ... Although she barely said half a dozen words.

TEMPLE: Can you remember the words?

CONRAD: Yes. She said something like ... "All right, I'll see you there."

STEVE: Can't you persuade Betty to confide in you, Doctor? Have you tried?

CONRAD: Have I tried? Oh, Mrs Temple, if only you knew ... (*After a moment*) You see, after her mother died Betty used to tell me everything, then when I married again things became difficult. She grew independent. At the time I thought maybe that wasn't a bad thing, that she should stand on her own feet, I mean, but it's different now – she's not just independent. She's ... so very remote.

STEVE: Can't her stepmother help at all?

CONRAD: I'm afraid Betty took a dislike to my wife right from the start. She was devoted to her own mother and deplored the idea of my marrying again. That's a fairly common reaction, of course. I thought she would grow out of it. Ruth has always been nice to her, and she's very upset about this business.

STEVE: Have you ever heard them quarrel?

CONRAD: Not for some time. They have very little to do with each other. I suspect they rather got on each other's nerves. That was the reason why I sent Betty to a finishing school.

STEVE: I see.

CONRAD: Doctor, what time did Betty go out this evening?

STEVE: Now let me see – about a quarter past eight.

TEMPLE: And it's now a quarter to ten …

CONRAD: Yes. I've been hanging about all evening waiting for her. I felt so desperate that I did rather an unpardonable thing.

TEMPLE: Oh? What was that?

CONRAD: I searched her room. I thought I might possibly find a clue as to who had telephoned her.

TEMPLE: And did you?

CONRAD: No. But I found this – which rather puzzled me.

STEVE: What is it, Doctor?

CONRAD: It's a membership card for a club – the Groove Club, Soho.

STEVE: The Groove Club!

CONRAD: You know it?

TEMPLE: (*Casually*) We've heard of it. I believe it's a jazz club in Soho.

CONRAD: Yes, so I understand. And that's what's so puzzling. You see Betty isn't that type – she hates jazz, always has done. She's keen on classical music.

TEMPLE: People change, you know. Tell me, did your daughter ever mention a girl called Gerda Holman?

CONRAD: No, I don't think so. Why?

194

TEMPLE: She was found murdered in Garmisch. In fact, the police actually thought it was Betty when the body was discovered.

CONRAD: (*Apparently very surprised*) Really? This is the first I've heard of it … It's rather terrifying … Why was this girl murdered, do you know?

TEMPLE: No. The police are still working on the case.

CONRAD: Do they think it had anything to do with Betty – with her disappearance, I mean?

TEMPLE: We don't know – not yet.

STEVE: Dr Conrad, did your daughter ever mention a young bank official called Denis Harper?

CONRAD: Denis Harper? Why yes. She seemed quite friendly with him at one time.

STEVE: Do you think he could have been the person who telephoned her this evening?

CONRAD: But surely he's in Munich?

TEMPLE: No, he's returned to London rather suddenly. He's been transferred to a branch in Kensington.

CONRAD: Well in that case – I suppose it could have been Denis Harper … Still, if it was, why didn't the silly girl tell me so? She's mentioned him before …

TEMPLE: I'll have a word with her about it tomorrow morning – you know I'm seeing her at Scotland Yard?

CONRAD: I know you've got an appointment with her. I only hope she keeps it. Not that you'll get much out of her, I'm afraid, if she does. I'm a psychiatrist, as you know. I'm used to problems of all kinds, but this one has beaten me.

STEVE: That's probably because you're dealing with your own daughter.

CONRAD: I hope that's the reason, Mrs Temple.

TEMPLE: Being a writer, I'm interested in psychiatry, Doctor. Have you written any books on the subject?

CONRAD: Yes, I've written two. One on Analytical Psychology, the other a study of Jung.

TEMPLE: Are they published abroad, by any chance?

CONRAD: Yes, they've done rather well on the Continent. Particularly in Sweden and Germany.

TEMPLE: I see.

CONRAD: Well, again, I'm sorry to have troubled you, Mr Temple. Forgive me if I seem a little overwrought …

TEMPLE: It's understandable, Doctor. Even a psychiatrist is human.

CONRAD: (*With a flicker of a smile*) Yes, indeed!

STEVE: Goodnight, Dr Conrad …

CONRAD: Goodnight, Mrs Temple …

TEMPLE: I'll see you out, Doctor.

The door opens and closes.

There is a pause.

STEVE: (*Calling*) Charlie!

The door opens.

CHARLIE: Yes, Mrs Temple?

STEVE: We shall want the car …

CHARLIE: What? Now? Tonight?

STEVE: Yes, Charlie – tonight. Mr Temple's had an urgent call. We're going to Bloomsbury.

CHARLIE: (*Fading on this speech*) I'll pop down to the garage. Shan't be five minutes, Mrs Temple.

FADE.

FADE IN the noise of a car engine.

TEMPLE: You know, Steve, you look tired. You shouldn't have come.

STEVE: I feel fine, darling. (*Unable to control a yawn*) I'm as lively as a cricket.

TEMPLE: Some cricket!

A pause.

STEVE: I was sorry for Dr Conrad, weren't you, Paul?

TEMPLE: I don't know about Dr Conrad – I'm certainly sorry for his daughter.

STEVE: Do you think she'll turn up tomorrow morning, Paul?

TEMPLE: I rather doubt it.

STEVE: (*A sudden thought*) You don't think she's disappeared again?

In the background, the sound of an approaching ambulance can be heard.

TEMPLE: Disappeared? No, I feel sure she hasn't … (*He hesitates*)

STEVE: What is it?

TEMPLE: You know, Steve, you have some pretty good ideas, darling. Thank you very much.

STEVE: (*Faintly exasperated*) What do you mean – I have some pretty good ideas, thank you very much!

TEMPLE laughs.

STEVE: Oh, Paul, you've developed some of the most exasperating habits. (*Suddenly*) Darling, pull over … there's an ambulance!

FADE IN the noise of an ambulance racing past TEMPLE's car.

TEMPLE: By Timothy, they're in a hurry!

FADE the noise of the ambulance and the car.

FADE UP the noise of the car.

TEMPLE: I think this must be the hotel …

197

STEVE: No, this is the Commodore – there's the name on that light over the door.

TEMPLE: Oh, Lord, I must have been thinking of the wrong hotel!

STEVE: No, I'm pretty sure the Coronet is in the Square, darling. Drive round the block …

TEMPLE: All right …

FADE UP the noise of the car.

FADE DOWN the noise completely.

FADE IN the car again.

STEVE: There it is! On the other side of the road …

TEMPLE: Yes – and there's the ambulance, Steve.

TEMPLE's car draws to a standstill.

The car door opens.

STEVE: There's quite a crowd round the entrance – and isn't that a police car?

TEMPLE: Looks like it. You'd better stay here, darling – I won't be long.

STEVE: Yes, all right.

FADE.

FADE UP noises of a crowd gathered round the hotel entrance.

FADE voices down to the near background.

MAN: (*With a Cockney accent*) They won't let you in, guv'nor …

TEMPLE: What's happened?

MAN: A woman shot herself about a quarter of an hour ago. They'll be bringing her out any minute …

TEMPLE: Oh, I see. Thank you.

DIGBY: (*Approaching*) Hello, Mr Temple! What are you doing here?

TEMPLE: Inspector Digby! How are you?

DIGBY: I'm all right, sir – only rather busier than usual.

TEMPLE: Yes, I can see that.

DIGBY: I thought you were in Germany, Mr Temple.

TEMPLE: We got back this afternoon, Inspector. I've an appointment here with a Mrs Dekker.

DIGBY: Mrs Dekker! You don't say!

TEMPLE: Good Lord! Is she the woman who tried to commit suicide?

DIGBY: That's right, Mr Temple. Is she a friend of yours?

TEMPLE: Not exactly. We met in Germany several days ago. She telephoned this evening and said she wanted to see me.

DIGBY: Well, she must have shot herself shortly after the telephone call, sir.

TEMPLE: Inspector, I've a feeling this business may have a bearing on the case Sir Graham and I are investigating. Do you mind if I ask the Hall Porter a few questions?

DIGBY: I can't see any objections to that, Mr Temple. Come this way, sir …

FADE UP the noise of the crowd.

FADE the noise of the crowd to the background, and then FADE completely.

DIGBY: This is Johnson, sir, the Hall Porter.

TEMPLE: Good evening, Mr Johnson.

JOHNSON: Good evening, sir.

DIGBY: This is Mr Temple. He'd like to ask you a few questions, Johnson. See if you can help him, would you?

JOHNSON: I'll try, sir.

TEMPLE: When did Mrs Dekker arrive, Johnson?

JOHNSON: About four o'clock this afternoon, sir.

TEMPLE: Had she made a reservation?

JOHNSON: No, sir. She simply called on the off-chance, and we happened to have a room vacant. She signed the book and went straight to her room. I haven't seen her since.

TEMPLE: Had you ever seen her before?

JOHNSON: No – never set eyes on her.

TEMPLE: And when did the accident happen?

JOHNSON: About twenty minutes ago.

TEMPLE: You heard the shot?

JOHNSON: Yes, sir. Her room is directly above this office. I ran upstairs immediately, opened the door with my key and found her lying on the bed with a revolver in her hand. It wasn't an accident, Mr Temple, it couldn't have been.

TEMPLE: Go on …

JOHNSON: I tried to get hold of the manager, sir, but he's out at the theatre somewhere …

DIGBY: Excuse me, Mr Temple – they're bringing her down now.

TEMPLE: Has she recovered consciousness?

DIGBY: Well, it's difficult to say.

TEMPLE: I'd like to see her, Inspector – is that possible?

DIGBY: Well – come on over here, Mr Temple. We'll have a word with the doctor.

FADE.

FADE UP voices of a small crowd in the hotel vestibule.

DIGBY: (*Approaching*) Excuse me, Doctor – just a moment please …

DOCTOR: (*A man in his late sixties – abrupt and bad-tempered*) Yes, what is it?

DIGBY: I'd like to see if the patient recognises this gentleman.

DOCTOR: It's hardly likely, she's only semi-conscious.

DIGBY: It won't take a minute – if you don't mind, sir.

DOCTOR: Well, I do mind. However, if you insist. (*To the STRETCHER BEARERS*) Rest the stretcher here for a moment, will you?

BEARER: Right, Doctor.

The stretcher is put down.

DOCTOR: All right – get on with it …

DIGBY: Mr Temple …

TEMPLE: Thank you. (*A moment*) Countess Elsa – this is Paul Temple …

ELSA: (*Faintly*) Mr Temple …

TEMPLE: Remember you telephoned me …?

ELSA: Yes.

TEMPLE: What is it you wanted to say?

ELSA: (*Faintly*) I wanted to tell you … The Groove Club … Soho … Captain … Smith …

ELSA becomes unconscious.

DOCTOR: You satisfied?

TEMPLE: (*Quietly*) Thank you, Doctor.

DOCTOR: (*Curtly*) Right, get her down to the ambulance!

BEARER: Yes, Doctor, right away … Take it, Bert … Right …

FADE UP voice from the background.

DIGBY: Mr Temple, did I hear you call her Countess?

TEMPLE: Yes, you did. Her name is Countess Dekker – she lives near Garmisch in Germany. Sir Graham and I know all about her.

DIGBY: Then you may have some idea as to why she tried to commit suicide?

TEMPLE: No, Inspector, I'm afraid I haven't! Because I don't think she did try to commit suicide!

FADE SCENE.

FADE UP the opening of a car door.

TEMPLE: (*Grimly*) I'm glad you didn't come in, Steve. You saw the stretcher.

STEVE: Yes.

TEMPLE: It was Countess Dekker – someone shot her about twenty minutes ago. If only Conrad hadn't called round to see us, I'd have probably been here in time to prevent it.

STEVE: Is she –?

TEMPLE: No, but she's very seriously hurt. Start the car, Steve.

The starter is pressed.

STEVE: Where are we going now – home?

TEMPLE: No, darling, we're going to Soho. We're going to take a look at the Groove Club.

The car starts.

FADE on the car engine.

FADE UP the car driving along a narrow road in Soho.

STEVE: (*Driving*) It's dark down here. Is it a cul-de-sac?

TEMPLE: No, I think there's a passage at the end.

The car stops.

STEVE switches off the engine.

STEVE: Will it be all right to leave the car here?

TEMPLE: Yes, I think so. Come on.

The car doors open and close.

We hear the sound of footsteps.

STEVE: I wonder if that's the place over on the other side …

A pause.

From inside the building a dance orchestra can be heard.

TEMPLE: Yes, I should imagine this is it … Come on, Steve.

A slight pause.

202

A door opens.

STEVE: Oh dear – it's very dark, Paul.

TEMPLE: Careful, darling – watch the steps.

FADE UP the sound of the orchestra.

STEVE: This is it … look – the Groove Club …

TEMPLE: Take my arm, Steve …

STEVE: I suppose we go through that curtain …

FADE UP of music.

HARRY: (*A young man, tough, slightly Cockney*) Good
              evening, can I see your membership card,
              please?

TEMPLE: (*A little taken aback*) Membership card? … Oh,
              yes, yes, of course …

HARRY: If you haven't got the card, chum – you've had
              it. We're very particular these days. This is a
              properly conducted club.

TEMPLE: Yes, I'm sure it is. Well, I've got the card
              somewhere …

TEMPLE proceeds to feel in his pockets.

STEVE: Have you looked in your waistcoat pocket,
              darling?

HARRY: You haven't got a card, chum – you're just
              trying it on …

STEVE: (*Suddenly*) Oh, Paul, look – there's Denis
              Harper! – Just coming out of the cloakroom.

TEMPLE: (*Calling*) Harper!

STEVE: He's seen us …

HARPER: (*Approaching*) Why, Mr and Mrs Temple! I
              didn't know you went in for this sort of thing.

TEMPLE: Hello, Harper! How are you?

HARPER: Oh, I'm all right, I suppose. A bit depressed …
              But what are you doing here? Getting local
              colour for one of your whodunnits?

203

TEMPLE: You can put it that way if you like, Harper. By the way, do you happen to be a member of this establishment?

HARPER: Of course. Why, do you want me to sign you in?

TEMPLE: If you'd be so kind.

HARPER: It's a pleasure. Let's have the book, Harry.

HARRY: Okay, Mr Harper.

A slight pause while HARPER signs the book.

TEMPLE: Have you been a member here long?

HARPER: Oh, about a year, I suppose. It's a pretty dim sort of place – but they all are in this Godforsaken city. Come along, Mrs Temple, let's go inside.

FADE UP the sound of the dance orchestra, loud and hot.

HARPER: I'll lead the way, Mrs Temple. I've got a table over there in the corner …

The dance orchestra continues: there are background noises of chatter and people dancing.

A pause.

HARPER: Sit here, Mrs Temple, – you can see the whole zoo from this corner.

STEVE: (*Laughing*) Thank you.

HARPER: Now, what can I get you to drink?

STEVE: Well – something fairly harmless, please.

HARPER: They have a rather pleasant fruit juice cocktail.

STEVE: Are you serious?

HARPER: (*Laughing*) Yes, quite serious.

STEVE: All right – fruit juice.

HARPER: And you, Mr Temple?

TEMPLE: I think I'd like a brandy and soda.

HARPER: Hey, waiter! Waiter!

WAITER: (*Approaching*) Yes, Mr Harper?

HARPER: Two of those atomic fruit juice things, and a brandy and soda.

WAITER: Right away, sir.

HARPER: When did you both get back from Germany, Mr Temple?

TEMPLE: This afternoon.

HARPER: I suppose the case is pretty well tied up now Betty's safe and sound, as it were?

TEMPLE: Up to a point, Harper – but unfortunately another girl, about Betty's age, was found murdered near Garmisch.

HARPER: When was this?

TEMPLE: The body was discovered on Thursday afternoon.

HARPER: But has this got anything to do with the Conrad affair?

TEMPLE: That rather depends which way you look at it.

HARPER: How do *you* look at it?

TEMPLE: I think it has. But whether Herr Breckshaft and Scotland Yard will agree with me or not, remains to be seen.

HARPER: Well – who was this girl?

TEMPLE: Her name was Gerda Holman. She came originally from Munich – you may have met her?

HARPER: Holman? No, I've never heard of her.

STEVE: But you know her employer, Mr Harper – Madame Klein. She runs a dress shop in Garmisch.

HARPER: I don't recall a Madame Klein.

STEVE: But surely – I saw you having tea with her one afternoon.

HARPER: (*Politely*) Really, Mrs Temple? Madame Klein, did you say? No, I'm sorry, you must be mistaken.

WAITER: (*Approaching*) The drinks, Mr Harper.

HARPER: Thank you, Bert. Put them on my account.

205

WAITER: Okay.

HARPER: Go on, Mrs Temple … try it …

STEVE picks up her glass and takes a sip.

STEVE: Whoa! (*With a laugh*) What sort of juice is this, Mr Harper?

HARPER laughs.

TEMPLE: Skol!

HARPER: Well, here's to a brighter London! (*He drinks*) I was rather depressed tonight, that's why I came here, to cheer myself up.

TEMPLE: Harper, forgive my asking, but did you ring Betty Conrad this evening?

HARPER: Why no. Why do you ask?

TEMPLE: Her father told me that someone telephoned her and he had the idea that perhaps it might be you.

HARPER: No, I haven't seen her, Mr Temple – not since she reappeared, as it were. As a matter of fact, I've purposely given her a wide berth. So far as I'm concerned she's dynamite.

STEVE: Why do you say that, Mr Harper?

HARPER: Well, I've had nothing but bad luck ever since I met Betty. After all, if it wasn't for this Conrad business I'd still be sitting pretty in Munich.

TEMPLE: Yes, I see your point, Harper. By the way, is this one of Betty's favourite haunts?

HARPER: What do you mean?

TEMPLE: (*Pleasantly*) I mean – does she come here, to the Groove Club?

HARPER: I've never seen her here. I should think she's a bit young for this sort of thing.

STEVE: They all seem a bit young for this sort of thing!

HARPER: You see that chap over there – the best dancer of the lot?

TEMPLE: Yes?

HARPER: Well, he could tell you whether Betty's a member or not. He's here practically every night.

STEVE: You mean the man with the red hair?

HARPER: Yes. Paddy, they call him.

STEVE: Well, he can certainly dance – if you can call it dancing.

HARPER: Would you like to have a word with him, Mr Temple?

TEMPLE: Yes, I would.

HARPER: Okay – wait till they finish and I'll get him.

The music continues, the dance eventually reaching a climax. There is a storm of applause and excited voices: as the laughter and clapping dies down HARPER calls across the floor to PADDY.

HARPER: Paddy! … Paddy! Here a minute …

A slight pause.

PADDY: (*With charm and a very slight Irish accent*) Ha, Mr Harper! Well now – I thought you were in Germany?

HARPER: Got back this week, old boy. Paddy, I want you to meet two friends of mine – Mr and Mrs Paul Temple.

STEVE: How do you do?

TEMPLE: We've been admiring your dancing …

PADDY: Delighted, Mrs Temple. Delighted, I'm sure … (*Suddenly*) Paul Temple, did you say? Mr Temple, did you write a book called East of Algiers?

TEMPLE: I did.

PADDY: I enjoyed every minute of it.

TEMPLE: Thank you very much. I hope you bought a copy.

PADDY: Why no, I borrowed it, of course! Whoever buys detective stories?

HARPER: Paddy, Mr Temple is rather anxious to know if a young girl named Betty Conrad ever came here.

PADDY: Betty Conrad? No, she isn't a member. I'm sure of that. Of course, she might use another name – some of the girls do, you know.

The band starts to play another dance number.

TEMPLE: No, I think that's unlikely.

PADDY: (*Thoughtfully*) Betty Conrad? … No, I've never heard the name before … (*To STEVE*) Would you care to dance the next one, Mrs Temple?

STEVE: (*Horrified*) I'm afraid not, Mr … I'm not wearing the right shoes and I'm rather tired … We only got back from Germany ourselves this afternoon.

PADDY: (*Laughing*) Sure – sure, I understand, Mrs Temple. Well, if you'll excuse me now – there's a young lady over there I've promised this dance to.

STEVE: (*Amused*) Well, what would have happened if I'd accepted?

PADDY: I should probably have danced with the pair of you, Mrs Temple … Well, goodbye now …

PADDY goes.

STEVE: (*Laughing*) He's quite a character!

HARPER: Yes, but people like him.

TEMPLE: I should imagine he's all right if you don't have to dance with him.

HARPER: (*Laughing*) That's about it, Mr Temple.

WAITER: Excuse me, sir. There's a telephone call for you.

HARPER: Oh – are you sure it's for me?

WAITER: Yes, sir – Mr Harper.

HARPER: Thank you. I shan't be a minute, Mr Temple.

TEMPLE: That's all right.

A pause.

208

TEMPLE: How's your fruit juice, Steve?

STEVE: Horrible. What's the brandy like?

TEMPLE: Warm.

STEVE: Darling, do you think we might leave fairly soon?

TEMPLE: Yes, as soon as Harper gets back we'll make our excuses and slip away.

STEVE: Paul, he's a strange chap, isn't he?

TEMPLE: Harper?

STEVE: Yes.

TEMPLE: (*Quietly*) Yes, he's strange all right …

FADE.

FADE UP the sound of footsteps on the pavement.

STEVE: Oh, thank goodness for some peace and quiet!

TEMPLE: I'll be even more thankful for a bed! By Timothy, I'm tired! This has been one of our hectic days, Steve.

STEVE: (*Yawning*) I don't know what was in that cocktail, but it certainly wasn't fruit juice.

The car door opens.

TEMPLE: Jump in.

They get into the car.

The sound of car doors opening and closing.

TEMPLE starts the engine.

The car begins to move, then after a moment, bumps to a standstill.

TEMPLE: Hello, what's wrong with the car?

STEVE: It feels as if we haven't got any shock absorbers!

TEMPLE: Wait a minute, darling …

TEMPLE gets out of the car.

There is a pause.

TEMPLE: (*From the background*) Well, by Timothy! …

STEVE: Paul, what is it?

209

TEMPLE: Come and have a look at this, Steve!

STEVE gets out of the car and joins TEMPLE.

STEVE: What is it, darling?

TEMPLE: Just look at the tyres.

STEVE: Good heavens! They've been slashed to ribbons.

TEMPLE: Yes, they certainly have.

STEVE: Paul, who on earth would do a thing like this?

TEMPLE: I don't know, but they've certainly made a first class job of it.

STEVE: What are we going to do?

TEMPLE: Well, we'd better pick up a taxi, and I'll phone a garage when we get home. There's no point in my messing about with this – in any case I've only got one spare wheel.

PADDY: (*Approaching*) Hello, Mr Temple! Are you in trouble?

STEVE: It's Paddy!

TEMPLE: Hello, there …

PADDY: What's the matter? Is there anything I can do?

TEMPLE: Yes indeed, Paddy. Someone slashed my tyres to pieces …

PADDY: No! You're joking.

TEMPLE: It isn't my idea of a joke …

PADDY: Let's have a look!

A moment.

PADDY: By Jupiter, they certainly have slashed them, Mr Temple! Well, well, that's a damn fine thing to happen, I must say!

TEMPLE: Have you got a car near here?

PADDY: Yes, I have. Would you like a lift?

TEMPLE: Well, I don't want to take you out of your way, but …

PADDY: That's all right, man! Don't be silly …

TEMPLE: Once I get home, I can ring my local garage about it.

PADDY: Why, yes, of course. Come along, Mrs Temple … My car's just round the corner …

FADE on footsteps.

FADE IN the sound of a large American car travelling fairly slowly.

PADDY: You did say Eaton Square, Mr Temple?

TEMPLE: That's right – about half way down the south side.

PADDY: Are you quite comfortable in the back, Mrs Temple?

STEVE: (*Sleepily*) Yes – I'm fine.

PADDY: (*After a moment*) That's a nice car you've got, Mr Temple. It's a pity about the tyres.

TEMPLE: Well, we'll soon get some new ones …

PADDY: Yes. (*A moment*) What do you think of this jalopy?

TEMPLE: Large – but very comfortable.

PADDY: All the Yankee stuff is like that … I like 'em.

TEMPLE: Yes. Are you in the car business?

PADDY: I've a finger in a lot of pies, Mr Temple. Yes, I'm in the car business in a small way. If ever you're looking for a bargain I might be able to put you on to something good.

TEMPLE: Thank you very much.

PADDY: I've a small showroom in Great Portland Street – just opposite the post office.

A slight pause.

PADDY: Drop in any time, I'll be glad to see you. Just ask for Captain Smith …

END OF EPISODE SIX

EPISODE SEVEN

COFFEE FOR
MISS CONRAD

OPEN TO: *The noise of a car.*

PADDY: I've a small showroom in Great Portland Street – just opposite the post office. Drop in any time. I'll be glad to see you. Just ask for Captain Smith.

STEVE: Captain Smith?

PADDY: (*Amused*) That's right, Mrs Temple, but everyone calls me Paddy 'cos I'm Irish.

TEMPLE: Take it you're not in the Service now, Captain Smith?

PADDY: No. I just keep the old title to remind me of the high times we used to have. And of course, it's a help in my car business. It inspires confidence, if you see what I mean.

STEVE: Do they know you as Captain Smith at the Groove Club?

PADDY: Well – some of 'em know I'm called Smith, of course, but they all call me Paddy.

TEMPLE: Do you often go to the Groove?

PADDY: Well, yes, quite a bit. I enjoy it. The band's tip-top and I like the kids …

STEVE: Doesn't it ever get a bit too rowdy?

PADDY: Occasionally. But I don't mind a rough and tumble every now and then. Shakes up the old liver … I say, do you mind if I stop here for a minute?

TEMPLE: (*Surprised*) This is Berkeley Square, isn't it?

The car draws to a standstill.

The engine remains running.

PADDY: Yes. I've got a little pied-a-terre over one of the office buildings, and I've left my key. The caretaker will let me have a duplicate, then I

215

needn't trouble him again when I get back later on …

TEMPLE: You're very lucky to find a flat in Berkeley Square.

PADDY: Yes, I got it through a pal of mine. You can get anything if you know the right people.

TEMPLE: So they tell me.

The car door opens and PADDY gets out of the car.

PADDY: I'll be back in a minute …

There is a pause.

The car engine continues to tick over.

STEVE: So that's Captain Smith! He seems harmless enough, darling. (*With a little laugh*) Almost moronic!

TEMPLE: (*Seriously*) Don't you believe it! We've had two warnings from Joyce Gunter about Smith, and I'm inclined to take them seriously …

STEVE: Perhaps you're right. Anyway, he does himself well – Berkeley Square.

TEMPLE: (*Imitating PADDY*) You can easily do well for yourself if you know the right people.

STEVE laughs.

A moment.

STEVE: The price of petrol doesn't seem to worry him … He's left the car running.

TEMPLE: (*Thoughtfully*) I wonder if there's a reason for that?

STEVE: What possible reason could he have …

TEMPLE: I'm going to switch it off.

TEMPLE switches off the car engine.

There is a pause.

STEVE: Paul, what's the matter?

TEMPLE: I'm thinking about the plane and the time bomb … Someone obviously intended to put a time

bomb on that plane, Steve, and they failed to …
(*Suddenly*) Steve, listen! Do you hear that
ticking noise?

STEVE: It's the dashboard clock, surely?

TEMPLE: The clock's stopped … Look – twenty past six
…

TEMPLE opens the car door.

TEMPLE: Come on, Steve! Get out! Quickly!

TEMPLE and STEVE get out of the car.

TEMPLE: Come on, across the street!

FADE DOWN footsteps.

FADE IN the sound of an approaching taxi.

TEMPLE: Our friend Smith should have been back by now
… and there's no sign of him … Here's a taxi –
we might as well grab it and get back home …
(*Calling*) Taxi!

The taxi draws to a standstill near TEMPLE and STEVE.

DRIVER: Where to, guv'nor?

TEMPLE: Eaton Square, please.

*As TEMPLE speaks there is the sound of a loud explosion in
the background.*

DRIVER: What the blazes was that?

TEMPLE: Steve – look at the car … Just look at it!

STEVE: Oh, Paul!

TEMPLE: (*To the DRIVER*) Take us to Eaton Square …

DRIVER: Blimey! Just look at my door …

TEMPLE: Don't worry, driver. I'll pay for the damage. Just
take us to Eaton Square.

DRIVER: Okay, guv'nor. Cor, what a night!

STEVE: (*Getting into the cab*) You can say that again!

FADE.

FADE IN incidental music.

FADE music.

FADE IN a door opening.

The door closes.

STEVE: Have you spoken to Vosper?

TEMPLE: Yes. I told him the whole story. He's showing me some photographs tomorrow, to see if I can identify our Irish friend.

STEVE: Paul, what a day! I believe it's the most exciting …

STEVE is interrupted by the telephone ringing.

STEVE: Oh, no!

TEMPLE laughs.

TEMPLE: It's probably Vosper again!

TEMPLE lifts the receiver.

TEMPLE: (*On the phone*) Hello?

CONRAD: (*On the other end of the line*) Mr Temple?

TEMPLE: Yes?

CONRAD: This is Dr Conrad …

TEMPLE: Oh, hello, doctor. Is there any news of your daughter?

CONRAD: Yes, she arrived home about ten minutes ago.

TEMPLE: Good. Have you any idea where she'd been?

CONRAD: No. She won't tell me. She's in a very difficult mood, I'm afraid. She refuses to see you tomorrow morning. She says she simply won't go to Scotland Yard again.

TEMPLE: (*After a moment*) Ask her to come to the telephone …

CONRAD: I don't think she will …

TEMPLE: Listen, doctor – tell her that Countess Dekker is dangerously ill. Tell her I have some news about the Countess …

CONRAD: All right, hold the line …

There is a pause.

218

BETTY: (*On the other end of the line; softly*) Hello? Mr Temple? …

TEMPLE: (*Kindly*) Hello, Betty. Are you feeling any better?

BETTY: (*Slowly*) What is it you want to tell me – about Countess Dekker?

TEMPLE: Someone tried to murder her this evening. She's very ill.

BETTY: (*Tensely*) Who tried to murder her? Where is she?

TEMPLE: She's in London, but I'll answer all your questions tomorrow morning, Betty.

BETTY: No, I can't see you tomorrow morning …

TEMPLE: If you're fighting shy of going to Scotland Yard again, I'll see you here in Eaton Square. Your father can bring you along.

BETTY: (*Reluctantly*) Well …

TEMPLE: No one else need know you've come here, I just want to ask you one or two simple questions, that's all.

BETTY: (*Softly, still nervous*) Questions – it's nothing but questions …

TEMPLE: In return you can ask me about Countess Dekker. I'll probably have some more news by then.

BETTY: (*After a moment*) All right, Mr Temple …

TEMPLE: Good. Tell your father to have you here by ten o'clock. Good night.

BETTY: (*Hesitantly*) Good night.

TEMPLE puts down the receiver.

TEMPLE: She's coming here tomorrow morning …

The door opens.

CHARLIE: Excuse me, sir. Inspector Vosper's here.

TEMPLE: Show him in, Charlie.

CHARLIE: (*From the background*) This way, sir …

TEMPLE: Come in, Vosper! You've certainly lost no time.

The door closes.

VOSPER: My men checked the place in Berkeley Square. Your friend simply walked in at the front and out at the back. There's a caretaker, but there's no top flat. And of course the caretaker had never heard of Captain Smith, or Paddy, or whatever he likes to call himself.

TEMPLE: That's pretty much what I expected.

VOSPER: I had a quick look through our records for a Captain Smith. There's a notorious character using that name. He's also known as Major Spalding and Lord Wensley. Seems to be able to turn on English, Scots, or Irish background, according to his fancy.

TEMPLE: What's his line?

VOSPER: Drugs – smuggling – confidence stuff – anything that pays off.

TEMPLE: I'll check his photographs tomorrow morning.

VOSPER: Good. If it is the same man we'd like to get our hands on him.

TEMPLE: Any news of Countess Dekker?

VOSPER: Yes. She's had an emergency operation and she's on the danger list – but they think there's a chance. By the way, I phoned Munich and passed the word on to Breckshaft about her.

TEMPLE: I'm sure Herr Breckshaft will be interested.

VOSPER: Yes. Well, he's over here tomorrow and he's calling round to see you.

TEMPLE: Oh good. Now, Inspector, I insist that you have a drink – and, Steve, I insist that you go to bed, darling!

STEVE: (*Yawning*) All right, Paul. Good night, Inspector!

VOSPER: Good night, Mrs Temple.

FADE.

FADE IN incidental music.

FADE music.

A door opens and closes.

VOSPER: Mrs Temple looks rather tired.

TEMPLE: Well – we've had quite a day, Inspector. Now what would you like to drink?

VOSPER: Could I have a whisky and soda, please?

TEMPLE: Wouldn't you prefer a Groove cocktail?

VOSPER: (*Laughing*) No, thank you! I'll stick to the whisky and soda!

FADE.

FADE IN a door closing.

STEVE: (*From bed, sleepily*) Darling, I was nearly asleep. Has the Inspector gone?

TEMPLE: Yes, he's just left.

A pause.

STEVE: Paul … Do you think this man Smith is the man behind everything?

TEMPLE: Everything?

STEVE: The whole case – the disappearance of Betty Conrad – the murder – of Gerda Holman – the attempt on the Countess …

TEMPLE: He's deeply involved, there's no doubt about that. But there's someone else behind Smith – and that's the person I'm really after, Steve.

STEVE: You know who it is?

TEMPLE: I've a pretty shrewd idea. And since I don't believe in underestimating one's opponent, we've got to be very much on the alert, darling. So wherever you go I want you to take Charlie with you for the next two or three days.

STEVE: Poor Charlie! (*Laughing*) I've got two fittings this week, and a hair-do!

TEMPLE: Steve, we've had two narrow escapes since this case started …

STEVE: (*Still amused*) Yes, but really, darling …

TEMPLE: You know I'm beginning to think there's only one way to deal with this affair. So far I've been pretty orthodox in my methods. Now I think I'll change my tactics and be a little unorthodox.

STEVE: How do you mean?

TEMPLE: Steve, do you ever see that old school friend of yours, the dress designer with the cottage near Tenterden?

STEVE: Gwen Thompson?

TEMPLE: Yes.

STEVE: I had lunch with her about a month ago. Why?

TEMPLE: Well, I want you to get in touch with her tomorrow morning. And this is what I want you to do …

FADE.
FADE IN incidental music.

FADE music.
A door opens.

TEMPLE: Hello, Steve! Everything all right?

STEVE: Yes, I phoned Gwen. Everything's fixed.

Voices can be heard in the hall.

TEMPLE: (*Quietly*) I think this is Betty Conrad and her father.

STEVE: All right, I'll leave you. I'll be in the drawing-room if you want me, Paul.

The door opens and closes.

A pause.

The door opens again.

CHARLIE: Dr Conrad, sir.

TEMPLE: Hello, Dr Conrad! Come along in …

The door closes.

CONRAD: Good morning. This is my daughter Betty …

TEMPLE: Hello, Betty! Come and sit down over here …

BETTY: I'd rather stand, if you don't mind …

CONRAD: Betty, Mr Temple's only trying to help you, remember.

TEMPLE: Yes, well, don't worry too much about that, Betty. I've had some news of your friend Countess Dekker.

BETTY: (*Tensely*) Oh! Is she …?

TEMPLE: She came through the operation remarkably well.

BETTY: Have they found out yet who tried to kill her?

TEMPLE: Not yet. That's one of the things I want to talk to you about …

BETTY: I know nothing about it …

TEMPLE: Dr Conrad, I'd rather like to talk to Betty alone, if you don't mind?

CONRAD: (*Faintly surprised*) No, of course not …

TEMPLE: I'll put her into a taxi as soon as we've had our talk.

BETTY: I've told you, I've got nothing to say –

CONRAD: You see, Mr Temple, you're wasting your time, I'm afraid.

TEMPLE: I'm a writer, I'm used to wasting time. Now listen, young lady, you may have nothing to tell me, but I've an awful lot to tell you. And if you don't listen to me, I think you'll be sorry – very sorry.

223

BETTY: (*After a moment, sullenly*) All right – I'll stay.

CONRAD: I'll be at Harley Street, Betty. Good morning, Mr
           Temple. I'm very grateful to you.

The door opens.

TEMPLE: No, I'm grateful to you, Doctor, for bringing
           your daughter to see me. Goodbye.

The door closes.

A pause.

BETTY: Well, what is it you want?

TEMPLE: At the moment I want some coffee. I don't know
           about you. (*Calling*) Charlie! (*After a moment*)
           Do you smoke?

BETTY: No – no, thank you.

The door opens.

CHARLIE: Yes, sir?

TEMPLE: Can you bring the coffee now, Charlie?

CHARLIE: Very good, Mr Temple.

CHARLIE goes out.

TEMPLE: I hope you didn't mind my sending your father
           away. There are times when one can say things
           to a stranger that might be embarrassing in front
           of a parent. (*After a pause*) Are you really going
           to stand there the whole time?

BETTY: Very well, I'll sit down. But that doesn't mean
           …

TEMPLE: It means you're going to sit down, that's all!

BETTY: I haven't the slightest intention of telling you
           what happened to me.

TEMPLE: I know what happened to you!

BETTY: (*Obviously surprised*) You do …?

TEMPLE: Yes, I do …

CHARLIE returns carrying a tray.

TEMPLE: Ah, here's the coffee! Put it on the table, Charlie
           – over here …

224

CHARLIE puts down the tray.

CHARLIE: Anything else you want, Mr Temple?

TEMPLE: No, thank you.

CHARLIE: Very good, sir.

The door closes.

There is a pause.

TEMPLE pours the coffee.

TEMPLE: Here you are, Betty …

BETTY: No, thank you.

TEMPLE: (*Laughing*) My word, you are in a difficult mood. Don't you like coffee?

BETTY: Yes, I do, but …

TEMPLE: (*Laughing at BETTY*) Well … here you are.

There is a pause.

BETTY: Could I have a little sugar?

TEMPLE: Oh, I'm so sorry! Yes, of course … Help yourself.

There is another pause.

BETTY drinks her coffee.

TEMPLE: … Now I'm not going to ask you a lot of questions about why you suddenly disappeared from Mrs Weldon's.

BETTY: I didn't dislike the school, if that's what you're thinking.

TEMPLE: No, that's not what I'm thinking. I'm more interested in what you can tell me about Gerda Holman.

BETTY: Gerda Holman?

TEMPLE: Yes.

BETTY: I don't know anyone of that name.

TEMPLE: Are you sure? She worked at a dress shop in Garmisch – she was found murdered the day before yesterday.

BETTY: I've – I've never heard of her …

225

TEMPLE: All right, then – you've never heard of her. It was very nice of you to be so concerned about Countess Dekker. Is she a great friend of yours?

BETTY: I went to her house several times – she used to invite the girls from the school.

TEMPLE: Yes, I know – but was she a <u>particular</u> friend of yours?

BETTY: No …

TEMPLE: And yet you seemed very upset when I told you that she'd been shot.

BETTY: Well, naturally, I …

TEMPLE: Were you upset because the Countess had been shot, or because you thought you knew who had shot her?

BETTY: (*Tensely*) I don't know what you're talking about, Mr Temple!

TEMPLE: All right, Betty. Let's go back to Gerda Holman.

BETTY: I've told you, I've never heard of Gerda Holman.

TEMPLE: But you saw her when you went to Madame Klein's to order your coat.

BETTY: Madame Klein? I tell you I don't know any of these people.

TEMPLE: No? We found a card from her in your room, saying that the coat was ready. Betty, I'm going to tell you something which I think will interest you. When you first went to Germany – your father took you to Munich to arrange about the publication of one of his books.

BETTY: Yes?

TEMPLE: You and your father had dinner one night with a book publisher, called Kurt Holman. That's when you met his daughter Gerda. A gay sophisticated girl of about your own age.

BETTY: (*Sullenly*) Oh, was that Gerda Holman?

TEMPLE: Yes, that was Gerda. You also met Madame Klein at that dinner party. She was arranging for Gerda to enter her dress business.

BETTY: I was a stranger there … They spoke German … I didn't really know what was going on.

TEMPLE: Didn't you? Anyhow, you can see I've made quite a thorough investigation of this affair.

BETTY: (*Tense, near to tears*) And what good has it done you?

TEMPLE: It's brought us a little nearer to the truth, Betty, and it hasn't been easy to discover the truth about this affair. You see, some people – people like yourself – are being loyal to the wrong person.

BETTY: I don't know what you mean.

TEMPLE: I'm not blaming you. When you're young, it's not easy to discriminate.

BETTY: I've had enough of this. If you don't mind, I'd rather …

TEMPLE: (*Quietly; yet with authority*) Sit down and finish your coffee. (*After a moment*) Now supposing we forget Gerda Holman and Countess Dekker and talk about another friend of yours – Elliot France. He is a friend of yours, isn't he?

BETTY: (*Hesitantly, a little embarrassed*) I know Mr France of course, but – (*A moment*) he was very kind to me …

TEMPLE: When was he kind to you?

BETTY doesn't answer.

There is a slight pause.

TEMPLE: Was it after you left the school?

BETTY:	Yes, after I left the school. You see it was Mr France who … (*Sleepily*) I don't feel very well …
TEMPLE:	Are you sleepy?
BETTY:	Yes, and I feel as if … was there something in the coffee?
TEMPLE:	It tasted all right to me …
BETTY:	I feel so … sleepy …
TEMPLE:	(*After a moment*) There's nothing to worry about, Betty …

There is a pause.
The door opens.

TEMPLE:	(*Calling softly*) Steve!

A moment.
STEVE enters.

STEVE:	(*Quietly*) Is she asleep?
TEMPLE:	Yes, have you got the rug?
STEVE:	Yes, it's here.

CHARLIE enters.

CHARLIE:	Everything's okay, Mr Temple. The car's at the door …
TEMPLE:	All right, Charlie. Now you take hold of her shoulders … Ready, Steve?

FADE.
FADE IN incidental music.

FADE music.
FADE IN the sound of a typewriter.
A telephone bell starts to ring and the typewriter stops.
TEMPLE lifts the receiver.

TEMPLE:	(*On the phone*) Hello?
BRECKSHAFT:	(*On the other end of the line*) Mr Temple?
TEMPLE:	Yes?
BRECKSHAFT:	Breckshaft here …

TEMPLE: Oh – hello, Breckshaft! Where are you?
BRECKSHAFT: I'm at St Matthew's Hospital. I've just been seeing Countess Dekker.
TEMPLE: Oh, how is she?
BRECKSHAFT: She's a little better. She can't talk to anyone yet … I'd like to see you, Temple.
TEMPLE: Come along straight away, if you want to.
BRECKSHAFT: Thank you. I'll pick up a taxi.
TEMPLE: You've got the address?
BRECKSHAFT: Yes, I have it.
TEMPLE: Right! See you soon.
BRECKSHAFT: Goodbye.

TEMPLE puts down the receiver and starts to type again.
After a moment, the door opens.
The typing stops.

TEMPLE: Steve! I didn't expect you back yet!
STEVE: I was lucky, the roads were very clear.
TEMPLE: Was everything all right?
STEVE: Perfect. No trouble at all.
TEMPLE: Did she recover consciousness?
STEVE: Yes, just as we got her into the cottage. Gwen and I talked to her – we assured her she was perfectly all right and there was nothing to worry about.
TEMPLE: How did she take it?
STEVE: I think she'll be all right, Paul.
TEMPLE: You've explained everything to Gwen?
STEVE: I gave her a rough idea of what the poor kid's been through. She'll take care of her. If there's any difficulty, I've told her to telephone us.
TEMPLE: Good. Well, I suppose I'd better finish this letter.

The typing starts again.

229

FADE on the noise of the typewriter.

FADE IN a door closing.

A pause.

TEMPLE: Can I offer you a cigar, Breckshaft?

BRECKSHAFT: No, thank you.

TEMPLE: What about a drink?

BRECKSHAFT: First, I would like to talk.

TEMPLE: Yes, of course. Did you find out anything from Countess Dekker?

BRECKSHAFT: No, she's too ill to talk. But one thing I am certain of, the attempt on her life – the murder of Gerda Holman – are all part of the same case.

TEMPLE: I'm interested to hear you say that, very – interested.

BRECKSHAFT: But you yourself do not think there is any connection?

TEMPLE: As a matter of fact, I do, but I didn't want to mention it to you until you'd explored the other likely channels.

BRECKSHAFT: Ah yes, I see what you mean.

TEMPLE: Tell me, have there been any more developments about Gerda Holman?

BRECKSHAFT: We have searched the room at her lodgings. Everywhere there were pictures of this man Elliot France – mostly cut from continental magazines.

TEMPLE: You think Gerda was friendly with him, then?

BRECKSHAFT: Well, she had many copies of his novels, and also a press cutting book devoted to his activities.

TEMPLE:	(*Pleasantly*) Well, things begin to add up, don't they?
BRECKSHAFT:	Do they?
TEMPLE:	I think so. Now what about that drink?
BRECKSHAFT:	Perhaps just a little whisky …
TEMPLE:	Certainly.

TEMPLE mixes the drinks.

A pause.

TEMPLE:	Have you seen anyone from the Yard yet?
BRECKSHAFT:	Inspector Vosper was kind enough to meet me at the airport.
TEMPLE:	Oh, good. He's a nice chap, isn't he? And very efficient. Don't underrate him, Breckshaft …
BRECKSHAFT:	(*Seriously*) Why should I underrate him?
TEMPLE:	(*Amused*) I wasn't suggesting that you … well, here's your drink.
BRECKSHAFT:	Thank you.
TEMPLE:	Skoal!
BRECKSHAFT:	Your very good health.

They drink.

A pause.

BRECKSHAFT:	The Inspector told me about the car incident – about this so-called Captain Smith …
TEMPLE:	You've heard of Captain Smith?
BRECKSHAFT:	Yes, I think perhaps I have. But I'm waiting to check from photographs. But tell me, why did you get out of the car? What made you suspicious?
TEMPLE:	I suppose it was just – intuition.
BRECKSHAFT:	Ah, yes! I always say intuition is worth a thousand clues.

TEMPLE: My wife would agree with you. (*A moment*) Has anyone else seen Countess Dekker today?

BRECKSHAFT: Yes, as a matter of fact Mr France and Mrs Weldon have seen her. They flew over with me this morning. They were most upset when I told them about the shooting and insisted on coming.

TEMPLE: I see. (*A pause*) There was something else I intended to ask you, Breckshaft … now, what was it? … Oh! Yes! About Fritz Gunter and his wife …

BRECKSHAFT: You mean the people who run the hotel at Oberammergau?

TEMPLE: Yes. Tell me, do you know anything about them?

BRECKSHAFT: Only what I've already told you. I believe Gunter was once an actor. Of course his wife's the business woman – she runs the hotel.

TEMPLE: Yes, I rather gathered that.

There is a slight pause.

BRECKSHAFT: (*A shade cautious*) Temple, there's something I'd like you to know, about Gerda Holman …

TEMPLE: Well?

BRECKSHAFT: After the post-mortem we made several tests. Gerda Holman was a drug addict.

TEMPLE: Heroin?

BRECKSHAFT: (*A little surprised*) Yes, heroin. That doesn't surprise you, then?

TEMPLE: Not entirely. Have you had reason to believe that there's a drug smuggling organisation in Bavaria?

BRECKSHAFT: We've had our suspicions for some time. Why do you ask?

TEMPLE: Because I discovered that June Jackson was a potential drug addict.

BRECKSHAFT: (*Surprised*) June Jackson? The American girl? – The one who disappeared ...?

TEMPLE: Yes. I taxed her with it and finally persuaded her to go home.

BRECKSHAFT: Go home! So that's what happened. (*A slight touch of sarcasm*) Well, thank you for telling me. Things are beginning to fall into place. (*After a moment*) On the way back from the airport the Inspector told me that you'd seen Betty Conrad today.

TEMPLE: Yes, I saw her this morning.

BRECKSHAFT: And how was she?

TEMPLE: Difficult – extremely difficult. She just refuses to talk.

BRECKSHAFT: I expect she will in time.

TEMPLE: I don't know, she's a pretty obstinate girl, and I doubt very much whether ...

TEMPLE is interrupted by the ringing of the telephone.

TEMPLE: Excuse me.

TEMPLE lifts the receiver.

TEMPLE: (*On the phone*) Paul Temple speaking ...

CONRAD: (*On the other end of the line*) This is Dr Conrad.

TEMPLE: Oh, hello, Doctor ...

CONRAD: I'm very anxious about Betty. She hasn't returned home yet.

TEMPLE: She left here about twelve o'clock.

CONRAD: Twelve o'clock! Why, that's extraordinary, I just don't understand it.

TEMPLE:	Look, Conrad, – don't worry. Give her until eight o'clock, then if she hasn't turned up ring me again.
CONRAD:	Yes, all right, Temple.
TEMPLE:	Remember she was pretty late turning up last night.
CONRAD:	Yes, I know, but … (*Wearily*) All right, I'll ring you again later. Goodbye.
TEMPLE:	Goodbye.

TEMPLE replaces the receiver.

TEMPLE:	Well, it rather looks as if Betty Conrad's disappeared again …
BRECKSHAFT:	Again! I'm glad she's not my daughter.
TEMPLE:	Yes – well, we shall see what happens. There's a meeting tonight, isn't there? At Scotland Yard?
BRECKSHAFT:	Yes, at six o'clock. (*Surprised*) Are you going to be there?
TEMPLE:	Sir Graham's asked me, but I don't know whether I shall make it or not.
BRECKSHAFT:	It might be a very good idea if you could. After all, it was you that Countess Dekker telephoned just before she was shot.
TEMPLE:	Yes. Well, I'll try.
BRECKSHAFT:	I must be off. Thank you for the drink.
TEMPLE:	Not at all. Goodbye, Breckshaft. See you later, perhaps …

FADE SCENE.

FADE IN a door opening.

FORBES:	Ah, hello, Temple! Come in!
TEMPLE:	They told me to report here, Sir Graham.
FORBES:	Yes, the meeting's in Vosper's office. I thought we'd go down together.

TEMPLE:	Who else is attending this meeting?
FORBES:	Mrs Weldon, Elliot France and Breckshaft.
TEMPLE:	Quite a gathering.
FORBES:	Yes. Before we go down, Temple, you'll be interested to hear we've checked on that Smith character. Vosper was right. He uses half a dozen aliases – we've been on the lookout for him for several months.
TEMPLE:	What about the car showroom?
FORBES:	That was nonsense, of course. They've never heard of him. Incidentally, it's our opinion that Smith was responsible for the Dale Black murder.
TEMPLE:	(*Puzzled*) Who's Dale Black?
FORBES:	He's the dead man you found in the house at Oxted just before you left for Germany. According to the F.B.I. Black was mixed up in the Tennessee drug scandal – he came over here on a false passport.
TEMPLE:	And he was an associate of Smith's?
FORBES:	Yes, we believe so, and according to all accounts they had a frightful row. Anyhow, we'll sort Captain Smith out when we pick him up.
TEMPLE:	When you manage to pick him up, Sir Graham.
FORBES:	(*Smiling*) Don't worry, Temple, we'll pick him up. Come along, let's join the others …

FADE.

FADE IN of VOSPER's voice.

VOSPER:	Ah, good evening, Temple. You know Breckshaft, of course, and I think you know Mrs Weldon – and Mr France.
TEMPLE:	Yes, of course. Good evening, Mrs Weldon.
MRS WELDON:	Good evening, Mr Temple.
TEMPLE:	Hello, France.
FRANCE:	Good evening, Mr Temple.
VOSPER:	Well now, I think the best plan, Sir Graham, is for Mr Temple to tell our visitors what happened last night. Then we can go on from there.
TEMPLE:	Well, quite briefly, I had a telephone call from Countess Dekker last night, asking me to go to see her at the Coronet Hotel in Bloomsbury. When I got there I found someone had tried to shoot her, and they were just taking her to hospital.
BRECKSHAFT:	Could you tell us please, a little more about the telephone conversation?
TEMPLE:	She seemed to be in a very nervous state, and she said she'd come over to London specially to give me some news about the Conrad case. Naturally I agreed to see her.
VOSPER:	Did she mention anyone, Mr Temple – anyone in particular?

There is a slight pause.

TEMPLE:	Yes, she mentioned Mr France.
VOSPER:	What did she say?
FRANCE:	(*Irritated*) Come along, Temple – let's have it. What did she say about me?
TEMPLE:	Well, I gathered that she was not very pleased with you, Mr France.

236

FRANCE:	Yes, that's true. As a matter of fact we'd had a row. There's no point in concealing it. She flounced out of the house in a fit of temper. But I assure you I hadn't the least idea she intended coming to London.
VOSPER:	And you've no idea who tried to kill her?
FRANCE:	No, of course not. I can't imagine who it was. (*To TEMPLE*) You say the Coronet Hotel in Bloomsbury? That seems a rather odd place for Elsa to stay. Was she at the hotel under her own name?
TEMPLE:	No, they knew her simply as Mrs Dekker. Well, that's about all there is to my story, except that just before she became unconscious she warned me about a certain Captain Smith …
FRANCE:	Captain Smith?
TEMPLE:	Yes.
BRECKSHAFT:	Do you know anything about this Captain Smith, Mr France?
FRANCE:	(*Hesitantly*) No, I've never heard of him.
BRECKSHAFT:	Mrs Weldon?
MRS WELDON:	Nor have I.
VOSPER:	The bullet that wounded Countess Dekker came from a Caussen. It's a German army revolver, now out of use. (*To MRS WELDON and FRANCE*) Have either of you ever seen one?
MRS WELDON:	I certainly haven't.
VOSPER:	Mr France?
FRANCE:	(*Still irritated*) I've seen one of course, but I don't possess one, Inspector, if that's what you're thinking.

MRS WELDON:	You think it was this man Smith who tried to murder Elsa?
VOSPER:	We don't know, Mrs Weldon, but we suspect that it might have been. We're after him on two other charges.
TEMPLE:	Mrs Weldon, may I ask what brings you to London?
MRS WELDON:	Well, of course. I came when I heard poor Elsa was at the point of death. She's been a good friend of mine for a long time.
TEMPLE:	And that goes for you too, Mr France?
FRANCE:	Well, naturally, I was very anxious about Elsa. We've been living … We've been very close friends for years.
TEMPLE:	Yet you quarrelled?
FRANCE:	People do quarrel, you know. Even when they're very good friends.
TEMPLE:	What did you quarrel about – Betty Conrad?
FRANCE:	Why should we quarrel about Betty Conrad?
TEMPLE:	Because Betty was rather fond of you, and I thought perhaps …
FRANCE:	(*Interrupting TEMPLE*) It was just a schoolgirl crush, nothing else. I certainly didn't take it seriously.
TEMPLE:	But did Countess Dekker take it seriously?
FRANCE:	(*A moment, reluctantly*) Perhaps …
MRS WELDON:	(*Surprised: turning towards FRANCE*) Elliot, you're not seriously suggesting that Elsa thought Betty was in love with you?

238

FRANCE: (*Irritated*) I'm not suggesting anything –
it's Mr Temple who's making all the
suggestions …

As FRANCE finishes speaking there is a knock on the door.

VOSPER: (*Calling*) Come in!

A SERGEANT enters.

SERGEANT: Sorry to interrupt you, sir, but this
message is most urgent.

VOSPER: Thank you, sergeant. That's all right.

VOSPER looks at the note.

VOSPER: (*After a moment*) This is a message from
the hospital. Countess Dekker's
recovered consciousness. She's asking for
Mr France.

FRANCE: (*Immediately rising from his chair*) I'll go
round at once.

MRS WELDON: I'd like to come with you, Elliot …

VOSPER: One of my men will drive you to the
hospital.

FRANCE: There's no need for that – we can easily
pick up a cab …

VOSPER: I'm sorry, sir – I'd like someone to be
with you. If Countess Dekker's very
much better, she may wish to make a
statement.

FRANCE: Yes, of course, I hadn't thought of that.

The door opens and closes.

BRECKSHAFT: You know, I think Elliot France is holding
something back …

VOSPER: Yes.

BRECKSHAFT: You think the girl was really – what do
you say – really sweet on him?

TEMPLE: I do.

VOSPER: Did she give you that impression this morning, Temple, when you questioned her?

TEMPLE: She didn't tell me anything this morning. I mentioned France, of course, but she didn't volunteer any information about him.

BRECKSHAFT: Incidentally, is there any news of the girl, Temple?

FORBES: (*A little surprised*) News? What do you mean, Breckshaft?

TEMPLE: (*Casually*) Her father telephoned me earlier this evening – apparently she hadn't arrived home from our interview – but you know what these girls are, Sir Graham. She's probably home by now.

VOSPER: She wasn't a quarter of an hour ago.

TEMPLE: How do you know?

VOSPER: Her father telephoned <u>me</u>. (*With the faintest suggestion of a smile*) You should take better care of your visitors, Temple …

TEMPLE: (*Without thinking*) I can assure you, Inspector, I …

VOSPER: I was only joking.

TEMPLE: Oh yes – yes, of course …

TEMPLE and VOSPER laugh.
TEMPLE's laugh is a shade uneasy.
FADE SCENE.

FADE UP the sound of a key being inserted in a lock.
The front door opens.

STEVE: Oh, hello, Paul.

TEMPLE: Sorry, darling, it was rather a long conference. Has anyone called?

STEVE: Yes. Denis Harper, and – he insisted on waiting for you. He's in your study.

TEMPLE: Is anything the matter?

STEVE: He won't tell me. But he's obviously upset about something.

TEMPLE: All right, I'll go in and see him.

A door opens.

A pause.

TEMPLE: Good evening, Harper. Sorry to have kept you so long.

The door closes.

HARPER: That's all right. I hope you didn't mind my waiting?

TEMPLE: Not at all. Sit down, Harper. Let me get you a drink.

HARPER: Oh, thank you.

TEMPLE mixes a drink.

TEMPLE: My wife seems to think you've got something on your mind?

HARPER: Well, yes – I have. I read about that bomb explosion in this morning's paper. It said that the car was owned by a Captain Smith, so I was worried in case you thought that … I was in some way involved.

TEMPLE: Why should I think that?

HARPER: Well, I introduced Paddy – Smith – to you at the Groove Club, if you remember.

TEMPLE: So you did! But it was obvious to me you hardly knew the chap.

HARPER: (*Relieved*) Well, that's it exactly. He's just one of those chaps you bump into every now and again. You know how it is.

241

TEMPLE: Yes, of course. Here's your drink. Don't give it another thought. The police are pretty hot on his tail, anyway. Is there anything else?

HARPER: Well, yes, there is.

TEMPLE: Go on.

HARPER: I telephoned Dr Conrad's house this evening to see if there was any chance of meeting Betty. I spoke to her father. He said she'd disappeared again.

TEMPLE: Certainly no one seems to know where she is at the moment, but there's no need for you to upset yourself.

HARPER: I don't know about that. I mean, she disappears while I'm in Germany – and now I'm back in England she disappears again. The police are bound to think I'm concerned in some way or other.

TEMPLE: I can reassure you on that point. I've just come back from a session at Scotland Yard. Your name was hardly mentioned.

The telephone rings.

TEMPLE: Excuse me.

TEMPLE lifts the telephone receiver.

TEMPLE: (*On the phone*) Hello?

VOICE: (*On the other end of the line: identical with HARPER's voice*) This is Denis Harper, Mr Temple. I'd like a word with you …

TEMPLE: Just hold on a minute, will you? (*To HARPER*) This is rather interesting. You appear to be on the telephone.

HARPER: What do you mean?

TEMPLE: Precisely what I say. You appear to be on the telephone.

HARPER: But I don't understand …

242

TEMPLE: (*Smiling*) Wait a moment. (*On the phone*) Sorry, Harper … I had a glass in my hand. Now, what can I do for you?

VOICE: Can I see you this evening, Mr Temple? It is rather important …

TEMPLE: (*Lightly*) Yes, I shall be delighted to see you …

VOICE: I want to talk to you about the disappearance of Betty Conrad – the murder of Gerda Holman …

TEMPLE: You suggest the time and place and I'll meet you, Harper.

VOICE: I want to avoid London, if possible.

TEMPLE: I'll meet you anywhere you say.

VOICE: I'm down at Barnes.

TEMPLE: All right, I'll meet you there.

VOICE: I have to see someone at a small factory on the river, on the north side about a hundred yards below Barnes Bridge. It's owned by a firm called Ryder and Taylor …

TEMPLE: Ryder and Taylor?

VOICE: Yes. They're paper merchants … Could you meet me there, Mr Temple – say at 12 o'clock?

TEMPLE: I don't see why not.

VOICE: Use the side entrance, in Feltham Road.

TEMPLE: All right, Harper. I'll try and be there.

VOICE: And don't mention this to anyone – please …

TEMPLE: I wouldn't dream of it. Goodbye.

VOICE: Goodbye.

TEMPLE replaces the receiver.

TEMPLE: (*Amused*) Well, that's the first time I've ever had a telephone conversation with a man who was in the room with me at the same time.

HARPER: You really mean to say that there was someone on the line actually pretending to be me?

TEMPLE: No doubt about it.

HARPER:	But who on earth would do a thing like that?
TEMPLE:	I'll give you three guesses.
HARPER:	(*Obviously confused*) But I haven't the faintest idea.
TEMPLE:	(*Still amused*) Haven't you? Well, in that case I suggest …
HARPER:	(*A shade tense*) Yes?
TEMPLE:	I suggest … that we both have a drink, Harper.

FADE.
FADE IN incidental music.

FADE music.
FADE IN the sound of a motor launch.

FORBES:	Did you say you know this place, Vosper?
VOSPER:	Yes, Sir Graham. The factory's just a bit further along … Easy now, Sergeant … Cut the engine …

The engine stops.

VOSPER:	… No point in advertising ourselves.
TEMPLE:	The man on the phone told me to use the Feltham Street entrance, so I doubt if he'll be expecting us to approach from the river.
VOSPER:	All right … just about here, Sergeant.

The launch comes in.

BRECKSHAFT:	There is nothing like an element of surprise … I'll go first.
TEMPLE:	Don't use torches if you can help it.
BRECKSHAFT:	No, there's no point in advertising ourselves.

FADE OUT of motor launch.

FADE IN noises of footsteps inside of the warehouse.

FORBES: (*In a low voice*) The place seems to be empty, Vosper. What sort of a factory is it?

VOSPER: I think it's used as a warehouse nowadays, sir. Ryder and Taylor are paper merchants …

TEMPLE: I thought I heard something … probably a rat.

VOSPER: Plenty of them about.

SERGEANT: I think I heard something too, sir.

FORB ES: (*Suddenly*) Quiet, everybody.

A pause.

A faint moaning sound can be heard in the near background. The moaning continues; someone is obviously in pain.

TEMPLE: I think it's coming from over there.

BRECKSHAFT: There's a door over here, Sir Graham.

FORBES: Be careful, Breckshaft.

The door slowly opens.

BRECKSHAFT: There's some stairs through the door …

SERGEANT: Let me go first, sir, just in case.

BRECKSHAFT: It's all right, Sergeant, don't worry. I can take care of myself.

They ascend the staircase.

VOSPER: No torches until I give the word.

A pause.

The moaning noise is nearer and louder.

VOSPER: Alright, we'd better have some light now.

SERGEANT: (*Slightly off*) Inspector, there's a man over here, sir – he's very badly hurt, looks to me as if he's been beaten up!

The moaning is now quite near.

VOSPER: (*Shocked*) Ye Gods, he certainly has!

FORBES:	Stand by, Sergeant, while we take a look at him.
SERGEANT:	Yes, sir.
VOSPER:	Poor devil! …
FORBES:	Yes. It's hard to identify him with his face in that mess …
SERGEANT:	He looks a goner to me …
TEMPLE:	Just a minute. I think I recognise that suit … Yes, he was wearing it last night. It's Captain Smith.

END OF EPISODE SEVEN

EPISODE EIGHT

PERSON UNKNOWN

OPEN TO: *FADE IN the voice of SIR GRAHAM FORBES.*

FORBES: Captain Smith! Are you sure, Temple?
TEMPLE examines the injured man.
TEMPLE: I'm positive, Sir Graham.
SERGEANT: He's trying to say something, sir.
PADDY: (*Hardly audible*) Get … get … doctor …
VOSPER: Yes, all right, Smith. Sergeant, get to a telephone and see if you can get a doctor here as quickly as possible.
SERGEANT: Yes, sir …
FORBES: Are you sure it's Captain Smith?
TEMPLE: I'm positive, Sir Graham. Sergeant, wait a moment.

A pause.

TEMPLE: Smith … Paddy …

A second pause.

TEMPLE: He won't need a doctor, Sir Graham. He's dead.
VOSPER: Phone for an ambulance, Sergeant.
SERGEANT: Yes, sir.

The SERGEANT goes.

BRECKSHAFT: I do not understand this, Sir Graham. What is this Captain Smith doing here?
FORBES: That's something we have to find out, Breckshaft.
BRECKSHAFT: You think perhaps the man who telephoned Mr Temple – who impersonated Harper – you think perhaps he also asked Captain Smith to come here?
TEMPLE: I think he ordered Captain Smith to come here.
BRECKSHAFT: So? This means that Smith is not the man you are looking for?

VOSPER:	We were looking for him all right, but …
BRECKSHAFT:	But he is not – what shall I say – the Top Man?
TEMPLE:	(*Quietly*) That's right, Breckshaft.
BRECKSHAFT:	Then this mysterious person unknown …
TEMPLE:	Obviously left before we arrived.

In the background there is the sound of a police whistle.

VOSPER:	That sounds like trouble, sir …
FORBES:	The Sergeant may have seen someone.
VOSPER:	There's a police car out in the road …

The SERGEANT approaches.

He is breathless and obviously a little frightened.

SERGEANT:	It's a fire, sir ... near the main entrance, and the wind's blowing it this way. There's barrels of linseed out there, sir – they'll go up like petrol.
FORBES:	We'd better make for the river.
SERGEANT:	The front way's already cut off, sir. (*He starts to cough*) I had a devil of a job getting back …

In the distant background the first sound of the fire can be heard.

VOSPER:	Then, come on, we'll go back the way we came.
BRECKSHAFT:	And what about Smith?
SERGEANT:	(*Coughing*) Inspector, believe me – there's no time to lose, sir.
TEMPLE:	He's right, Vosper.
FORBES:	We'll just have to leave him.
VOSPER:	Lead the way, Sergeant … (*He starts to cough*) This smoke's getting worse.
FORBES:	Keep close behind …
VOSPER:	Quickly, everybody … Watch the stairs, Sir Graham.

They begin to descend the stairs.
FADE.

FADE UP the noise of the fire.

SERGEANT: The fire's really gaining ground now, sir …

VOSPER: Get a move on, Sergeant.

FORBES: My God! This heat …

SERGEANT: Careful, Sir Graham …

VOSPER: We're all right … This leads back to the river … Down here, Sir Graham …

FORBES: Wait a minute! Where are Temple – and Breckshaft?

VOSPER: (*Stopping in his tracks*) I thought they were following.

SERGEANT: Get on, sir … we can't stay here.

FORBES: But Temple …

SERGEANT: Perhaps there's another way down to the river, sir. They're probably in the launch by now.

VOSPER: Anyway, I don't see what we can do, sir … (*Very concerned*) Come along, Sir Graham …

FADE UP the sound of the fire and the noise of falling timber.
FADE UP the sound of the river.

FORBES: Here's the launch … There's no sign of Temple or Breckshaft!

VOSPER: Well, maybe they've got out on the other side. Jump in, Sir Graham …

SERGEANT: Quickly, sir …

SIR GRAHAM, VOSPER and the SERGEANT climb into the launch.

The SERGEANT starts the engine.

SERGEANT: I'll have to take the launch out into midstream, sir – it's too dangerous here.

FORBES: Yes, all right, Sergeant.

We hear the sound of a fire engine in the distant background.

SERGEANT: There's the fire engine …

VOSPER: (*Quickly, tensely*) There's Temple! – on the roof! – with Breckshaft.

A moment.

FORBES: Well, they can't stay up there long, the roof will fall in. They'll have to jump for it! Haven't you got a speaker on board, Sergeant – a microphone thing?

SERGEANT: Yes, sir.

FORBES: Give it to me.

SERGEANT: Just a moment, sir …

A pause.

VOSPER: Be quick, Sergeant.

SERGEANT: Here we are. Ready, sir …

FORBES takes the microphone and uses it: his voice booms across the river.

FORBES: Temple, can you see us? Temple!

A moment.

VOSPER: Yes, he's waving, Sir Graham.

FORBES: (*Using the microphone*) You'll have to jump for it! You'll have to jump into the river! We'll stand by, Temple.

Halfway through SIR GRAHAM's speech the perspective switches and we hear his voice as from the roof.

The fire effects are very much nearer.

BRECKSHAFT jumps, after a moment there is a splash as he hits the water.

CROSS FADE back to the motor launch.

FORBES: There's Breckshaft!

VOSPER: Over to the right, Sergeant …

FORBES: To the right, Sergeant … Quickly now!

FADE.

FADE UP the noise of the launch and TEMPLE being dragged over the side of the launch.

FORBES: Give me your hand, Temple.

TEMPLE: Phew! Thank you, Sir Graham …

FORBES: What on earth happened to you?

TEMPLE: We lost sight of you, turned through a sort of tunnel and the fire was right ahead – we had no choice, Sir Graham. We had to go up on to the roof …

BRECKSHAFT: Well, thanks to Sir Graham and Inspector Vosper, we are safe, Mr Temple.

TEMPLE: Yes, if a trifle wet.

BRECKSHAFT: I shouldn't have liked anything to have happened to you.

TEMPLE: Thank you, Breckshaft. I shouldn't have liked anything to have happened to you, either …

FADE.

FADE IN the sound of liquid and of glasses.

TEMPLE: Let me fill your glass, Breckshaft …

BRECKSHAFT: Thank you – just a little …

STEVE: Are you sure you feel all right, Paul?

TEMPLE: Don't worry, darling! I've had a nice hot bath and three whiskies …

FORBES: All the same, it was a pretty grim business.

STEVE: Oh, Paul – Dr Conrad telephoned. He said there was still no news of Betty. He wondered if we'd heard anything?

TEMPLE: You told him we hadn't?

STEVE: Yes, of course.

BRECKSHAFT: It is very strange that this girl should disappear again. Who was the last person to see her?

TEMPLE: Well, I suppose I was.

BRECKSHAFT: And did she not say anything, about meeting someone perhaps?

TEMPLE: No – nothing.

BRECKSHAFT: I suppose it's possible that whoever impersonated Harper to you, Mr Temple – may have done the same to Betty Conrad.

TEMPLE: Yes, that's quite possible.

BRECKSHAFT: And you have no idea who this man might be?

TEMPLE: I have a very good idea.

FORBES: (*Surprised*) You have?

TEMPLE: Yes, I think it's Fritz Gunter.

FORBES: Who is Fritz Gunter?

BRECKSHAFT: He is the proprietor of the Hotel Reumer at Oberammergau. But what makes you suspect Gunter, Temple?

TEMPLE: I've made some enquiries about him at various studios and theatres. Before he became a regular actor he used to tour the Music Halls as an impersonator, in other words, a mimic.

STEVE: Oh, that explains quite a lot. But what about that Bavarian accent of his?

TEMPLE: That was part of his act. He really spoke English perfectly.

FORBES: Yes, but what makes you think he's in this country?

TEMPLE: Well, I haven't actually seen him, but I know he comes here quite frequently.

FORBES: He still acts in films, then?

TEMPLE: No, he's after bigger money, Sir Graham – and more excitement.

FORBES: What sort of excitement?

TEMPLE: I suspect that he's an agent for an organisation concerned with drug smuggling and blackmail. (*A moment*) Am I right, Breckshaft?

BRECKSHAFT: You are perfectly right, Temple. I had a report to that effect from Madame Klein just before I left Munich.

STEVE: (*Surprised*) Madame Klein?

BRECKSHAFT: I did not tell you sooner because she asked me to remain silent. But now you had better know. Madame Klein is an agent for Interpol.

TEMPLE: That doesn't surprise me in the least.

STEVE: (*Surprised*) But I never dreamt … Madame Klein …

BRECKSHAFT: She is a very capable agent, Mrs Temple. She has been helping us to try to trace the source of this drug smuggling, but it has not been easy. This organisation has covered its tracks very well indeed. They use many people who are outwardly respectable.

STEVE: So you think Joyce Gunter is involved as well as her husband?

BRECKSHAFT: No, I have reason to believe that Mrs Gunter is much troubled about him. She is also very much troubled about her little boy.

STEVE: Oh! I didn't know she had a child. Why is she worried?

BRECKSHAFT: Because she has been threatened by this organisation that if her husband did not obey orders then the child might suffer.

TEMPLE: I expect it was Smith who threatened her – and that's why she warned me against him …

BRECKSHAFT: Most probably.

FORBES: You don't think this man – Fritz Gunter – is the man we're after?

BRECKSHAFT: No, Sir Graham …

FORBES: What about you, Temple?

TEMPLE: I agree with Breckshaft. (*A moment, looking at BRECKSHAFT*) I don't think so, either …

FADE IN incidental music.

FADE music.

FADE IN a telephone ringing.

After a moment, TEMPLE lifts the receiver.

TEMPLE: (*On the phone*) Hello?

VOSPER: (*On the other end of the line*) Is that you, Temple?

TEMPLE: Oh, hello, Vosper!

VOSPER: You feel all right this morning?

TEMPLE: (*Patiently*) None the worse, thank you. What's new?

VOSPER: Fritz Gunter is staying at the Crescent Hotel in Knightsbridge. I've got two men tailing him.

TEMPLE: Good.

VOSPER: You think we'll be able to pull him in soon?

TEMPLE: Yes, I do, Inspector – on a murder charge …

VOSPER: Murder charge!

TEMPLE: Yes. The murder of Gerda Holman.

VOSPER: (*After a moment*) I see. All right, I'll keep in touch. Goodbye.

TEMPLE: Goodbye.

TEMPLE replaces the receiver.

STEVE: What was all that about?

TEMPLE: Fritz Gunter's in London.

STEVE: By himself?

TEMPLE: I imagine so. His wife wasn't mentioned. By the way, I'm expecting Denis Harper.

STEVE: What does he want?

TEMPLE: It isn't what he wants. It's what I want, for a change. By the way, darling – I think I'd better see him alone.

STEVE: All right, Paul …

The door opens.

CHARLIE: Morning papers …

TEMPLE: Oh – thank you, Charlie.

CHARLIE: Got yourself on the front page again, I see, Mr Temple.

TEMPLE: You mean the fire in Barnes last night?

CHARLIE: And a lot more besides! Here it is in the Daily News … There aren't 'arf going to be a clean-up according to this!

STEVE: Let me see, Charlie …

TEMPLE: And Charlie – remember what I told you yesterday about keeping an eye on the door. That still goes.

CHARLIE: You bet, Mr Temple. Don't worry – I'll be on the job!

The door closes.

STEVE: They've got the whole story, Paul … Betty Conrad … finishing school in Bavaria … Harley Street psychiatrist …

TEMPLE: I wonder who on earth managed to get the story?

STEVE: It says it's by the Daily News Crime Reporter … a man called Howard Ross …

TEMPLE: Let me have a look, Steve …
STEVE: He's a bit hazy on facts, but he's made some
          pretty good guesses … And he's got pictures of
          practically everybody – including poor Mrs
          Weldon …
TEMPLE: Yes, so he has … By Timothy, that's a terrible
          picture of Breckshaft!
STEVE: The one of you isn't so hot, either!
TEMPLE: (*With a little laugh*) It certainly isn't …

A slight pause.

TEMPLE: You know, I don't agree with you, Steve.
STEVE: What do you mean?
TEMPLE: His facts are pretty good, considering … He's
          got the whole story … The Countess … the
          attempted murder … he even mentions – Elliot
          France …

The door opens.

CHARLIE: Mr Harper's here, sir.
TEMPLE: Yes, all right. Ask him in.

A pause.

STEVE: How do you think this man Howard Ross got
          hold of the story?
TEMPLE: Someone gave it to him – that's obvious … He
          couldn't have ferreted this out on his own …
CHARLIE: Mr Harper.
TEMPLE: Come in, Harper …
HARPER: Good morning, Mrs Temple.
STEVE: Good morning, Mr Harper. (*To TEMPLE*) I've
          got a hair appointment, darling. I'll see you later.
TEMPLE: Yes, all right, darling.
STEVE: (*To HARPER*) Excuse my rushing away like
          this, Mr Harper …
HARPER: Yes, of course, Mrs Temple.

The door closes.

TEMPLE: Well, Harper …
HARPER: You sent for me.
TEMPLE: Yes, I did …
HARPER: Well – I hope it won't take long. I'm due at the office at nine-thirty …
TEMPLE: This is more important than your office.
HARPER: (*A little surprised*) Oh?
TEMPLE: Harper, we're coming to the end of this case and it isn't going to be a very happy ending as far as you're concerned.
HARPER: I don't follow you.
TEMPLE: How long have you known Howard Ross?
HARPER: Howard Ross?
TEMPLE: The Crime Reporter on the Daily News.
HARPER: I don't know what you're talking about.
TEMPLE: Listen, Harper. I've known Ross for years. He's a first-class journalist and a man of integrity. I've only got to pick up that telephone …
HARPER: Look – I had nothing to do with that newspaper story, Temple.
TEMPLE: No? There's a photograph of everyone concerned in this affair, splashed right across the front page – a photograph of everyone – except you. That was part of the arrangement, wasn't it?
HARPER: (*Without thinking*) No, it wasn't. That was just a coincidence. I told …
TEMPLE: Go on …
HARPER: (*Tensely*) I've got nothing to say. I don't know why the devil you got me here this morning. I'm going to the office …
TEMPLE: Sit down …
HARPER: Now look here, Temple, you can't threaten …
TEMPLE: Sit down!

259

There is a slight pause.

HARPER: (*Nervously*) What is it you want?

TEMPLE: How long have you been taking drugs?

HARPER: Taking drugs? You must be out of your mind to suggest …

TEMPLE: Do you think I can't recognise the symptoms after all these years?

HARPER: You're bluffing! You've got no proof that …

TEMPLE: Haven't I? Your friend Paddy – Captain Smith – died last night …

HARPER: I know that.

TEMPLE: Before he died, he talked – quite a lot. He mentioned several names – yours was one of them …

HARPER: (*Nervously*) Good heavens, Temple – you know Smith! You know what a liar he was …

TEMPLE: A dying man doesn't usually tell lies. You know, Harper, I don't think you realise exactly what you're up against.

HARPER: What do you mean?

TEMPLE: Unless you cooperate with us, you're liable to find yourself facing a murder charge.

HARPER: (*Stunned*) What the devil are you talking about?

TEMPLE: I'm talking about the murder of Gerda Holman …

HARPER: (*Tensely, frightened*) I'd nothing to do with the Holman murder!

TEMPLE: But you know who had, don't you?

HARPER: Yes, but … (*He hesitates*)

TEMPLE: Go on …

HARPER: I think it was Fritz Gunter …

TEMPLE: Thank you. Now, if you take my advice you'll see Inspector Vosper and make a complete statement.

260

HARPER: I can think of pleasanter ways of committing suicide.

TEMPLE: We'll take care of you until we pick up the person behind all this – the person you're frightened of …

HARPER: (*Bitterly*) You'll never do that, Temple.

TEMPLE: What makes you so sure?

HARPER: Because you don't know who you're after!

TEMPLE: Take a look at this newspaper. (*A pause*) You see those photographs on the front page?

HARPER: (*Tensely*) Yes?

TEMPLE: (*Pointing*) Well, that's the person I'm after, Harper! Am I right?

HARPER: (*Staggered*) Yes … yes, you're right! …

TEMPLE: Now, perhaps you'll come to Scotland Yard with me and make a statement …

FADE IN incidental music.

FADE music
FADE UP the noise of a car engine.
FADE the engine noise to the background.

FORBES: I think we'll stop here for five minutes, Temple …

TEMPLE: Yes. Better pull into the lay-by, Vosper.

The car slows down and gradually comes to a standstill.
The engine is switched off.

FORBES: That's it … Now, Vosper, let's make sure we've got the details right. You say you've seen the hotel manager and everything's laid on?

VOSPER: Yes, Sir Graham, everything – I even tested the microphone myself. It'll pick up every word.

FORBES: Good.

TEMPLE: I hope they're not too obvious, Inspector?

VOSPER: No, they're the new type, not much bigger than an overcoat button.

FORBES: (*To VOSPER*) Did you tell the hotel manager exactly what was happening?

VOSPER: Well, I had to confide in him to a certain extent. I'm pretty sure he's trustworthy.

FORBES: Right. We'll have to take your word for it, Inspector.

VOSPER: You don't think it would have been better to have confronted our friend, Harper, instead of …

TEMPLE: No, I don't, Inspector.

FORBES: You can always produce Harper's statement, if it's necessary.

TEMPLE: Yes, I agree, Sir Graham.

FORBES: (*After a moment*) How are we for time, Vosper?

VOSPER: We've about an hour to go, sir. And we're about twenty minutes from the hotel, I should say.

FORBES: Then I think perhaps we'd better get moving. Just in case our friend decides to arrive early …

TEMPLE: Yes, that might be a little awkward, to say the least.

The car engine starts.
FADE.

FADE IN noises associated with the entrance hall of a small country hotel.
FADE the noise to the background.

FRANCE: Good morning.

WOMAN: Good morning, sir.

FRANCE: Mr Temple is expecting me. My name is France – Elliot France.

WOMAN: Mr France! Oh, yes, of course, sir. That's room number 4, on the first floor. The lift is over there, sir.

FRANCE:	It's quite all right, thank you, I'll walk.

FADE.

FADE IN voice of DENIS HARPER.

HARPER:	Where can I telephone, please?
WOMAN:	There's a box just outside the smoke room.
HARPER:	Oh, thank you.

A long pause.

WOMAN:	Good morning, sir.
BRECKSHAFT:	(*Apparently irritated*) I have an appointment with a Mr Temple.
WOMAN:	Oh yes! Could I have your name, please? Then I'll phone Mr Temple and see if …
BRECKSHAFT:	There's no need to phone Mr Temple. He's expecting me. He told me to go straight up. My name is Breckshaft.
WOMAN:	Very well, sir. It's on the first floor. Room number five.
BRECKSHAFT:	(*Impatiently*) Room five – thank you.

FADE background noises completely.

FADE IN a knock on a door.
The door opens.

FRANCE:	(*Surprised*) Conrad!
CONRAD:	Shut the door.

The door closes.

CONRAD:	You're late!
FRANCE:	Late? I don't understand. I didn't even know you were coming here.
CONRAD:	Stop talking nonsense, France. (*Angrily*) Now, where's Betty?
FRANCE:	I haven't the slightest idea where she is! I haven't seen her since she left Bavaria!

CONRAD: (*Extremely annoyed*) You're lying! You kidnapped her before and kept her with that damned Countess woman, and now you've done it again! Now where is she?

FRANCE: Conrad, talk sense – you know why I kidnapped Betty in the first place. To get those letters from you – to get out of your clutches!

CONRAD: Yes, well, I gave you the letters and the documents. Now you've double-crossed me. What's the idea, do you fancy yourself as a blackmailer?

FRANCE: (*Interrupting CONRAD, annoyed*) Conrad, listen – I know nothing about Betty. I haven't the faintest idea where she is.

CONRAD: (*With sarcasm*) No?

FRANCE: No …

CONRAD: Then why did you send me this note with Betty's glove?

FRANCE: (*A moment*) What note?

CONRAD: Since you want to play fun and games, I'll read it to you – (*Reading*) "This glove will prove that Betty is with me – and is quite safe. If you want your daughter back meet me at the Cygnet Hotel, Pangbourne, Room 4, at 11.30 tomorrow morning. Elliot France."

FRANCE: May I see the signature?

A pause.

CONRAD: Well?

FRANCE: It's certainly very much like my signature – but I didn't send the note.

CONRAD: Now look, France, you were awkward with me once before – in Bavaria – remember?

FRANCE: What do you mean, I was awkward?

CONRAD: You refused to do what I wanted.

264

FRANCE: Of course I refused. You used my case history to blackmail me. I was prepared to pay money but not to work for you. That still stands.

CONRAD: I'm not asking you to work for me now. I'm simply asking you to release Betty. If you don't …

FRANCE: (*Curious*) Well?

CONRAD: I've got photostat copies of those letters of your case history. I could sell them tomorrow to any newspaper in the world.

FRANCE: Look, Conrad – I can only tell you the truth and hope to God you have the sense to believe me. I've not seen Betty since the day she was released – and I'm completely in the dark as to where she is now.

A pause.

CONRAD: (*Quietly*) Is that the truth?

FRANCE: I swear to you, it's the truth!

CONRAD: (*After a moment*) Then what about this note?

FRANCE: I don't know … I only know that I didn't send it.

CONRAD: Well, if you didn't send it, why did you come here?

FRANCE: I was asked to meet Paul Temple here. He telephoned me and suggested that we …

FRANCE stops speaking, a sudden thought has occurred to him.

CONRAD: Temple …?

FRANCE: Yes …

CONRAD: He telephoned you?

FRANCE: (*Puzzled*) Yes – last night.

CONRAD: (*A note of desperation in his voice*) My God …

FRANCE: What's the matter?

CONRAD: He sent this note … He intended we should meet
… He knew that as soon as we came face to face
we'd start talking about … (*He stops*)

FRANCE: (*Tensely*) What is it?

CONRAD swings an armchair away from the wall, turns over
a table and throws a standard lamp to one side.

CONRAD: (*Desperately*) It's in the room. It's here
somewhere …

FRANCE: What are you looking for?

CONRAD: (*Searching the room*) There's a microphone in
this room somewhere …

FRANCE: Nonsense!

CONRAD: It isn't nonsense! Why the devil do you think
Temple … (*He stops*)

FRANCE: What is it?

CONRAD: (*Quietly*) I've found the wire. It's in the corner
… My God, they must be in the next room!

CONRAD pulls the wire away from the wall.

FRANCE: (*Tense*) What are you going to do?

CONRAD: What do you think I'm going to do? I'm getting
out of here …

CONRAD crosses and tries to open the door.

It is locked.

He shakes the door handle.

CONRAD: The door's locked!

FRANCE: Of course it isn't locked! Let me try …

CONRAD shakes the door handle, desperately.

CONRAD: It's locked, I tell you! It's locked from the
outside …

The door opens.

TEMPLE: Good morning, Dr Conrad! Now don't be stupid,
put the gun down …

FORBES: You'd better give me that gun, doctor.

266

CONRAD: (*Desperately*) Stand back – all of you! I warn you, I shan't hesitate to shoot! Get out of the way, France!

FRANCE: Conrad, for heaven's sake – you're only making things worse!

VOSPER: Look out – he's going for the window!

FORBES: He's jumped from the balcony – it's only a short drop.

VOSPER: He's done it.

TEMPLE: He's making for the car park!

VOSPER: Blast!

FORBES: What's the matter?

VOSPER: My men are over on the other side, sir …

COMPLETE FADE.

FADE UP of footsteps and the sound of excited voices.

VOSPER: He's doubled back into the road! Hey, Weston! Stop him! Charters!

TEMPLE: Where's his car?

FORBES: That's it over there, near the entrance … He's going to make it all right.

TEMPLE: Yes, it looks like it …

VOSPER: His car's facing this way – he won't have time to turn …

FADE UP of excited voices.

FADE UP the sound of a car starting.

VOSPER: He's coming this way!

FORBES: But surely this is a cul-de-sac?

TEMPLE: The road ends at the river, he'll have to turn …

VOSPER: Look out!

The car roars past.

FORBES: The man must be crazy.

TEMPLE: He'll never brake at that speed …

FORBES: Well, if he doesn't, he'll find himself in the river
           ...

*As FORBES speaks there is the distant scream of brakes and
the sound of impact as the car strikes the bank.*

VOSPER: He's hit the bank!

We hear the sound of the car plunging into the river.

TEMPLE: He's gone over the top, Vosper! (*Urgently*)
           Come on, Sir Graham!

FADE UP the sound of footsteps and excited voices.

FADE.

FADE UP the noise of water.

*A detailed search is being made for the car and the body of
CONRAD.*

VOSPER: It's no use, Sir Graham, the car nose-dived into
           the river ... The bonnet's wedged deep into the
           mud ... If the impact didn't kill him, he's
           drowned by now ...

FORBES: Yes – well, we've got to make sure, Vosper.

DIVER: (*In the background*) All right – wind her in ...

VOSPER: The diver's fastened the cable to the car ... It
           should be coming up any minute now ...

*In the background the sound of a crane operating and the car
is dragged out of the water.*

FORBES: Did your man phone for a doctor, Vosper?

VOSPER: Yes, he should have been here by now.

TEMPLE: There's his car ...

DIVER: (*From background*) Easy! Up she comes! All
           right now ... Steady ...

The crane stops.

*We hear the sound of water and the car being dragged out of
the water.*

VOSPER: Well, there he is ... Conrad's still in the driving
           seat, Sir Graham ...

TEMPLE: Not exactly a pretty sight …

FORBES: No. (*Quietly*) You know the drill, Vosper?

VOSPER: Yes, sir.

FORBES: Come along, Temple – let's leave them to it …

FADE IN incidental music.

FADE music.

A door opens.

NURSE: Would you wait here, please, and I'll tell Countess Dekker?

STEVE: Thank you. Perhaps you'd like to take these flowers, Sister …

NURSE: Oh, thank you, Mrs Temple. Aren't they lovely?

The door closes.

TEMPLE: Steve, did Countess Dekker give you any idea as to why she wanted to see me?

STEVE: No, she wouldn't tell me. But she seemed very anxious when she telephoned. I promised to bring you along as soon as I could.

TEMPLE: Did she sound fairly normal?

STEVE: Oh yes, apparently she'd made a marvellous recovery. She'll be up and about in a week or so.

The door opens.

NURSE: Countess Dekker will see you now, Mr Temple.

TEMPLE: Thank you, Sister.

NURSE: This way, please.

FADE.

FADE IN the voice of COUNTESS DEKKER.

ELSA: Ah, Mr Temple … Mrs Temple … What lovely roses! Thank you very much, Mrs Temple …

TEMPLE: You're looking a great deal better than I expected, Countess.

269

ELSA:	Yes. I'm very much better … Please sit down both of you …
TEMPLE:	Thank you.
ELSA:	I was anxious to see you because I heard on my radio that Elliot France was being questioned by the police.
TEMPLE:	(*Slightly amused*) I thought you were not very friendly with Mr France?
ELSA:	That was just a little – what do you say? …
STEVE:	A little tiff?
ELSA:	Yes, that's right … But Elliot is a good man, Mr Temple. Please believe me, he's not a criminal …
TEMPLE:	He appears to have been rather deeply involved with one.
ELSA:	Conrad?
TEMPLE:	Yes. We know he was the man behind the whole business.
ELSA:	Thank heaven you know that.
TEMPLE:	But how exactly did Elliot France come into it?
ELSA:	Well, after Elliot had stayed with me for some time, I could see there was something on his mind. One night I persuaded him to tell me about it. Then it all came out – how this psychiatrist – Dr Conrad – had been blackmailing him because of his past weaknesses and how Conrad now wanted him to take charge of his organisation in Bavaria for distributing illegal drugs. Elliot was desperate –
TEMPLE:	So you suggested a way out?
ELSA:	Yes. I said the only way to deal with such an unscrupulous man like Conrad was to get some sort of hold over him.

270

TEMPLE: And France remembered that Conrad had a
           daughter?

ELSA: Yes. And there she was – almost on our
           doorstep. It was not difficult to devise a little
           plot to kidnap Betty Conrad.

STEVE: Then she really did come to your house that
           afternoon?

ELSA: She did. Though it was not very easy for anyone
           to prove it. Naturally, Mrs Weldon reported
           Betty's absence to the police. Elliot told Conrad
           that Betty would be sent back as soon as the
           papers and letters he was blackmailing him over,
           were returned to him. Dr Conrad came to
           Germany and tried to reason with Elliot, but I
           made Elliot be firm. Conrad's only weak spot
           was his daughter, and indeed, it's not surprising.
           Betty is a very attractive girl.

TEMPLE: And you found her a little too attractive?

ELSA: Oh, so Elliot told you about that?

STEVE: He said you'd had a quarrel, and you'd walked
           out on him.

ELSA: Yes, it was very silly of me. I can see that now.
           Betty developed a schoolgirl passion for Elliot.
           Although I was jealous, I must confess now,
           Elliot didn't take it very seriously.

TEMPLE: I'm glad you're able to feel so detached about it.

ELSE: I've had time to think, Mr Temple, since I've
           been in hospital. Elliot and I looked after Betty.
           She had everything she wanted – we treated her
           as one of the family. Perhaps it would have been
           better if we hadn't.

STEVE: Why was that?

ELSA: Because she overheard a conversation between
           Elliot and myself about Dr Conrad. She heard

271

the truth about her father. How he was trying to extend his organisation half way across Europe. It was a dreadful shock for the child. Anyhow, after Betty left us, I had a letter from Conrad saying that she was pining to see Elliot again.

STEVE: Conrad was trying to make trouble between you?

ELSA: Yes, and he did his utmost to get us involved. Do you remember when June Jackson's ring and a cocktail stick were found in my car?

TEMPLE: Yes. You see, June had started taking drugs and she gave Conrad her ring in return for a supply of heroin. Conrad made Harper put the ring in your car to throw suspicion on to you and France – he wanted the police to think that one of you was responsible for the disappearance of June. He didn't realise of course that I'd taken the law into my own hands and packed her off to America.

ELSA: So that's what happened to June.

TEMPLE: Yes.

STEVE: Countess, when did you decide to come to England – was it after you received Conrad's letter?

ELSA: Yes, it was. Although I knew Conrad for what he was, the letter made me jealous of Betty. I had a row with Elliot and decided to come to London and tell you the whole story.

TEMPLE: And you were very nearly murdered by Captain Smith?

ELSA: Yes. I'll never forget that man coming from behind the curtains with a gun in his hand. I tried to scream, but …

STEVE: Now you mustn't think about it.

272

ELSA:	No. I must try to think about Elliot. I must try to think what's best for him.
TEMPLE:	I shouldn't worry too much about Mr France, if I were you. The police merely questioned him about a recording of a conversation between himself and Dr Conrad.
ELSA:	(*Relieved*) Oh! Oh, I see …

There is a knock on the door.

ELSA:	(*Calling*) Come in.

The door opens.

FRANCE:	(*Softly*) Elsa, my dear, how are you?
ELSA:	(*Surprised and delighted*) Elliot! …
TEMPLE:	Steve, I think this is our cue, darling …
STEVE:	That's just what I was thinking. Exit Mr and Mrs Temple … Goodbye, Countess.
ELSA:	Goodbye.

FADE IN incidental music.

FADE music.

TEMPLE:	(*After a moment*) Would you like a light, Sir Graham? Your cigar seems to be …
FORBES:	No, it's fine, Temple. (*Contented*) And I'm very comfortable … My word, it's been quite a day …
BRECKSHAFT:	Yes, and I cannot tell you how grateful I am to you, Sir Graham – and Temple, of course. We were getting very concerned in Munich about the drug traffic.
FORBES:	Well, now you can get concerned about the Gerda Holman murder. That's your pigeon, thank goodness …
BRECKSHAFT:	She was unquestionably killed by Fritz Gunter, acting on orders from Conrad. The

	doctor suspected that Madame Klein was an Interpol agent. He was afraid she'd question Gerda and the girl would break down.
TEMPLE:	Yes. I don't think there's any doubt about that. Madame Klein had already got her eye on Conrad. That's why she was interested in Betty.
STEVE:	But why did they put a blue coat on the dead girl?
TEMPLE:	Because Conrad wanted us to think that Madame Klein and the dress shop were involved in the murder – he wanted us to continue our investigations in Bavaria, and not in London.
STEVE:	I see.
BRECKSHAFT:	Is there any news of Gunter, Sir Graham?
FORBES:	Not yet, I'm afraid.
STEVE:	And what about Denis Harper?
FORBES:	We've had to arrest Harper, of course – but I should imagine he'll get a fairly light sentence.
TEMPLE:	Conrad found him a useful accomplice, but, like most drug addicts, he couldn't screw himself up to tackle the really big jobs.
STEVE:	How do you mean?
TEMPLE:	Well, when Gunter lured us into that trap at Innsbruck, Harper hadn't the nerve to finish the job – he used blank cartridges. Ever since he's been scared that Conrad will cut off his supply of dope. When we saw him at the Groove Club he was there to pick up some more of the stuff from Smith.

FORBES: Yes, Conrad's been using the Club as a distribution centre.

STEVE: Then why did Conrad send us there? Don't forget he produced the membership card which was supposed to belong to Betty. That's why we went to the club.

TEMPLE: He wanted us to go for two reasons. One to scare the pants off Harper, and two the bomb incident – and Captain Smith …

STEVE: But it couldn't have been Harper who forced our car off the road on the way to Oberammergau.

TEMPLE: No. I imagine it was Fritz Gunter. He'd been tipped off by Conrad that we were in Garmisch.

FORBES: Temple, I don't get the significance of the cocktail sticks?

TEMPLE: They were presented by Fritz Gunter to various members of the ring, and used as a means of identification …

FORBES: So that they would be able to contact each other?

TEMPLE: Exactly.

STEVE: But what about that time we went to Pointers?

TEMPLE: That was an ingenious idea of Conrad's to get us down to the cottage at Oxted – the idea being that we should be murdered by his American associate, Dale Black. Luckily, for us, Smith was jealous of Black and that very afternoon murdered him.

FORBES: And you think it was Conrad himself who killed Smith?

TEMPLE: Yes, because Smith had bungled the bomb incident. Don't forget when Smith was dying he said … "Get – doctor …" What he was trying to say, of course, was Doctor Conrad.

STEVE:	And the postcard, Paul – the one we found in Oxted?
TEMPLE:	That was a copy of the card addressed to Betty Conrad. The Doctor paid a servant of the school to send him copies of all her correspondence. The letters and cards were sent to Oxted and addressed to Mrs Ruth Conrad.

As TEMPLE finishes speaking there is a knock on the door.

STEVE:	Come in!

The door opens.

TEMPLE:	Come in, Vosper!
VOSPER:	I thought you'd like to know we've picked up Fritz Gunter, Sir Graham.
FORBES:	Oh, good man! Where was he?
VOSPER:	In a telephone box, sir – giving an imitation of you.
FORBES:	What! Of me? What on earth do you mean?
VOSPER:	Yes, it appears he spoke to Digby at the Yard, and ordered him to call off the hunt. It was such a good imitation that it fooled Digby, and the message was sent out to all squad cars.

TEMPLE and BRECKSHAFT both laugh.

FORBES:	Well, I'm blowed!
TEMPLE:	I imagine you'd like a drink, Inspector?
VOSPER:	Thank you very much. A very large whisky!

TEMPLE laughs.

STEVE:	(*Quietly*) Paul, there's just one more question …
TEMPLE:	(*Still amused*) No more questions, darling, please! No more!

BRECKSHAFT: Does that include me? Because I have a question I would like to ask Mrs Temple.

TEMPLE: (*Surprised*) Steve?

STEVE: Me, Herr Breckshaft?

BRECKSHAFT: (*Smiling*) Yes, Mrs Temple. (*After a moment*) During the course of these investigations, I have had many talks with your husband. He has told me about your previous cases. Always, during those investigations you – yourself – have had a certain intuition …

STEVE: (*Laughing*) Oh, my intuition!

BRECKSHAFT: No, I'm serious! You have always suspected one particular person.

STEVE: Yes, but I haven't always been right.

BRECKSHAFT: I know that, Mrs Temple.

STEVE: Well – what was your question, Herr Breckshaft?

BRECKSHAFT: (*With a twinkle in his eye*) Tell me – honestly – did you think I was the unknown person? Did you ever suspect me, Mrs Temple?

STEVE: (*Apparently horrified: with great charm*) You, Herr Breckshaft? Good gracious, no! Whoever would have suspected you?

TEMPLE: (*Aghast*) By Timothy! By Timothy, Steve!

They all laugh.

FADE.

FADE IN a door opening.

CHARLIE: Excuse me, Mr Temple. Do you want anything before I go?

TEMPLE: No. Good night, Charlie. I hope you win.

STEVE: Win? Win what?

TEMPLE: The South of England cha-cha competition, darling. Our Charlie's in the final.

CHARLIE: Was in the final, Mr T. Beryl's got the flu.

TEMPLE: Oh, bad luck, Charlie. Well, if you want a partner there's always Mrs Temple.

CHARLIE: Oh, this is modern stuff, Mr T. None of your polkas and gavottes.

STEVE: Oh, really, Charlie.

TEMPLE: I was only joking.

STEVE: Where is this competition, Charlie?

CHARLIE: Why, it's at the Groove Club, Mrs Temple.

STEVE: The Groove?

TEMPLE: Steve, what are you thinking?

CHARLIE: Mrs Temple – you wouldn't, you couldn't –

STEVE: Couldn't I? Three of those atomic fruit juice things and I'll be the new cha-cha champion. Lead the way, Charlie, lead the way.

They all laugh.

THE END

ALTERNATE
ITALIAN
ENDING

Why and how did an alternate Italian ending to *Paul Temple and the Conrad Case* come about? Here, Italian superfan Antonio Scaglioni gives a possible explanation:

In Italy fiction on the radio has always played a subordinate role to other genres, such as music programmes, variety or news. Then from the second half of the 1960s it underwent a further downsizing, remaining relegated in practice to only a quarter-hour more or less in the morning, with an audience almost exclusively composed of housewives and retirees, and for Francis Durbridge there was no exception. Despite the great success that Durbridge was experiencing in Italy through television, in the same period only four radio serials featuring Paul Temple were produced in about a decade, from 1967 through 1977 before his name disappeared permanently from Italian radio schedules, each divided into ten episodes of about fifteen minutes and broadcast Monday through Friday invariably around ten o'clock in the morning. The four stories were, *Margò* (*Paul Temple and the Margo Mystery*) in 1967; *Chi è Jonathan?* (*Paul Temple and the Jonathan Mystery*) in 1971; *La ragazza scomparsa* (*Paul Temple and the Conrad Case*) in 1975; and finally *Cabaret* (*Paul Temple and the Spencer Affair*) in 1977. This is just to explain how little impact radio dramas had in the ratings both in terms of air times and the length of the broadcasts themselves. Then knowing that the original British serials had for each episode double the length one can easily guess that the stories had to undergo careful editing to adequately summarize the events. Real adaptations that, however, did not sacrifice any major plot elements, starting with the cliffhangers that closed each episode. Anyway, some changes and actualizations (some of the original stories were even twenty years old) were physiological, such as replacing the disk in *The Spencer Affair* transformed from an unknown, at least in Italy, "My

281

Heart and Harry" into "Cabaret," the famous musical soundtrack. But these were always or mostly small changes that did not affect the development of the events. Except in two cases: in both *The Margo Mystery* and *The Conrad Case*, the guilty party who was unmasked by Paul Temple in the finale turned out to be different from the one in the original serial. How was this possible?

There were only two possibilities: either it had been an initiative taken arbitrarily by those who had adapted the stories (in this case the Italian translator Franca Cancogni with the directors of the two serials, Guglielmo Morandi for *Margo* and Umberto Benedetto for *Conrad*), or the changes had been made by Durbridge himself, which by the way he had done already in the past especially in his adaptations for Germany. But why should the Italian adapters have taken the burden and risk of changing without permission the endings of these two stories alone? (Let's recall here that Franca Cancogni was the translator of almost all the Italian radio versions of Durbridge's scripts, and never on any other occasion do the endings turn out to be changed from the originals.) Besides, unlike television serials, where millions of viewers and constant media attention justified any expedient to protect the secrecy of the ending, the interest aroused in the public and the press by radio serials was not so great as to require such major interventions.

So, it doesn't seem very likely that the translator or the director took the trouble to change the ending on their own. Moreover, as I mentioned above, Durbridge was no stranger to even heavily tweaking his earlier scripts that did not convince him, and it would not be the first case for Italy either. It had already happened in 1960 for an hour-long radio drama, *Preludio al delitto*, which had been rewritten from scratch with several changes and new names for the characters, when the plot had clearly come from a 1946 work of his for the BBC, *The Caspary Affair*, published by Williams & Whiting in *Three Plays for Radio - Volume 1*.

So the change of ending made by Durbridge himself is the most likely scenario, particularly in the first of the two cases, *Margò*, which we will discuss in more detail in the appendix to a forthcoming volume in this series, *Paul Temple and the Margo Mystery*.

Instead about the alternative ending of the other serial mentioned above, *La ragazza scomparsa* based on *Paul Temple and the Conrad Case*, published in this volume, the situation is a little different. First of all, it should be mentioned that one of the main characters of the story, Countess Elsa Dekker, is replaced by Nicole Dubrewskoja, a French woman (but the surname sounds more like it originated in Eastern Europe), former ballet étoile, and dance teacher in the college where Betty Conrad, the "missing girl" of the Italian title, was studying. Then subject to the necessary adaptations to reduce the four hours of the original version into the two hours of the Italian version, everything more or less proceeds as established in the original script until a few minutes from the end, when in the last episode immediately after the car crash of the alleged criminal, which I hope you have previously read about in the original version, everything turns around and, out of the blue, Temple accuses another person.

I must say that in revising the whole thing carefully to translate it here into English, doubts run high. The explanation comes too abruptly, Temple churns out a series of clues that one cannot quite understand either where they come from or when he collected them, since by his own admission he suspected someone else until a few minutes before (namely, the one who is actually the guilty party in the original version).

In short, this time the Italian ending appears rushed and much less convincing than the original. This doesn't mean it can't be Durbridge's work. In fact, the same objection made above applies: why should the Italian adapters have taken on the burden and risk of inventing another ending on their own? And probably even this eventual new ending, if it was really Durbridge who wrote it, would have undergone the same heavy editing as the entire script, perhaps losing passages that would have made it less rushed and apparently unwarranted. However, in this case, the doubt remains and it seemed fair to point it out.

But now you can judge for yourselves.

LA RAGAZZA SCOMPARSA (THE MISSING GIRL)

(from *Paul Temple and the Conrad Case*)
Translated by Franca Cancogni
10 episodes aired daily
from February 17th to February 28th 1975,
length: about 15 minutes each episode.

Cast:

Paul Temple . . . . Alberto Lupo
Steve Temple . . . . Lucia Catullo
Inspector Breckshaft . . . . . . Max Turilli
Nicole Dubrewskoja . . Josette Celestino
Betty Conrad . . . . Antonella Della Porta
June Jackson . . . . . . .Cecilia Todeschini
Sir Graham Forbes . . . . Carlo Ratti
Elliot France . . . . Vittorio Sanipoli
Mrs. Weldon . . . . .Gabriella Genta
Madame Klein . . . . Ingrid Schoeller
Gerda Holman . . . . .Ilaria Guerrini
Dr. Conrad . . . . Claudio Gora
Dennis Harper . . . . . . .Enrico Bertorelli
Fritz Gunther . . . . . . Carlo Hintermann
Joyce Gunther . . . . Grazia Radicchi
Ruth Conrad . . . . . . Ombretta De Carlo
Paddy Smith . . . . Nino Dal Fabbro
Inspector Vosper . . . . . Giuseppe Pertile

Directed by Umberto Benedetto

The following scene between Paul and Steve, with a quick phone call from Vosper, was inserted in the Italian version, and it is included here to explain the other very short scene that closes this version. It takes place after the rescue of Paul and Inspector Breckshaft from the river just before Elliot France and Dr Conrad meet at the hotel.

TEMPLE: Atchoo! Atchoo!

STEVE: Paul, are you sure you haven't caught a cold?

TEMPLE: I'm quite sure. I've had a hot bath and three whiskies …

STEVE: Well, I think you need a fourth one.

STEVE laughs.

STEVE: But if Scotland Yard find out that we're hiding her, won't that be dangerous?

TEMPLE: Atchoo!

The phone rings.

STEVE: Oh, you poor thing! It's all right – I'll get it.

STEVE lifts the receiver.

STEVE: (*On the phone*) Hello … Yes, all right, I'll get him. (*Softly; to TEMPLE*) It's Inspector Vosper.

TEMPLE takes the receiver.

TEMPLE: (*On the phone*) Hello, Vosper!

VOSPER: (*On the other end of the line*) Just to let you know, you were right, Temple. Fritz Gunther is in London.

TEMPLE: Can't you arrest him? Isn't Harper's testimony sufficient?

VOSPER: Yes, for Gerda Holman's murder. In any case, we'll keep you informed. By the way, how's the cold doing?

TEMPLE: Oh, not so bad. Atchoo!

TEMPLE replaces the receiver.

STEVE: What did he want?

TEMPLE: He just wanted to confirm that Fritz Gunther's in town. They're going to arrest him.

STEVE: That poor woman – his wife … What is she going to do? Paul, tell me, did you suspect Gunther just because of the photograph we saw in the restaurant?

TEMPLE: Well, the photo reminded me of some of his movies and his being an actor – someone who can mimic everyone's voices. And as soon as he realised we'd seen it he replaced it.

STEVE: And to think I like him. (*A pause*) Paul, do you now know who the head of the organization is? Did Harper tell you?

TEMPLE: I already knew it. Harper only confirmed it to me.

STEVE: I think I know that too. Tell me, is it …

STEVE whispers in TEMPLE's ear. Her whisper is inaudible.

TEMPLE: Yes.

STEVE: But then …!

TEMPLE: Yes, but first we must prove it! Harper's testimony is not enough. He's so scared at the moment that he might well retract everything tomorrow.

The following scenes start right after DR CONRAD's car crash and end the story.

SERGEANT: Stop! Stop! Don't come any closer!

STEVE: Is he dead?

SERGEANT: Apparently not, not yet.

STEVE: Better for him if he were.

TEMPLE: You never can tell, Steve.

We hear the sound of an ambulance approaching.

FADE IN incidental music.

FADE music.

NICOLE: You do understand why Conrad tried to kill
            me, don't you? Because he knew that if he
            continued with his hateful blackmailing of us,
            Elliot and I would end up talking, even at the
            cost of a scandal.

TEMPLE: I suppose the evidence, that is France's
            medical records, are in your possession?

NICOLE: I destroyed them.

TEMPLE: Conrad was more far-sighted. A copy of that
            file is now in the hands of Sir Graham Forbes
            at Scotland Yard.

NICOLE: If there is a copy, it's a forgery.

TEMPLE: Conrad's file is not a medical record. It
            contains recordings of phone calls, copies of
            letters, prescriptions, the operations of the drug
            trade that you set up using Dr Conrad's clinic,
            his name, even his patients.

NICOLE: That's a lie!

TEMPLE: Madame Dubrewskoja, until five years ago,
            you were quite a well-known dancer in Paris.
            But suddenly you stopped dancing.

NICOLE: What does that have to do with anything?

TEMPLE: Let me explain. Five years ago in Conrad's
            clinic, a young patient committed suicide
            under the influence of a drug administered by
            mistake. That patient's name was Helene
            Tessier and she was your sister. I'm right,
            aren't I?

NICOLE: Yes.

TEMPLE: It all started from there. First for revenge, and
            then for money. You started blackmailing
            Conrad. To make public what happened to
            your sister would have ruined him and meant

the end of his career. Conrad went along with you for a while but then started to get in touch with the right people. The various Dale Blacks, Fritz Gunthers, Captain Smiths ... Finally, you met Elliot France who had been ill with a rather severe psychic form of illness, but you, for your own purposes, made him believe himself to be a maniac murderous sort of person, with a compromising medical record that Conrad threatened to send to the newspapers. It was a way of tying him to yourself and hiding your real activity from him. You had Betty kidnapped not to save France, but to silence Conrad, who by now had accumulated enough evidence to blow the whole thing wide open. And before that, even to the same end, you had tried to push into drug trafficking through Gerda Holman, through Harper, even by means of June Jackson. Everything I have told you, dear Madame, is proven, and when we bring you to the dock, there will be another witness against you – the most important one ... Conrad!

NICOLE: Conrad is dead. You told me ... (*She breaks off*) No! You lied to me ...

TEMPLE: Conrad is alive, and he will testify against you. I lied to you about him dying to see how far you would go. No, you have no way out, I'm afraid. Even the false assault in the hotel is evidence against you. You fired two shots to show that you had an enemy, but your only enemy is yourself.

FADE IN incidental music.

FADE music.

STEVE: Cheers, darling!
TEMPLE: Cheers, Steve!
They clink their glasses.
STEVE: But, Paul, you really are the limit! When I said
            that I thought Dr Conrad was the boss of the
            organization, why did you say yes?
TEMPLE: (*Laughing*) Because, my sweet, up until that
            moment, I thought so too ...
STEVE joins in the laughter.

THE END

Printed in Great Britain
by Amazon

41016969R00179